The Hi

Experi

Laurie B

CW00539475

The Hidden Experiment

Laurie Bowler

Published by Blackhawk Publishing, 2023.

THE HIDDEN EXPERIMENT

First edition. July 30, 2023.

Copyright © 2023 Laurie Bowler.

ISBN: 979-8223021407

Written by Laurie Bowler.

Table of Contents

Prologue

D r Foster rushed up to the glass chamber after he saw it happen. He grabbed the sides of the wall with his breaths wild and looked at the floor. "Daniel?"

All that was left of him was ash.

The man remained frozen for all of twenty seconds before running back to his computer to try to do something, anything, to reverse what had just happened on his account. *Shit.* He thought intensely as his fingers moved quickly across the keyboard.

Nothing he did seemed to be working.

The man swallowed thickly as he turned back to the glass chamber of ash and the floating purple rock inside of it. Despite the calamity, the rock did not seem fazed at all. It was just there, floating like it had been before it turned Daniel into a pile of ash before it disintegrated a human being into absolutely nothing. The exact opposite of what it was engineered to do.

"Oh my God," Foster continued trying desperately to reverse what had happened by tampering with the rock's programming, but nothing was helping. In fact, all of his tamperings seemed to be aggravating the entity.

The dark rock with purple lights shining through its cracks released sparks after he pressed a few buttons. There was actually a metal rod sticking out of the glass chamber connected to the back of it. That was how he was able to adjust it using his computer.

LAURIE BOWLER

But adjusting seemed to be futile at the moment because nothing he pressed seemed to be able to bring the child back. *Shit*. He thought it with an air of sadness and desperation this time, tears welling up in his eyes. This was not something that often happened to him. He was usually much more level-headed.

"James, you're still here?"

He gasped when he heard the automatic door close after that voice spoke to him. He had not heard it open. What was . . .

He turned and saw his partner walking up to him. *No*. "Christopher," he whispered. His eyes were wide with stun.

"Why so surprised to see me? I'm the one who usually leaves last. Except when Dave gets carried away once in a while, but that only happened twice," his voice sounded casual, for he knew not what he was walking into. "What are you doing? Making some adjustments to the prototype?" Christopher scratched his head while looking around.

James could not speak. He did not know how to say what needed to be said.

"I actually came in here looking for Daniel since he ran off earlier to explore the lab. You know how he is," he shook his head before making eye contact with his friend. "Have you happened to see him anywhere?"

James' mouth was dry. "Christ-"

Christopher turned to the glass chamber resting against one of the walls. "That's strange. Why is it sparking so much?" he walked over to it to get a closer look.

Their creation continued to release purple sparks, which indicated instability.

Christopher rubbed his chin as he observed it before examining the chamber to see if anything within it might have caused this. "Did you interfere with the set- ash?"

James could not keep it secret any longer, now could he? "Christopher, he came in here, and he was asking about the prototype. He-he seemed so excited and eager, so I told him all about how it could enhance human beings. We were so close to the perfect model, and we were in the final stages of testing, so it looked as if it would work, so I allowed him as a treat to go in there to be our final test subject but then he-it-"

Chris turned to him with bulging eyes. "What are you saying?" he rushed in a short whisper.

James grabbed the sides of his head. "Daniel disintegrated! I'm so, so, *so* sorry!"

Christopher did not seem to know what to say. "He . . ." he faced the chamber again, then beat both hands on the walls while staring in horror at the ashes.

"I've been trying to bring him back. That's why . . . Chris, I'm so sorry. Please forgive me. Maybe we can still do something. Yes. There must be a way. I'll just keep working, and eventually, experiment 810 will bring Daniel back to us, and we can continue testing so that we can save mankind. I just know it," he rushed over to his computer to keep pressing buttons, but it only made the rock spark more. He had been doing any and everything while trying to bring Daniel back, so the settings were now a mess. "It will work eventually. I-I just need to undo everything I'd been doing before-"

"No."

James heard the tone. It sounded like one of defeat. He faced his partner. "Christopher, we can bring Daniel ba-"

"No," Christopher seemed serious as he turned to James again. "Stop this now. *All* of it," His voice was dripping with disdain.

James gulped. "What do you mean?"

"It was doomed from the start. We were stepping too much into unfamiliar territory, and now-"

"But we're not like other researchers. Our brilliant minds can save-"

"Look what this did to my son! Do you really believe that this can save anyone? We were stupid to think that it would," Christopher faced the ash in the chamber again, his chest tight and his throat aching. His son . . . "We shouldn't have tampered with something so unknown, unheard of. They all warned us, but we were too ambitious and now look."

James disagreed. "This is just one setback-"

"One setback- listen to yourself!"

"It doesn't make sense to just drop everything because this happened. We worked too hard. We've been working for years! Do not let your grief blind you!"

"What else do you want me to do! Things were risky from the start, and now this proves that it will ultimately bring more suffering than anything else," Christopher was gesturing to the chamber behind him, his eyes filled with tears.

James stepped back.

Christopher cursed, then stared at his feet. "I was wrong to even bring Daniel near any of this. Agh!" he started screaming while holding his head.

"Don't give up. We can bring him ba-"

"How? Stop arguing with me!"

"You're just emotional!"

"My son is dead!"

"I know, but let's keep our heads on and think of a way to bring him back-"

"Bringing the dead back to life is a whole other thing. Let's just stop this now. All of it. It's too dangerous. *Especially* experiment 810. We knew it from the start, but we were too stubborn. Give it up, James. We can't force mankind to evolve unnaturally,"

James looked at his partner's face without an expression on his own for a moment but slowly, his face changed to a look of disappointment and anger. "You sound like all the naysayers now," he appeared disgusted.

Christopher was equally so. "Maybe they were right all along," he wiped his eyes, then turned to the remains of his only child in the chamber. "You got nothing to lose, Foster. That's why this doesn't hurt you. But me . . ." he chuckled, but it hurt. "Well, this just took away a part of me, but if I continue, it may steal the whole thing," he frowned at the other man. "I don't want that to happen,"

James scoffed before walking to the exit.

Christopher's eyes followed him.

The automatic door opened, and James stepped through it. "I'm sorry about Daniel. You've reacted better than many grieving fathers would but seeing that you've lost him, it appears as if you will no longer be able to think logically," he looked over his shoulder. "I need logic if I want to continue this experiment-"

"You're going to continue? James, it's too-"

"To achieve greatness, we sometimes need to take risks and accept that we may lose what we know and love in the process," James sounded different.

Christopher frowned sternly. "Don't you dare hurt more people with this madness,"

"You don't get to tell me what to do anymore. From now, we are no longer partners," James nodded once and then walked away, letting the door close after he did so.

Christopher sighed after he left but decided to talk to him later.

He ran up to the chamber and looked down at the ashes that were his child.

Painful tears came to the surface of his eyes and squeezed themselves out after he squinted them.

The father rested his forehead against the glass and wept heavily, painfully, his soul breaking with every sob.

He started banging on the glass in an effort to break it, but nothing he did could.

Christopher eventually yanked the door open in a fit and made a grab for the unstable component.

He pulled it away from its rod and brought it to a metallic desk in the centre of the lab despite all of its sparking and spazzing.

It floated over the desk and continued to behave unstably.

Christopher did not care, though. He went to the sidelines to get something heavy and ended up finding a metallic toolbox.

He inhaled deeply, then held it over his head. This strange element was the reason why his son was no longer with him. It had once seemed like a blessing to him, but now it looked like a curse. Its sparking and twitching were not helping that fact.

I will destroy you. He cried out as he forcefully slammed the heavy metal toolbox against the rock.

CHAPTER ONE

"Welcome to Reymond High. We truly hope that you enjoy your time here and that you'll find ways to use your gifted mind to better mankind," a peppy girl handed Jun a flyer after he stepped out of the office with his dad.

"Ah, thank you. What's this?" the man took the piece of paper from his son to examine it.

The girl kept smiling as she started explaining. "Consider it an invitation to our meet and greet on Friday for the new school year," she looked at Jun.

He held tightly onto the straps of his backpack and tried to avoid eye contact, but she somehow found his eyes anyway.

Her smile remained on her face. "It may be your first year here, but it doesn't mean you have to be scared of mingling. We're all friendly over here. Gifted minds must unite," she did a gesture with her arms where one was held down as her hand cuffed into a fist and the other shot up. It resembled a superhero pose, and her face became serious as she struck it.

Jun watched as she smiled again and then hurried off after doing so.

"Mmm. Nice place, nice place. The secretary was nice when she handed you your schedule just now, and everybody we met over the summer while getting you settled had been nice too. This place is amazing," his dad chuckled as they walked down the hall away from the office.

Jun tried to ignore all the people dressed in similar clothing. He had never been to a school that required uniforms in the past, but he supposed that Reymond High was just extra. "I don't know about that," he started walking down the stairs with his father.

"Ah, come on. Are you still in a bad mood 'cause you have to transfer?" his dad grabbed his shoulder while they walked. Some students were coming up as they moved. It was the official first day of school after a long summer break, so a busy environment was expected. "This is a gift, Jun. *You* have a gift. Do you know how many kids your age wish they were born with an incredible brain like yours?" he faced his son once they were at the bottom of the staircase.

Jun thought of his old school and all the friends he had left right before one of their final years together. *All because of some stupid regional test scores.* Why didn't he get a say in whether he came here or not? This school wasn't even old enough to demand that students who got above a specific grade should be transferred to it. How long had it been in existence? *All the pamphlets said something like eighteen years.* He was not impressed by it despite the good reviews and high-tech building. The uniforms just screamed 'prestigious' as well, and being here almost felt like something out of a comic book. A school for geniuses with top-notch technology and professors? Something crazy was bound to happen here, right? *If Trevor got transferred with me, that's definitely what he'd be thinking.* He smiled briefly to himself, but it faded when he realised that he was now living in a completely different state from one of his best friends. This school felt like another world. It was even isolated from other buildings.

"Not many. Most teenagers just wanna hang out and have a good time," his hands were in the pockets of his blazer. It was a royal blue colour while the tie was a bright yellow. He wore brown dress pants and black shoes to go with it. The girls wore navy blue pleated skirts with plaid lining on the fabric. A lot of them seemed to wear it short.

His dad rolled his eyes. "Well, when they get older, they'd aspire to have a brain like yours because being as gifted as you apparently are, makes things a tad bit easier in this crazy and unfair life," he exhaled while looking down the main hall to the exit. "Anyway, I don't wanna keep you," he patted his son's shoulders. "You got everything right?"

Jun was beginning to feel an awful sensation in his chest. This was a boarding school, so at the end of a day of classes, he couldn't go home to have dinner with his parents like he was used to. His dad would be leaving in a bit, and when he did, he would not see him in person for a pretty long time. "Yeah, Dad, I'm okay. We've been double and triple-checking since you and I set out to come here. Mom wouldn't let us get this far without having everything packed. It's all there and in my room," the dorms were in a different section of campus.

"Okay, good, good," his father looked at him.

Jun felt a bit emotional, but he fought it with all his might. "You okay, Dad?"

"Yes, I am. Don't worry. I just . . . it feels like I'm sending you off to college at only sixteen years old," he laughed painfully before shaking his head.

Jun had laughed too, but now he was putting up a battle with his tears like his father was. Were people staring? He didn't want to be caught becoming emotional because his parent was leaving. This wasn't preschool.

The father opened his arms, and Jun went in to embrace him.

They patted each other's backs for a bit before parting and giving a firm nod.

"Bye, Jun. I think you're gonna do great here," the man held him firmly by the shoulders before nodding another time and then releasing him to begin walking away.

Jun watched the way he left through the entrance when he arrived at it and breathed out. "It's officially begun, huh?" he said softly to himself.

"Try not to cry *too* much," a mocking voice called from his side.

Jun turned and saw a guy standing with a group of others near a classroom.

He frowned and rolled his eyes before starting to head for his first class. Whoever that guy was, he would try to stay clear of him. There was no way that he would let the freaks at this school mess around with him. All he wanted to do here was finish what he came to do and never look back. *Exactly.* And if anyone or anything tried to get in the way of that . . . well, he would be pretty pissed off.

HIS FIRST CLASS HAD gone okay, and now he was heading over to his second with hands in his pockets.

The halls felt wide and unfamiliar, and every student he glanced at looked like an alien to him. His mind kept juxtaposing things with his old school, but all that did was make him homesick. He could not afford to let his emotions blind him from what he needed to do. *Get out.* If he got too caught up in his feelings, he might end up spending more time here. This school was for the best of the best. No one he had spoken about it with had shied away from explaining how difficult it could be. The lessons were on a whole other level, and the tests were challenging as well. *That's why I need to stay focused as much as possible.* He inhaled deeply as he walked up to his next class.

It was Chemistry.

"Alright, students, take your seats, get out what you need," the teacher said lazily from the front.

Jun took a seat next to a girl with dark brown skin and bleached locks.

She looked at him briefly but returned to looking forward.

He noticed that she had given him a glance, but he tried not to glance back. *I mean, it might be wise to make friends here, but I don't know.* After his actual friends had found out that he would be transferred to this place, they had not hesitated to share what they heard about the students who got in. They were all freaky geniuses who only talked about Math and Science. Jun did not know how true that was, but he would rather keep his distance than have to come up with a way to back out of a conversation about Pythagoras' Theorem.

The teacher proceeded to introduce herself and then asked the class to do so afterwards. It was the typical first-day routine that Jun usually found boring, but he didn't bother complaining.

He started taking notes when the teacher began giving them, and while doing so quickly, the point of his pencil broke.

"Shit," he shook his head and looked to his pencil case to get out a new one, but the teacher continued to teach rather quickly. He was missing quite a bit.

Just as he pulled out a fresh pencil, a plastic one rolled up to the side of his notebook and stole his attention away from his own.

Jun picked it up and pushed the eraser, which elongated the point. He had seen many of these being used these days but took no interest in them. Kids at his school preferred pens anyway, but over here, it seemed like things were much different. He saw a lot of students typing quickly onto tablets and others taking no notes at all. Could they just memorize?

"I don't think you should stay staring too long,"

He snapped out of his thoughts to turn to the person who spoke.

The same girl he had sat next to was writing feverishly into her own notebook. She was one of the few people using one, and he was also sure that she had been the reason why that plastic pen had been rolled towards his stuff.

Jun remembered what she had called herself during their introductions. Her name was Chantalle. "I was just-," and now he realised how much he was indeed missing.

Jun shook his head and decided to continue trying to take down notes.

"I'll give you my notes once we're done. I had her in freshman year. She just talks and talks and expects us to write. The real learning happens when we head to our rooms and read everything over," she spoke softly but was also somehow writing what was being said. "Then you'll realise that her words were actually pretty helpful. But if you don't take note, it won't stick, and you'd be pretty lost when it's time for finals," she tucked one of her locks to the back of her ear and kept writing.

Jun was surprised by how much she just shared and also her offer to give him notes. Should he say something? They were sitting towards the back of the class, so he doubted that anyone could hear them, but he usually preferred to not disturb them while classes were in session.

"You should write," she said.

"R-right. Thanks," that was all he told her before listening and deciding to keep taking notes. He wondered why she was so willing to help him for a moment but only for that long. A moment.

The class ended just as the bell rang, and their teacher started telling them what she wanted them to do as homework.

Jun felt a bit exhausted after this class. The others had not been too challenging, but this one? He could not put into words how he felt right now.

"Here. You can give it back to me at the end of the school day. Guess you can take some pictures whenever you have the time. My dorm room is room 57AW." Chantalle left her book with him and got up to leave with the other students, who did so rather quickly.

"Uh, thank y- whoa," Jun looked up to thank her but noticed that the room was empty right now.

Was there supposed to be another class here? He wondered.

"Hmm . . ." he shouldn't be late for his next class, but he kind of wanted to get taking a photo of that girl's notes out of the way before he went on with his day. *Don't wanna end up forgetting or something.* So he got his phone out of his pocket and held it at an angle to snap a picture.

"Okay," he said to himself as he put his phone away. He started packing up his stuff quickly to head out, but just as he ran to the door, he bumped into somebody.

"Crap!" the person he hit dropped what they had been holding in hand.

Jun noticed that it was something like a fan and some other stuff that looked like garbage. "Aw jeez, I-I'm sorry," he stooped to help pick the stuff up.

"No, it was my bad. I wasn't looking where I was going," the person he hit sounded like a boy. He tossed everything into the box he had been holding with Jun's help, then held it up against his chest. "Oh boy, this is heavy."

Jun frowned at him. He looked pretty short, and his voice sounded childish. "Uhh . . ." he was wearing a uniform, so he must have gone here, right?

The boy seemed to be confused by his staring. "Can I help you with some- wait, are you lost?"

Jun adjusted his bag straps and then checked his watch. He started off just being kind of late, but now he was really late. If his next class was anything like the one he just had, then he would be in serious trouble. "No, I'm just-"

"I'd help you to find where you wanna go, but I'm actually pretty new to this place. Heh heh. This is my first official year at Reymond High School for the gifted, so I'm pretty nervous, but I heard about this science fair they have at the end of the year where all students can join in and show their inventions. And the person with the best one gets to win a grand prize! They told us about that at orientation, and man, was I over the moon! I started working on my project right after I unpacked my things 'cause if I'm gonna make a good impression, then I'm gonna need all the time I can get. Who knows who'll be at that science fair? I need to make my mark, man . . ."

Jun just could not believe how much this kid could talk. He wanted to just walk away, but the boy seemed really excited to talk to someone about this. Had he just been holding all of this in since he moved here? *I should just go, shouldn't I?*

The kid continued talking about the science fair and what he had in mind for his invention and other stuff that Jun did not really have time to listen to.

The boy had brown hair and bright eyes. The colour of them was green. There were freckles across his nose, and he was a bit chubby. It was probably just baby fat. He looked about twelve for the most to Jun.

Okay, that's it. He cleared his throat. "Listen, I got a class to go to, and you and all your talking have kind of made me late so . . . I'm gonna just head off," Jun started walking away briskly but stopped to turn and look at the kid. "Don't you have a class?"

The boy shrunk for a moment before appearing mischievous. "Would you rat me out if I said I was skipping?"

This was interesting. "Skipping?" People around here skipped classes? "Why? On your first official day?"

The boy did a dance that made it seem as if he wanted to pee.

Jun was very lost in this movement. "Are you okay?"

"I just wanted to use this lab to build something while it was free. It'd be better to use it after school, but I don't know if that's even allowed with the kinda security we've got. And plus, it'd be creepy being here after dark," he shuddered. "I mean, I could ask the principal if I could use the lab during lunch, but I've heard that he's pretty picky about letting students use labs outside of classes. I don't know. Guess he doesn't want us messing with the supplies?" the boy shrugged.

Jun hummed to himself. "So you're basically doing something unauthorised?"

He smiled sheepishly. "Yeah? But don't tell anyone. Please. I'll do your homework. I know I'm a freshman, but I've seen the material for juniors, and it ain't that challenging. At least not to me," he sounded confident.

"Huh . . . okay, but I don't want you doing anything for me. I'll just keep your secret 'cause I don't care enough to let it slip," Jun shrugged, then started hurrying off.

"Wait!"

He slid after stopping abruptly, then turned to look back. "What?"

"What's your name?" the boy asked him.

Jun couldn't believe that that was what he wanted to know. "Jun," he shook his head and kept running.

"Alex! That's my name!"

He did not respond to that. He just kept moving as fast as he could to try to make it to his class before it ended.

IT WAS NIGHTTIME.

Jun left the bathroom on the floor of his room with a yawn.

"Hey, new guy, having trouble with the workload already?" a boy asked from his own room.

Jun stopped in the hall to look at him with a frown and noticed that he was the same idiot who had tried picking on him after his dad left. There was someone else in his room with him, but Jun ignored them both even though they laughed. *Is that their idea of bullying around here?* How pathetic?

He made it to his own room and sighed before looking into his mirror. It was from his room back home.

The first day wasn't so bad, I guess. He thought tiredly to his reflection. The classes had been pretty intense at the beginning of the school year, but he had adjusted pretty well. *I gave Chantalle her book back like she asked me to.* And he had even transferred her notes into his own notebook. It was midnight now. Transferring the notes and doing homework had taken a while. *And it's just the first day.*

Jun shook his head and went to lie in bed after turning off his lights.

He lay on his side and scrolled through his phone.

The kids in his former class group chat were asking him about the freaky genius school he was now enrolled in, so he proceeded to type a message to try to describe it to them. They all knew it was his first day.

He closed that chat and opened one between him and his best friend, Carter.

Carter asked him if he had encountered any colossal nerds yet.

Jun snickered, and the boy outside of his Chemistry class crossed his mind. *His name was Alex.* He started telling Carter about how Alex would not shut up about some weird science fair that he had literally only heard about during orientation since he was a freshman.

They laughed about the weird kid together, and Carter asked him if anyone else he met struck out. He started telling him about the annoying guy who just happened to be living on the same floor as him, and after he sent that message, he thought of Chantalle. *She wasn't that interesting or strikingly weird, so I won't mention her.*

He and Carter spoke for a bit longer before Jun told him good night and scrolled through Twitter until he fell asleep.

The school was challenging so far but also more exciting to him. He never really voiced this to his friends back home, but the regular school had been pretty boring to him since the pacing had been too slow. These were just thoughts that he kept to himself. No one needed to know that Jun, the star basketball player was the type to complain about lesson pace. That would make him annoying to the rest of the schoolgoers.

He still did not like the new arrangement, but he would try to make the best of it. What would make this more bearable would be if he could make some cool friends, but he already had it in his head that no one here was cool, so he would keep to himself. Having lunch alone while listening to music had not been so bad anyway. He had a lot of friends back where he was from, but he did not mind being alone. Before high school, he had been a loner anyway. But that was when he was a different person.

As his mind took him to dream land, he hoped that things would run smoothly as he stayed here and that he would do well and get into a good college afterwards. Carter was pretty smart, too, so maybe they could go to the same place.

Jun just wanted all this to be over and done with as soon as possible.

CHAPTER TWO

J un slammed his locker after getting out books for his next class during the transition period.

"Hey, you,"

He heard a voice call to him from down the hall and noticed the kid from yesterday. What was going on?

Alex jogged up to him happily and was standing at his side in no time. "Jun, right?"

Jun looked around in confusion and noticed some people who were most likely from his year staring at him. "Uhhh . . ." they were giggling too. It probably looked weird that he was interacting with a freshman, right? *Or maybe this kid has a reputation.* Alex had just started school, so that was unlikely, wasn't it? "Yeah, my name is Jun," he started walking off, but Alex followed him.

"Great, so I remembered," Alex kept smiling at him with his hands-on his backpack straps. "Thanks again for agreeing to not tell my secret,"

"I only did that because I didn't care enough to let it slip-"

"I just couldn't get that out of my head all day, you know?" Alex chuckled. "And now I happened to see you while on my way to class, so I thought that maybe-"

Jun did not like where this was going. "Maybe what?"

Alex seemed to be nervous. "I'm pretty new here, and this place is kinda intimidating. I wanna just focus on what I gotta do, but at the same time, the older kids are just . . . scary. You know, yesterday, on my way to the bathroom, this guy just blocked me. He and some other dudes. They must have been your age, a bit taller than you, so you can imagine how tall they were . . . anyway, I was kinda wondering if you might wanna be my mentor? Not for studying or anything; I got that in the bag. I meant like an older friend who protects me from danger and stuff? Back at my old school, I got beat up a lot, and I thought here that wouldn't happen 'cause everyone is gifted like me, but now I'm seeing that . . ."

Jun once again couldn't believe how much this kid talked. He rolled his eyes as he turned into a different hall but noticed the idiot who had been harassing him yesterday.

"Ah, that's him!" Alex pointed at the boy before hiding behind Jun.

Jun cursed in his mind. All of his drama drew attention to the two of them.

The guy had blonde hair and grey eyes and just looked like someone who was up to no good. He smirked when he saw Jun and started approaching him with his two pals at his left and right sides.

Jun tried to move away so Alex wouldn't hide at his back, but the kid kept behind him. "Hey. Beat it already,"

"Well, if it isn't a new guy and- what's this? The preschooler who got in for some reason?" the blonde-haired boy pointed at Alex and laughed with his friends.

"I'm not a preschooler. It's obvious that I'm fourteen. You're just being a jerk," Alex peeked from Jun's back to say this but then hid again.

Jun could not believe his position. People were staring at him, and it wasn't because he did something cool.

The guys laughed at Alex. "So sorry. You're just round and squishy like preschoolers, so I assumed!" the blonde one made a grab behind Jun's back and yanked Alex by the top of his head.

Alex screamed as he was pulled towards the older guys who laughed at him.

"That wasn't hard, was it?" the guy shoved Alex to the ground.

Jun watched this with a few other people in the hall. Should he do something?

Alex struggled to his feet. "What's your problem, man? I'm literally out here existing, and you're trying to pick fights with me," he frowned as he held tightly to his bag again.

"His backpack looks like something a middle schooler would wear," one of the other guys pointed, and they all laughed.

Jun cringed as other people joined in. *I should go.*

Alex's face reddened. "No, it's not! This is a state of the art-hey!" his bag was yanked off his back, and he was shoved. "What's your problem?" he tried to grab it from the blonde guy, but the boy held his forehead to keep him away, and it seemed effective.

The entire hall was laughing at this, it seemed.

Really? Aren't you all nerds? You should feel sorry for this kid. It could be any one of you going through this if you went to a different school. Jun groaned internally before walking up to the blonde guy and snatching Alex's bag.

"H-" the guy got mad, but Jun pushed him to the ground.

"Ohhh!" the hall was immersed.

His lackeys looked at their leader and then Jun.

Alex was just as surprised as everyone else.

"Knock it off. You call him a preschooler while you act like a preschool bully? Get over yourself, man," Jun stretched out his hand to give Alex back his bag.

Alex took it and kept staring with wide eyes at the guy on the ground.

The blonde boy got up in a huff and started marching away with his peeps.

Jun thought he would do something like that. All those guys were the same.

The bell rang, and he started walking quickly to his next class.

Alex was at his side again. "Thanks for that back there,"

"Don't mention it. I mean it," Jun didn't want to have anything to do with Alex and yet the kid was following him.

"See? That was a perfect example. I need someone like you helping me out," Alex nudged him. "You're tall, you seem fit, you're cool, so it can work. You can be like my body guard- ooo. You can come with me at night to work on my science fair project in the Chemistry lab! I still don't know what it's gonna be yet but what I do know is that all of the appliances in there help with inspiration," he stroked his chin. "Doing it at night would be tricky, but I think that nighttime is the best time for people to come up with good ideas. Did you know that the light bulb was invented at night?"

Jun frowned. "How would you know that?"

"I don't. I just made that up, but it would be funny, wouldn't it? That and practical. 'Cause, there's no light at night, so-"

Jun sighed heavily. "Alex," he stopped walking to face the short boy.

Alex shrunk. "Yeah?"

"If I agree to come with you to help out with your science fair project thingy tonight and only tonight, can you promise me that you will leave me alone for the rest of the school year?" Jun asked slowly.

Alex's shoulders fell, and he seemed to be disheartened. "Only tonight? Leave you alone for the rest of the school year?"

Jun felt people passing by them quickly. "That's what I said."

"But . . ." Alex frowned, appearing more angry than sad. "I don't wanna leave you alone for the rest of the school year. We have some-"

"Dude, we met like yesterday," Jun rolled his eyes.

Alex appeared hurt. He looked to his feet, then shook his head. "No. I don't want your pity," he turned his back and walked off.

Jun watched him go.

The younger boy disappeared among all the students, and it was as if he had never been there in the first place.

Jun clutched onto his bag strap and turned on his heel to go to his own class. That was easy. *Yeah. Glad I managed to get rid of him.* The last thing he wanted was to have to babysit a freshman all year. That would surely ruin his image.

As he walked away, though, he wondered how Alex would fare out working on his project without a lab for 'inspiration'. Would he go to the lab by himself, or was it too creepy? *The junk he'd been carrying yesterday looked like it could build something, actually.*

Jun entered his class and took a seat in the middle. As he did so, his brain started constructing something that Alex could make out of what he had been holding yesterday. *Yeah, that could work, but . . . I'm getting distracted.*

He decided to try to focus on the lesson at hand.

ALEX WOULD JUST DROP the idea of using the lab for this, but he felt that it would be a great location to create something amazing for the science fair.

I'm sure he'll say yes. I mean, it's not for classes, but it's for a school activity. Plus, I'm an ambitious young scientist. The school was still in session, but it was lunch time. He was walking up the stairs to head to the principal's office to ask for permission to use the lab tonight so he could work on an invention that would blow everybody away. *And then Stanford will instantly accept me. Heh heh.*

He went up to the secretary first and asked her if he could talk to the principal.

The woman told him to hang on as she called the man in charge. He was also the founder of this school.

Dr Reymond had been reading through some files when the phone on his desk rang. He set them down and picked them up. "Hello?"

"Sir, one of the students would like to see you directly. It's Alex Johnson,"

"Alex . . . okay. Let him in," he tried to make his desk look more presentable since someone would be entering, but that was difficult considering all of the stuff he had scattered about it.

By the time the boy entered, he was still putting stuff in his drawers. "Oh, you walk fast, don't you?" Dr Reymond asked.

Alex had never been here before. All the freshmen and new students usually went to the secretary when they were enrolling and getting their schedules and other information for the school. It had struck him as strange when he just came, but the secretary had simply said that Dr Reymond was a 'busy man' when his parents had asked why he was not the one meeting them when they first brought him here.

"Not really. Doesn't take that long to get here from the secretary's office," Alex looked at the two seats in front of the man's desk. *I heard he's a world-renowned scientist who gave up research to open his own school.* He was the type to geek out and look deeply into anything he was newly getting involved with. That was why he knew that about their school's principal. *But that's kind of all I know. A lot of information about him seems to have been erased.* The articles and newspapers he had found with information about his school's founder had felt vague and surface level. It mentioned that he used to work with several other scientists who were trying to better humanity through science, but there were never many details about the experiments. Alex had been very confused about that while digging into the school's founder, but he had lost interest in that aspect of the school pretty quickly since he'd been excited about their science programs. *But now that I'm here . . . it's all coming back.*

"True, true," Dr Reymond gestured to the seats before his desk, telling Alex to make himself comfortable.

The boy did so and exhaled. "Why are you available to chat during ordinary school days but not for big things like meetings with parents and new students?" he decided to just ask this now.

"Wow, is that why you came here? To ask that specific question?" Dr Reymond chuckled in amusement.

"No. It just came to mind now,"

"Well, Alex, if I had to meet with every single student who enrolled here when they did, then I wouldn't be able to take care of all of this paperwork. Being the principal of such a prestigious school isn't easy, you know," he replied fondly to the boy's question.

"Oh yeah. Guess that makes sense," Alex no longer cared about this topic. "Why I'm here actually is to ask if I could use Chemistry lab OW after school to work on my invention for the science fair. I heard them say that we're not allowed to use the science labs outside of classes during orientation, but this is school-related, so it's totally cool, right?" he really hoped that that rule had just been exaggerated during orientation. *Yeah, Dr Reymond seems pretty chill so far. Kinda reminds me of Santa Claus. Not that he's fat. Just the grey hair and glasses.* He supposed that a lot of older men could fit that description, so maybe Dr Reymond did not resemble Father Christmas all that much.

Dr Reymond's brightness dimmed after he heard the request. "Chemistry lab OW?"

"Uh-huh," Alex could sense a shift in his attitude.

"Chemistry lab OW . . ." the man appeared to be saying this to himself now more than anything. He looked up at the young boy again. "Why that lab specifically?"

"It can be any lab, but that one's the biggest," Alex expressed.

"Why would you need the biggest lab if you're the only one working on this?"

"Well, I just said it could be any lab, but I also kinda wanted to use the biggest one in case my invention ends up being huge. I'm thinking of leaning more toward my engineering skills for this one. Ever seen a dancing robot that moves on command?" Alex started doing a robot dance, consumed by his eagerness toward this science fair project. *Yeah, I don't need anyone with me while I do my work. Jun is so overrated.* He said this in his mind as if he had not been sulking over how Jun had treated him all day.

"I-I have, but-" Dr Reymond was still much more serious than he had been earlier. Maybe more contemplative than anything else? A lot was on his mind right now. "I don't trust students going in there unsupervised, so I think you should stick to working on this in your dorm room,"

Alex hated that. "What? But-"

"I'm sorry, Alex. I can see your ambition burning through your eyes, but . . . sometimes it's good to just settle for something smaller since hoping to do big, big things can prevent you from doing simple good things. Big isn't always better. Great isn't always superior," the doctor looked past his student.

Alex was trying to catch his eye, but it seemed as if the principal was staring in space.

"And sometimes . . . what's great can also be dangerous,"

Alex blinked at him as he paused after stating this.

The principal managed to get back to reality. "Anyway, students aren't allowed there outside of classes for their own safety,"

"What if a teacher came with me?" Alex was scared of going into the labs at night, but he really did want to use them.

"No. It's just our policy," Dr Reymond would not budge on this.

Alex inhaled deeply, then let it out. "Fine. I'm sure I'll be able to come up with something amazing in my tiny dorm room with barely any inspiration around me,"

"Don't put it like that. You're a boy genius, Alex. You'll do just fine in a smaller area," Dr Reymond smiled at the ambitious student.

Alex shrugged before climbing to his feet. "Thanks anyway. You're actually pretty easy to talk to. I haven't really been talking to anyone since I got here, but I guess it's kinda always like that with me,"

Dr Reymond tilted his head. "Well, it's only the first day. I'm sure you'll make some friends soon. Have you by any chance run into anyone who seems of interest to you?"

Alex's heart broke a bit, but he knew that he was creepy for feeling that way. Jun had seemed so cool. He never really felt a connection with anybody until meeting him, but Jun didn't like him, so he wouldn't beg for his acceptance. "Yeah, but that person's not interested in me, so I've decided to leave them alone," he smiled tightly at the principal before dragging his feet away from his office.

Dr Reymond felt sorry for the boy after he left but sat back after that feeling faded. *Chemistry lab OW . . .* He decided to just keep working.

CHAPTER THREE

J un lay on his back that evening with thoughts about his new school and his old life floating through his mind.

Today had been okay. He had adjusted pretty fine to the pacing of the lessons and had found it a lot easier to get around now that his mind had quickly adapted to the building. The only thing he didn't like about this place was that everybody seemed as bright as he was. It was exciting at first, but as he thought about it more, he realised that it meant he would have a much harder time standing out when exams and tests rolled around. *I'll figure it out, I guess.* He always did. That was something he was known for.

He sat up and decided to continue doing his advanced calculus homework since there was so much of it. The amount of work here really was something, but he could manage.

When he finished, he would text his friends from back home and then retire for the night. *Right. I don't have much reason to stay up late, so I'll retire when I'm done doing whatever I have to do.*

As he wrote into his notebook, though, he couldn't help but remember how his day had started. That Alex kid had been something else, hadn't he? *I kinda told him to beat it, though.* And because of Alex's reaction, Jun had been thinking of that encounter a lot all day.

He thought back to the junk in Alex's box and how his mind kept trying to build something with it. *I wonder if Alex has thought of something like that yet.* The kid seemed pretty smart but was he creative? *Hmm . . .* Where was Alex now? Would he be in the lab? *Maybe but why am I thinking about this?*

Alex was probably in his dorm room. Jun wondered if he would appreciate some input on his little science project. *Not that I wanna hang out with him. I just want to make sure that he's using his resources in the best way possible.* Right.

He stopped writing for a few seconds before groaning and climbing out of bed.

Jun stood in the doorway of the idiot who had been bugging Alex today.

The guy's door was always open, and he seemed to always have friends over too. Did he ever do homework?

He spotted Jun and frowned his way. "What do you want?"

Jun instantly noticed that he had ruined their vibe. *That somehow satisfies me.* He smiled a little. "You seem like the type of bully who'd be borderline obsessed with his victims."

"What?" The guy sat up straighter. He was in a rolling chair while his two pals sat on stools.

"Hey, don't talk about Devon that way. He's not obsessed with anyone," one of his henchmen defended.

Jun did not even take heed of him. "Would you happen to know where the kid you were bothering today is staying? Like . . . what dorm room is he in and where?"

Devon folded his arms. "I wouldn't know that. And why are you even asking? Wanna meet up with him to make out? You two looked like a couple earlier with how you defended him," he and his buddies laughed, and one of them high-fived him.

Jun did not bother countering that. His disses were equivalent to those of a third-grader. *How did he get into this school?* "I wanna talk to him,"

Devon looked right at Jun before groaning. "Didn't you get a tour when you first came here? The freshmen stay on the left wing of the building, so his room is probably around there. You can ask other people where he is 'cause I don't know. Half the time, I forget that kid exists. He just started going here, man,"

"Yeah, sure, but thanks," Jun started walking with purpose down the dorm hallway. *Left-wing eh?* Why was he so interested in Alex's silly project anyway? *I don't want him to waste his resources.* Right, that was it. And . . . he guessed he felt kind of bad for how he treated the younger guy earlier. *But I don't wanna think about that too much.*

He hurried his steps as he kept moving.

ALEX WAS SITTING AT his desk blandly, finishing up the easy Maths homework that their teacher had assigned.

"Okay. All done," he hardly seemed glad that he did so.

The boy put his books into his backpack next to his chair and then turned to the other side to pick up his box of potential gear for his project. "And now this,"

He looked at all of the things he had collected while snooping around the campus. Most of it probably looked useless to the average person, but Alex was not average at all. His brain could come up with something epic to make out of everything here right now. *Exactly but . . .* He sighed. *It would have been cooler to have an actual lab to do this in.*

Back home, he had only been allowed to use the lab belonging to the sole veterinarian in his small town. *And that was for an hour anyway, so it barely counts.* His dad had begged the vet to let him tinker around with things in there so he could live his dreams of being a scientist, and surely enough, he had been allowed.

But that place had been pretty small scale. The lab at my old school was too, and I was only allowed in there during classes. It was a lot like now, wasn't it? *Only that I expected more from a place like this.* How was he in the highest-ranking school for STEM subjects and still not allowed to use his scientific creativity however and wherever he wanted. *I wonder if Dr Reymond is hiding something . . .*

Someone knocked on his door, and it pulled him out of his thoughts. What was that about?

The teenager hopped to his feet and walked up to it, and opened it. "Oh," his voice was flat when he saw who was standing outside.

Jun deserved that greeting, didn't he? "Give me props for finding your room?" he smiled half-heartedly.

Alex was actually pretty excited to see Jun here, clearly back for him- *well, I hope he is anyway*- but at the same time, he didn't want to give the guy his joy. Not after how he treated him in the halls earlier.

Jun watched as the younger boy rested his side against the door frame. "Listen, Alex I . . ." he caught sight of the box of junk. " . . . wanna help you."

Alex frowned. *Coulda swore that was leading to an apology.* "Wanna help me?" he turned to look into his room and saw the guy fixated on his box. "Why?" he narrowed his eyes while looking up at the jerk.

Jun walked in without Alex's permission.

"Hey, what the hell? You're a little too forward here, man. You can't just walk onto my property like this. I didn't give you permission. Have you forgotten that you're the one who doesn't like me and asked me to stay away from you for the rest of the school year?" he walked behind Jun after saying all of this angrily.

Jun was standing next to the desk, rummaging through the box. "I saw this, this, yes this,"

Alex had no idea where this enthusiasm was coming from. "Dude, with how you were acting earlier, I coulda sworn that you were only a few sentences away from calling me a total nerd," he folded his arms. "Why are you geeking out now? Ready to drop your cool guy act? When no one is around is when you're comfortable showing your true self, huh? Typical. Spare me the drama Jun. I've seen enough movies to know how the rest of this will go. You're gonna only wanna work with me behind closed doors because you actually like me but are too ashamed to admit it to everyone and while we're out in public, you're gonna make fun of me. I'm not an idiot, Jun. I watch TV. A lot of i- hey, that looks pretty good," while he had been ranting, Jun had been assembling something quickly. "Is that a mini insulator fan? You made this out of plastic bottle shards, a pencil and what? A rubber band? Right before my eyes?" his mind was blown.

Jun set it aside and started looking for more stuff. "That's just one piece of a much bigger appliance. I think that if we're dedicated enough and if we look for more junk, we'd be able to make our own remote control speed boat,"

"Wait, so this isn't an insulator?" Alex was holding it in his hand.

"I had it in mind as the propeller, but we can see where it fits as we work," Jun was making something else now.

Alex watched him in admiration for all of ten seconds before shaking his head. "Hey, but you pushed me away. What changed your mind? I have literally no idea what's happening right now, and you're not explaining,"

Jun sighed and then looked at him. "Look, I was wrong for pushing you away like that. I just . . . I came here with a mind that said all the students here were freaky geniuses-"

"Ouch. Wait, the joke's on you. You're a student here too, so meh," Alex stuck his tongue out.

Jun rolled his eyes. "I thought everyone here was freaky, so I wasn't interested in making friends, but you came along and . . ."

Alex was very attentive.

"You're . . . I wanna help you with this so you can win that science fair, okay?" Jun put his hands in the pockets of his grey sweatpants.

Alex felt like this guy had trouble expressing his feelings. *Humph. I'll let it slide for now.* "Why?"

Jun wished this kid would stop asking so many questions. "Because you actually talked to me on my first day."

Wow, improvement already. Alex smiled a little. "Well, I guess that makes sense."

"So, do you wanna make a speed boat or something else?" Jun shook the stuff he held in his hands.

Alex hummed in thought. "Let's make a speed boat that changes the colour of the water it moves on top of. That would look so cool!"

Jun did not expect that idea at all. "Wow uh . . . okay- what would be the point of that?"

"It's fun. What would be the point of making a speed boat? It's not like it's anything groundbreaking," Alex challenged him.

"You mainly see Science as something fun, don't you?"

"Yup," Alex looked into the box. "Although, as creative and ingenuitive as we both are, I don't think anything in here is gonna be able to help us with the trail of colour that I want our boat to leave,"

Jun thought about it too. "There might be something in the Chemistry lab," he frowned. "Didn't you want to use it for all this?"

Alex sighed as if heartbroken. "I did, and I even asked the principal, but the guy seemed to really not want anyone to use it outside of classes. It was almost like he was afraid. What does he think is gonna happen? We'll blow the whole place up?"

Jun found that interesting, but Alex had already told him that the principal was against such things. "Well, Alex," he set the stuff down and then placed a hand on Alex's shoulder.

The younger boy did not know what this was about. "What?"

Jun smirked. "You're the same one who skipped one of your classes to try to figure this thing out on your very first day at this new school,"

"Yeah, so? Who cares?" Alex was lost.

Jun rolled his eyes. "If you were ballsy enough to do that, then I think you can just use the Goddamned lab now and for the rest of the nights that you need it to work on this project,"

Alex gasped. "What? I can't do that. There are security cameras and night guards all over the place,"

Jun gave him a blunt look. "Yeah. And we're geniuses,"

Alex couldn't believe he had used the label. "Well yeah, but . . . I don't know."

"I actually think that a lab would be the best place to construct what we're making for real. And well, it's got supplies so we can gain more inspiration. It's not fair that you go to this high-tech school with all of its up-to-date gadgets and gizmos, and yet you have to use literal trash to do your science fair project," Jun picked up a rusty metal rod.

Alex cringed. "You kinda got the point for real actually . . ." he twisted his mouth and looked at his feet before sighing with hands on his hips. "Okay, uh . . ."

Jun was becoming eager to make something. He would make small inventions when he was a kid and had won quite a few science fairs at elementary and middle school but he kind of abandoned that side of him when he got to high school because of certain events that led him to be who he was today. But being with Alex and seeing his passion for invention was awakening that side of him again. No one he knew was here, so he could do as he pleased.

"Fine. I can't even try to resist. It may be risky, but it's also a challenge, and I'm up for those, so let's do it," Alex appeared pained, but he was actually very excited.

Jun wanted to grin, but he controlled himself. "Awesome,"

CHAPTER FOUR

"Hey Jun, we should make something else instead. I think a boat may be too basic," Alex whispered as they both walked on quiet feet towards the lab in the dark halls.

Jun was in front of Alex and using his phone flashlight to see where they were going. *It took a while, but Alex found a way to hack into the security system to replace the footage of now with the footage of last night so they can't see us.* And as for the night guards? They had distracted them with a fake break-in to get them away from this area. It had been fun working out how they would sneak into the lab. "All of a sudden, you wanna change our idea?" Jun asked as he approached the lab door.

"Yeah. Colourful boats are cool, but I wanted to make a robot. AI's are what impresses people nowadays. Maybe *that* can leave a trail of colours . . ." Alex seemed mesmerised as he walked in behind Jun.

Jun sighed while moving further into the room. *We also hacked into the automatic door system.* The doors were supposed to be closed shut, but Alex got this one to open for their little activity. *What time is it?* "What's with you and colours, though- use your laptop to shut the doors again," he had been carrying the box of junk, so he placed it on one of the desks once they were in.

"Oh yeah," Alex opened his laptop and held it in one hand to do his thing to get the doors to close. "They shoulda thought of this, honestly," he laughed as the doors shut behind them. "And, of course, the security system in here is disabled, so we can go wild," he grinned at the guy who managed to come around. *He likes me but doesn't wanna admit it.* Jun was one of those guys, wasn't he?

"Yeah, they really shoulda," Jun placed his phone on the desk and shone the flashlight upwards so the ceiling could bathe with light. It illuminated the room a bit, but it was still dark. "So what were you saying? Robot with colours?" this kid was something else, wasn't he?

Alex hopped onto one of the stools. "Yeah. I don't know how we'll incorporate the colours, but we can think of it later,"

Jun shook his head. "Let's just stick to one thing. You don't want a boat- wait. What if we made a boat, right? But the boat wasn't the star of the show because our project would be all about letting AIs do thighs for us. Not a revolutionary concept, but hear me out. The robot will be manning the speed boat," it just came to him, and he loved it.

Alex's mouth hung open before he frowned. "What's with you and speedboats?"

"What's with you and colours and robots?" Jun shoved it back in his face.

Alex groaned. "Okay, fine, we can do that,"

"What? You don't like it?"

"I do, I do. I think it'll blow people away. Now let me just . . . ah, this is a chemistry lab, so it won't have what we need. Shoot. Why did we think of a project based on engineering anyway?" Alex hopped off his stool.

Jun climbed off his too. "Because that field is cooler and . . . I think there might be stuff in here that can help us if we look around enough," he looked from one storeroom door towards the back of the class and then to the other at the front next to the touch screen board. "Hold on," he picked up his phone and started moving to the one up front.

"Hey, you're taking the light with you," Alex followed him.

They were both looking into the store room with the aid of Jun's flashlight.

Alex gulped. "It's . . . bigger on the inside than it looks on the outside,"

"Yeah . . ." Jun breathed. This was actually pretty creepy to him, but . . . "There are lots of shelves and drawers so we might be able to find something. Come on and use your own flashlight to search," he walked in boldly.

Alex did not like the vibe of this place. "Okay," they had to do what they had to do, though.

Jun was shining his light into a drawer of gears he had just opened. "I can use this," he smiled while looking at it.

Alex was more towards the back. He had not opened any drawers yet. He was looking for spare plastic or metal. "Maybe it would be . . . here?" he walked up to the very back and saw a bunch of old bags stacked upon each other. "Hmm . . ." he stretched to feel one, and it was hard. *It must be steel in there.* That could work.

So he tried pulling that bag out from under the others even though it was incredibly heavy.

Alex struggled for quite a while before the bag dragged out, and with it came the other bags tumbling. He screamed.

"Alex?" Jun heard the noise and walked further down to find him. "What happened?" he saw all the bags and shook his head. "You're making a mess. Now we have to . . ." he trailed off when he looked up and saw something.

Alex felt ashamed. "I know, but I just wasn't thinking straight at the moment. Of course, if I pulled this one, the others would come to do-"

"Alex . . ." Jun walked past him.

Alex blinked in confusion before turning around to see what he was moving towards. "What is- oh . . . huh?"

Jun was looking at a silver door. The fallen bags revealed it.

"What's behind it?" asked Alex in awe and confusion.

"I-I don't know," Jun felt a force drawing him towards it, but he decided to step back. "Okay, maybe we should just pack everything back and continue what we were doing-"

"Wait, wait, wait . . ." Alex walked up to the door and moved the remaining bags away from it.

Jun's eyes darted to the left before he kept watching. "Alex, there's probably something dangerous behind that."

"I know but . . . but what?" Alex was feeling the door with his hands. It was in full view now, and he could see that it had a handle. "'It's cold, so maybe at the back of this is a freezer,"

"Yeah, definitely, now let's go-"

Alex grabbed the door handle and pulled it down to open up.

Shit. Jun did not like where this was going, but Alex seemed really curious. "Let's just go back to our rooms. We can use the engineering lab next ti-"

And now Alex was pulling the door open.

Jun closed his eyes when dust flew out of it along with cold air.

Alex was squinting too. "When was the last time this had been opened?" he rubbed his eyes of dirt, and when they opened, he saw a dark room. "Huh . . ." was there nothing in here? The room was about the size of a large closet but was practically void of furniture. It had an eerie vibe to it because of this, and the cold environment did not help.

Jun was relieved but disappointed. *It's empty.* The inside still seemed pretty creepy, though. *But why have a silver door leading to an empty space?* "All of that for-"

"Wait," Alex spotted a curtain hanging on the back wall and, behind it, something glowing.

And now Jun was officially freaked out by this. "Alex, let's go back now," he said sternly.

"This must have been what he was so scared of. Oh . . . but what is it?" Alex was walking into the cold, dusty, dark room.

Jun face-palmed. Alex was doing everything that one was not supposed to do in a sci-fi horror movie. *Fine.* If the kid died, it would be on his head. Devon already knew he went to see Alex, so Jun needed to step up and provide protection. "Alex be careful," he followed the boy in.

Alex's eyes remained fixated on the glowing coming from behind the curtain. It was almost as if it was calling him, telling him that it could bring good into his world if he dared to find out what it was.

Jun was able to catch up to him quickly and hold his shoulder with a firm hand once the boy was close enough to the curtain.

Alex snapped out of his trance-like experience and then looked at Jun's hand. His eyes slowly went up to Jun after that, and the light from the glow was the only thing illuminating the guy's face. From what he could see, Jun was not into this.

"Do you really want to find out what's glowing behind that curtain?" Jun gestured to the room. "This place was locked off from the rest of the school, so whatever's glowing there is probably bad news," that was right. He needed to convince the younger boy to drop this like he had been trying to earlier. There was something in Jun himself saying to move the curtain so they could see what was causing the glow, but he fought with it in the name of his and Alex's safety. *It could be a night light, though.* Then why would it be in an isolated room behind a silver door and a curtain? *These curtains are creepy up close too.* They looked old and torn, dusty.

Alex gulped before facing the light once more. "I know, but . . . it wouldn't hurt to have a look at what Dr Reymond's been hiding-"

"Who says that what's behind that is what he's hiding? It could be something he's holding onto for the government," Jun gulped. "Which in that case means we should leave this alone even more,"

Alex shook Jun's hand off his shoulder and rolled his eyes. "Quit being a baby. I'm gonna take just a little peek, alright? I mean, it's right there, and nothing is happening, so simply moving the curtain won't hurt, would it?" he smiled at Jun.

Jun gave him a frown in return but eventually gave in. "Okay, but just one look and then we're outta here," he felt uneasy in this setting.

Alex was so happy he agreed. "Okay, on a count of three," he raised his hand to hold the end of the curtain. "One . . . two . . . three!" he moved it quickly and immediately sharpened his eyes to see what was hiding.

Jun looked, too, even though he had been against this. "What . . ."

"-is that?" Alex finished as he watched in awe.

The thing they were looking at was a floating black rock with grooves all over it that made it glow purple. It also had an unstable purple field around it that seemed to be there as a result of the grooves. It was also releasing sparks as it just stayed there, suspended in the air.

Jun gulped. That thing looked like trouble. "So . . . they just have this . . . rock here, and it's . . . floating?"

"And glowing," a million questions were racing through Alex's mind as he reached for the specimen. Why was it here? What was it? It did not look like anything from this planet. Had it come from a different galaxy? What were its components? Why was it floating?

"Hey!" Jun stopped him from touching the weird thing by dragging him back. "You said you wanted to look at it, and now you looked, so let's go," he held Alex by the arm and tried dragging him off.

"But Jun, it looks so cool!" Alex managed to pull his arm away. "Check it out!" he did a pose next to the rock with his hands open. The curtain had been placed behind it so Alex could get a good look.

Jun folded his arms and shook his head. "We don't know what that thing is, and neither of us should be here, so let's just go before something weird happens,"

Alex was not listening to him. He was watching the rock with a finger stroking his chin. "Perhaps a new element? No, it seems like earth, so- but rocks aren't black, and they don't glow. It just looks like a rock, but that doesn't mean that it is one," he hummed in thought before pulling a pen out of his pyjama pocket to poke it.

"Alex, I said don't touch!" What was wrong with this kid? Jun was so freaked out, but Alex was using this as an opportunity to play a scientist. "If it's here, then that means it's dangerous- oh my God," he stopped talking when Alex poked the thing with his pen.

Alex drew his stationary back after it made contact with the entity and waited.

Jun had been holding his breath for a moment as he examined the item in wait for what it would do, but when he realised that nothing was happening, he breathed again. "Okay, you've had your fun, poked around at the thingy, so now can we please go?"

Alex poked it again.

Jun cursed. "Alex, you're insane," he grabbed the back of the boy's shirt and started dragging him out behind him.

"Wait, but Jun, I was trying to get a feel of what sort of material it is!" Alex cried as he watched the rock get farther and farther away. Jun was really dragging him, wasn't he?

Jun's back was to the specimen, and he had no intention of looking back at it. "Oh well. You can dream about it tonight if you're that desperate. We gotta clean this place up and head back. After all of that, I am exhausted,"

Alex was about to argue with him about what he was doing, but before he could, he noticed the rock glitching a bit more. "Uh, Jun?"

"Nope. I'm not letting you keep poking that hell rock-"

"Jun, I think it's gonna blow up!"

"Huh?" Jun stopped the dragging from turning around. "Oh my God,"

Alex stood straighter and backed up.

The rock kept glitching and spazzing where it floated, causing sparks to fly out of it.

Jun backed up more. "Let's go," he said in a soft voice.

"What? We can't go now. We have to try to fix it. What if it-what if it blows up the whole school?" Alex was finally reacting appropriately by whining with fear in his voice.

"I don't . . . uh, what do you propose we do? Throw it out?" Jun's heart was racing, and he was more than terrified of what he was seeing. The glitches kept getting stronger, and more and more sparks burst out of it.

"I-I guess. I don't know, I just-" Alex got cut off when he saw full-on lasers start shooting out of that thing! "Ahh!"

Jun started dragging Alex out again so they could close the door and forget they ever saw that thing.

He kept looking over his shoulder as they neared the exit, and right as he did, he saw a laser blast coming straight for Alex, who was behind him!

It was like it happened in slow motion.

Jun looked from Alex to the fast-approaching blast and dragged the boy to stand behind him so that he would not feel the impact of the laser.

Alex barely had time to notice what Jun was doing before he saw the older guy gets hit by a purple laser and jolt violently with his body blinking in purple before he fell to the ground!

The glitching stopped after that.

Alex's ears had been filled with noises from the malfunctioning rock, but now all he could hear were his own breaths.

Jun was down. The only guy to give him the time of day at this school was lying on the ground, completely motionless.

"J-Jun?" Alex whimpered.

Jun did not budge.

Alex immediately started crying. That blast was from some unknown weird thing. Jun was dead! It killed him, and it was all Alex's fault. "Juuuun!" he got on his knees and started shaking the older guy. "You gotta get up, man. Please! I'm sorry. I shoulda left it . . ." he looked forward at the floating rock that looked *very* creepy now that he was the only conscious person in this dark, isolated part of the school.

He felt Jun's chest for a heartbeat after rolling him onto his back and was so glad when he detected one. *But he probably needs a hospital.* How would he explain what happened? *I'm gonna get expelled.*

His eyes welled up with tears, but he knew that it would only be right to get Jun help and explain the crisis that had befallen the two of them because of Alex.

"It's okay, man. You'll get through this, alright? I just . . . let me-"

Jun's eyes suddenly opened wide, and his iris was completely purple.

Alex had never gotten a fright quite like this one.

He jolted back and scooted away from Jun, wondering if he was now a zombie of some sort because of what that thing did. "J-Jun you-you . . ." he was panting as he backed away in fear.

Jun's eyes eventually closed a bit more, and they returned to normal.

Alex gulped. What was that?

Jun was now sitting up slowly, groggily. "Oh man,"

He sounds normal. Was Jun okay or not?

Jun held his head and turned to look at Alex.

Alex saw purple electricity pulsing around Jun for a bit before it stopped. "Jun . . . you okay?" he asked slowly.

"I . . . yeah, but man did that hurt," he held his head.

Alex did not like how he had awoken a while ago. "You don't feel different? Strange? Zombie-like?" he had to be careful here. That thing was creepy, so it may lead to creepy events.

Jun rolled his eyes and then climbed to his feet.

Alex stood too, inspecting Jun. "You sure you're okay? 'Cause, you woke up with purple eyes a while ago,"

"Purple eyes?" Jun scratched his head.

"Yeah, and there was purple electricity," Alex informed. "What do you think it means?"

"It means we need to get out of here," Jun stepped back and shut the big silver door.

"Wait, but . . ." Alex saw him packing the heavy bags back. "But something could have happened to you. You were all purple and . . . and it was weird,"

"I feel fine right now, so let's just ignore it. I think the electricity and stuff were just an after effect of the blast," Jun was tired of this. When he finished packing everything, he patted Alex's shoulder and walked briskly to the adjacent lab.

Alex was left confused for a second, but he shook his head to follow the older guy. "Maybe we should try running some tests-"

"No," that was all Jun had to say about that. "You and I are going to go back to our respective rooms and never speak of this again, okay?" he pointed at Alex's chest.

Alex wanted to argue, but he had caused enough trouble for Jun in one night, hadn't he? "Okay,"

"Good, now come on," Jun began walking with purpose to the exit. He was pretty freaked out by what Alex described had happened to him when he woke up, but he preferred not to worry about that since he felt okay, and he didn't want to remember being zapped by that stupid rock thing. *Dr Reymond, what the hell was that?* He had so many questions but would ask none since he wanted to stay true to his motto at this school. *Get in and get out.*

So Jun ignored the tingling sensation in the palm of his hands as he and Alex made their way back to their individual rooms.

CHAPTER FIVE

D r Reymond sat in his office over some paperwork the next
morning.

He had already had his morning coffee and had felt energised
enough to get started on all that he needed to do, but right now,
something on his mind was taking him over and preventing him
from getting anything done.

Being the principal and founder of one of the newest and yet
most prestigious high schools in the country had a lot that came with
it. There were always people looking to him and asking questions
about how he managed to develop what he did and what he hoped
for the future of his school and its students, but these questions and
statements and even the paperwork that he constantly needed to
complete were not the things on his mind that made him anxious
or distracted. They were actually meant to serve as distractions from
other thoughts and worries.

The man sat back in his seat and used one hand to stroke the area
under his nose, his expression serious. Some parents complained that
he was not as available as the principal of a high school should be,
especially when it came to new students, but they did not understand
that he was a man of many secrets. One of them was that he did not
see his role as principal of a school for exceptionally bright students
as his most important one.

And while founding this incredible school was something that
he had come up with himself and was very proud of, there was

still another matter that took precedence over the school's smooth sailing. His intentions were not to be misunderstood. He did care for each student attending this school, but the other role that he had given himself was direr than ensuring that each student here was doing their best. And that was because if he did not view it as urgent, lives could be lost.

His phone started ringing, and it snapped him out of his thoughts.

Dr Reymond picked it up and held it to his ear. "Yes, Carla?"

"Dave, the head of security is here. Says he needs to have a word with you,"

His eyes widened. "What about? Is it-"

"No, not that kind of word. Something else. I guess he'll explain when he comes in?"

Dr Reymond's shoulders fell for a moment. *So still no headway in finding him. Humph.* He shook off that disappointment. "Let him in. I'm not too busy right now, so we can talk, especially if it's urgent,"

"Alrighty then," the secretary hung up.

A moment later, the head of security was standing before his desk. He wore a navy blue cap, a polo shirt of the same colour and grey pants. But that was just his uniform.

"David, what is it that you'd like to talk to me about that isn't about tracking him down?" he asked while watching the man take a seat.

Dave exhaled. "Sorry if I got your hopes up by telling Carla to call an 'urgent' meeting. You probably thought we'd found something, huh?" he smiled awkwardly.

Dr Reymond shook his head. "No, it's fine. It's been years, but if we'd actually managed to track him down now, I'd still say it was too soon. Me and him weren't labelled some of the most exceptional scientists in our field for years for nothing. He would never hide in plain sight. For all I know, he could be in space,"

"Not too far-fetched based on the old experiments," Dave clasped his hands before him. "Listen, Doc, one of my guys noticed that the security system had been hacked last night,"

Dr Reymond raised an eyebrow. "*Our* security system?"

"Yes. It must have been someone pretty skilled with computers 'cause, as you know, we designed that thing to be unbreakable, but I guess that someone with a highly intelligent mind could figure out how to get past the fire walls if they were determined enough," Dave sounded disappointed. "And well, this is a school of geniuses, so I'm thinking that one of the kids on the higher end of the IQ scores might have done it,"

"But why?" Dr Reymond was quite confused by this. Students weren't usually interested in hacking into the school's programs. What could be the reason behind this?

"Beats me. It's pretty odd . . . maybe they wanted to get up to mischief after hours and didn't want anybody seeing? I mean, the main halls are on lockdown at night, so they must have wanted to roam about them or pick up something they left in class after hours. That's all I can think of," Dave's arms were resting on the armrests of his seat.

"Hmm . . . perhaps," Dr Reymond locked eyes with his head of security and old friend. Dave wasn't just a security guard here. He had helped him to develop all the state-of-the-art programs at this school, including the security system. They had also worked on the student portal, the school website, learning hubs, the school email system and much more.

"So what are you gonna do? Try to sniff out who might have been behind this, or just leave it alone?" Dave asked.

Dr Reymond was not sure of how to address this actually. On the one hand, the student who had done this might have gotten into serious trouble while the cameras had been off, while on the other hand, it could have just been what Dave suggested. Someone wanted to pick up something they left in class and was too uncomfortable approaching a teacher at night to help them, so they just quickly messed with the security system to get what they wanted and headed back to their room. "My students aren't typically malicious. Usually, all they want to do is learn and challenge themselves, so I doubt that it's anything to worry about," for some reason, the young boy who had requested permission to use the lab after hours came to mind. *Alex was his name.* He frowned for a moment as something occurred to him but then quickly dismissed that possibility since that boy had a squeaky clean record. *Ambition can drive people to do insane things, though.* He frowned as memories came to mind, and then the boy's face popped up after.

"Great, so just ignore it?" Dave was standing again.

Dr Reymond shook his head. Would it make sense to call that boy in for questioning regarding this? *I have too much to do. I doubt that he did anything.* "Yeah, leave it alone for now. If anything else happens and it seems related to that, then we'll have to investigate, but for now, I don't have the energy,"

Dave laughed briefly. "Why? Being a principal is more taxing than working full time as a scientist?"

Dr Reymond chuckled. "It's sad to say, but yes. I love it anyway,"

"Then that's all that matters," Dave started leaving.

"Take care, okay, David?" Dr Reymond waved a hand.

"Yeah, you too and . . ." Dave held onto the door as he stood in the doorway. "We'll find him soon. I can feel it,"

Dr Reymond was silent as he looked at him.

"And when we do . . . we'll shut down whatever dangerous experiment he's been working on for all these years,"

Dr Reymond exhaled. "That's the plan, isn't it?"

"It is . . ." Dave stared at nothing for a moment before saying goodbye and leaving.

Dr Reymond kept an elbow on his desk and a hand at his chin as he thought of the last time he had seen the person in question. The one who had been on his mind for years and years since everything happened. *Where are you, and what are you up to?*

JUN . . . WAS NOT SURE how he felt.

"So the test next week will be on these topics, and I know it seems a little early for testing, but I just want to make sure that all of you have been listening closely and have everything cemented in your heads. We've done a lot over the past few days, and I plan on finishing this chapter by Friday, so there'd be enough to be tested on next week for sure . . ." his chemistry teacher was speaking up front.

The clock showed that it was almost time for the bell to ring, so there were no more notes to write or type. The teacher was just speaking to them about the test they would be having soon.

He kept seeing flashes of memories of last night when he had gotten blasted, and while he slept, all he had dreamed of was that creepy glowing rock. It somehow consumed his mind, and there was no way for him to shake it. *Woke up in cold sweats this morning, and my hands still feel weird.* He wanted to ignore it so bad, but it was there and kind of interfering with his day. *And by that, I mean it's distracting.*

Alex had kept asking him if he was sure he was okay on their way to their dorms, and this morning the younger guy had found him in the hall to ask him how he felt too. The kid seemed pretty worried about Jun, but Jun himself preferred to ignore everything that happened last night. *I told Alex to ignore it, too, but I guess he can't.* He took a deep breath and released it before trying to write down what the teacher had been saying about tests.

His hands felt hot as he held his pencil, and he had to release it because he was sure that something had come out of them in the process.

Jun frowned at his pencil after letting it go and looked closely.

It seemed a little charred. *What?* He gulped while staring at his hands, but they appeared normal right now and felt that way too. What was that about?

"Hey," the person next to him whispered.

Jun blinked, then turned to his side. It was Chantalle.

"You okay?" She asked softly, occasionally glancing at his hands.

Jun set them on his desk and tried to act normal. *Am I really out here causing a scene?* He was not one to have people give him strange looks, so from now on, he would ignore everything even more. "Yeah, I'm fine," he said dismissively before staring at the teacher again.

"Okay . . ." Chantalle's voice seemed sceptical.

Jun heard a sizzling sound as he rested his hands on his desk, and he pulled away to look for what might be causing it.

Someone in front of him sniffed audibly and then turned around to check. "Is something burning?"

Jun saw part of his notebook messed up like his pencil was, but he refused to believe what might be happening.

The guy faced forward again since no one answered him, and the smell died down.

Chantalle kept staring at Jun as the end of the lesson went on.

Jun noticed her and felt a tad bit annoyed. Couldn't she mind her business?

The bell rang a minute later, and he was the first to pack up his things and go, wanting to head to the bathroom to hopefully wash his hands and inspect what might be going on closer. *If things start going crazy, I may need to talk to Alex.* His hands were heating up, and things were burning? What was that supposed to mean? *I better not be transforming into a fricken fireball.* He just was not in the mood for that kind of drama.

He got to the bathroom quickly and was glad it was empty.

Jun rushed up to the sinks and started washing his hands. He did not really know if this would help, but they kept heating up and somehow burning things, so maybe cooling them down would stop this?

He had been acting pretty calm back in class while things kept happening but now that he was alone, the panic was sinking in. He had been zapped by some weird glowing rock last night, and now his hands were burning things? That could mean so many different things. Either he was going to become engulfed in flames and die, or he was going to start shooting fire out of his palms like some kind of superhero in a comic book. *Crap.* Maybe if he was someone else, the thought would be appealing, but he was himself, and all he wanted to do was live a simple life quietly with his friends from back at his old school and whoever else he might meet and like along the way. Nowhere in his future plans was it written that he wanted to become a mutated weirdo with fire powers.

Jun turned the handle of the pipe while breathing heavily and then stared at his palms.

They looked normal and felt cold from all the water, so he supposed that was a good sign. *Yeah, things are probably back to normal, but I don't know when it'll start acting up again.* He swallowed harshly as his heart rate increased. What was going on? He was freaked out but didn't know what to do. *I gotta tell Alex, but what could he even do about this?* Why was that rock even in that room? Was that really why the principal didn't want anyone in the labs outside of class time? Were there other dangerous glowing rocks in the other labs? If so, then that was *definitely* a hazard. Why would the principal keep stuff like that at a school filled with curious science geeks?!

If things start getting weird again, I guess I could probably tell an authority figure, but me and Alex might get in trouble. They had not only disobeyed the principal but had also hacked into the security system. That would not look good on his permanent record. *Yeah, and hot hands won't look good either, so it might be best to just keep this a secret.* He took a deep breath as he stared at his palms and then walked with hands in his pockets towards the exit.

Jun walked through the halls with eyes out for Alex and with a heightened awareness of the temperature of his hands. He felt pretty anxious right now but hid it by whistling.

As he walked to his next class, he saw people occasionally glancing at him. Did he look weird?

The girl that he and his dad had seen outside of the office on his first day smiled and waved at him when he walked past her and his friends. They reminded him of cheerleaders. *Does this school have a cheer squad?*

He smiled and nodded at them, but the girl spoke to him as he took a step away from them, and he had to stop to listen.

"So are you coming to the meet and greet on Friday? It would be the perfect opportunity to get to know the people at this school. There'll be lots of performances, snacks and drinks. It's kind of like a school dance but on the football field and way more fun. Oh! We'll have music too, of course," her hair was blonde, and the ends of it were dyed pink.

"Oh wow . . ." Jun was not really interested, but this was the second time she was bringing this up to him, so he decided to just respond.

"You should definitely come. You're new here, right? And you're not a freshman? I think that a lot of girls will be interested in getting to know you, tall guy," the girl's friend rested an elbow on her shoulder and gave him a smart nod. She had light brown skin and curly hair that reached her shoulders.

"Uhh . . ." Jun was blushing like crazy as the other girls giggled. There were two more. "I don't know if-"

"Jun!"

Jun turned around and saw Alex speeding up to him.

Alex started panting once he was at his side.

The girls stared in confusion as the shorter boy struggled to catch his breath. "Are you okay?" the one with the pink ends asked. She sounded genuinely concerned.

Alex had been bent over, but he managed to catch his breath and stand taller. "Yeah, I just . . . I- oh," he became mute.

Jun felt him drag his face down to his ear.

"I didn't know you knew girls," Alex whispered in fear.

Jun frowned at him. "I don't. They were just inviting me to a thingy. Why do you sound terrified?" he whispered back.

The girls were staring at them.

Jun smiled awkwardly before facing the nervous Alex.

"Because I'm afraid of girls. They-they . . ." Alex shuddered.

Jun had heard it all. "Okay fine. If you wanna talk, we can do it over there next to that fountain, but we should make it quick 'cause class starts soon. We don't have much time,"

"Good idea," Alex stared at the girls blankly before grabbing Jun's hand and dragging him to the fountain in question.

Why'd he have to grab my hand like that? Jun felt like an idiot as they faced each other at a corner in the hall.

Alex appeared relieved. "Okay, no more girls, so I can speak-"

The bell rang.

Jun threw his hands up. "Guess we weren't fast enough, huh?" he tried walking away, but Alex pulled him back.

"No, Jun, this is serious," Alex's eyes darted from left to right as the halls cleared. "Has anything . . . you know . . . freaky happened since the um . . . incident?" he fluttered his fingers on the word 'freaky'.

Jun could feel that he would be late, but Alex was here, and stuff had been happening, so this was the best time to address this. "Yes,"

"Oh, good. I was worried that- wait, did you say yes?" Alex gasped. "What? Like what? What happened?" he was looking all over Jun for signs of mutation or illness. "Your eyes aren't purple or anything, and you seem to be feeling fine, so is it like-"

Jun showed him his palms which were becoming warm right at this moment. "They keep heating up. Last night I said nothing changed, but my hands had been tingly, and now it's way worse. I even charred my pencil in class. I have no idea what's happening, but I want it to stop. As we speak . . ." his hands were heating up immensely, but it didn't hurt.

Alex felt guilt clutch his heart. What if something bad happened to Jun because of his own curiosity? Jun had basically sacrificed himself for him last night. He didn't want anything to happen to the guy. "As we speak, what? Do you think your whole body might heat up like an intense fever?" he was whispering quickly.

"No, my hands are crazy hot right now, but somehow it doesn't affect me. I don't feel hurt or . . ." Jun was concerned by the temperature he was sensing. He stared at his palms.

"They're- *gasp*- dude, steam! Steam is coming out of your palms," Alex backed away with wide eyes and a hand over his mouth. What did this mean? "Oh my God, it's like in the comic books. You got super powers!" he whisper shouted.

Jun growled. "Don't say that, man this is serious. I'm terrified," it took a lot out of him to admit that, but the steam was new, and it was very frightening. "How do I turn it off? What is this?" he couldn't go to class like this.

"Maybe you should wash your- oh my God!" Alex raised his voice when both of Jun's palms erupted into thick black flames with purple outlines. It was like something out of a sci-fi movie.

Jun started screaming. "A-Alex, what do I do? What do I do? Aren't the cameras on?"

Alex gulped while looking up at one of the security cameras. They moved around all the time, and it just so happened that the one responsible for this corner was turned away. *Good.* He thought fast and yanked his water bottle out of his bag before dousing Jun's hands with water and then shoving the guy quickly to the nearest bathroom.

Jun was relieved when the fire disappeared, but it came back and was even bigger. "Holy crap! Crap! Crap! Alex!" he looked at the younger boy desperately.

"Can't you control it or something? Maybe it's like this because you're on edge?" Alex set his empty bottle on the bathroom counter while looking on in terror at the huge fire balls in his friend's hands. "What the hell was that thing!" he wanted to act fascinated, but at the same time, his fear was too much right now.

"I don't know, but it made me a total freak! Ah!" Jun ran to the sink to try to wash.

"No, that can't- you're gonna set the sink on fire!" just as the words left Alex's mouth, Jun did exactly that by holding the pipe handle.

Jun staggered back after this happened and fell onto his butt. He was panicking so much that he was not thinking straight and ended up touching the ground and letting the fire spread all over the floor.

"Shit! Shit!" Alex was filling his bottle at a different sink to try to put out the thick flames.

"Alex, what do I do!" Jun struggled to his feet and tried to step away from where the floor fire was spreading.

"I-I don't know! Maybe uh . . ." Alex filled his bottle and tossed water onto the sink fire and then the ground.

Smoke filled the air as some of it went out.

Jun wanted to help put out the flames, but his hands were still lit up! "Alex, throw some water on me, please!" The fire would probably reappear a bit after that was done, but Jun could think of no other way to solve their temporary problem.

"Y-yeah, I'll do that right now," Alex refilled his bottle and tossed the water onto Jun's hands, but absolutely nothing happened.

And now Jun was hyperventilating. "What the hell?"

"Maybe the source is too strong?" Alex didn't know what to do.

Jun backed up into the wall and stared at the strong flames on his hands. "So what? What does that mean?"

"Maybe uh . . . hey try flashing it off or something. Maybe it can come off, and then I can out it wherever it lands?" Alex was just spitballing here. He had no idea what was happening.

Jun fearfully started to flash his hands, and tiny fireballs ended up flying all over.

One narrowly missed hitting Alex, but he moved away in time.

This was not working as far as Jun could see. *No.* All he wanted was to be normal. He had already been chucked into a school classified as a freak show by everyone he knew, and now he was actually a literal freak? *No.* He worked so hard to be considered what he was today. Just a chill guy that people could have fun with, but now he was . . . "Why? Why? Is this happening!" he shouted and ended up blasting a massive wave of flames right through the bathroom door!

Alex had felt the heat of it as it happened, but now that it was over, the heat was gone.

Jun breathed heavily as he watched the huge hole he had left.

Not just the door had blown out. A lot of the wall had gone too. There was a trail of fire left in its wake, but Jun's hands were back to normal.

Alex stepped up to him and looked at the hole and all the fire. He whistled low as he watched some of it spread and wondered how they could explain this.

Jun felt all the heat of his hands completely gone. He didn't even have the tingling sensation. Was that it?

"So . . . should I try to put out those flames too or . . ." Alex heard the fire alarm go off and then saw water spraying from the ceiling ahead.

"That took care of itself so . . ." Jun turned to him. "We should head to class,"

"Yeah, we should. This never happened?" Alex asked.

"What do you mean?" Jun was already playing the role.

The two guys ran as fast as they could away from the scene. The fact that they would be the only people late to class when this happened may lead people to believe that they were behind it, but it was hard to pin black and purple flames on two high schoolers when there was absolutely no explanation on how they could have created them.

"Wait, wait," Alex stopped at the staircase where they would part. They were quite far from the flames, but people were peeking out of their classes to see what all the commotion was about.

Jun wanted to be as far from all the drama as he could. "What?"

"Dude, we need to talk about this like for real. Can we meet tonight to try to figure out what's going on with all this and try to stop it?" Alex asked as he stared at Jun's hands which were completely normal now.

Jun looked at the classroom he was supposed to be in. It was close to the staircase, and he saw the teacher coming out to see what caused the fire alarm to go off. Many students were leaving the class too. Fires were a big deal. He and Alex were wet from the sprinklers, though. "Okay. That's a good idea. Hopefully, if we put our heads together, we'll be able to come up with-" a teacher approached the two of them, and he felt like hiding.

"There's a fire? Where is it?" The man asked, wearing a frown.

"Holy crap!" they heard a voice down the hall exclaim.

Jun knew what that meant. They must have caught wind of his flames. "Yeah, we were both kinda slacking off when we heard the alarm start up, but we didn't see what happened. I think whoever yelled just now might know, though," he was trying to get the man to leave.

It worked. The teacher walked towards the noises of commotion coming from the distance.

Jun sighed with relief.

"Isn't there supposed to be some kind of protocol for all of this?" Alex scratched his head.

"Apparently not at this school," Jun saw the halls filling up more and more.

People were asking questions and trying to find the source of the flames. Teachers came out to try to put order to everything.

"Try to blend in with the crowd, alright?" Jun whispered to Alex.

"Oh yeah, yeah," Alex started looking around in wonder like everyone else was.

Jun joined him and, in doing so, caught Chantalle again. She was still staring. *Ugh. Why?*

She continued for a moment before looking away and disappearing among the other students.

Jun's shoulders fell once she vanished. Had she heard his thoughts just now? Did she sense his weariness towards her concern? She had indeed seemed concerned for him earlier, but he just didn't want attention on the weirdness going on with him. *I'm reading too much into this.* He kept acting confused by the situation with everyone else and awaited more instructions from teachers.

CHAPTER SIX

The incident ended up on the news.

"Do we even know where the fire came from? Why were the flames all black and purplish? Did an experiment go wrong in one of the labs?" the secretary was looking at the TV in the principal's office that night.

Dr Reymond sat on his desk as he stared at the screen. It was perched up on the wall to the left of his office. He stroked his chin as he watched the news anchor speak on the matter before it switched over to a student being interviewed. The kid looked really excited to share what she had seen, and a few friends of hers had the same reaction. This would not have caught the attention of news stations if his students hadn't posted pictures of the dying black flames on the internet. Many people had seen it and were given information on what happened to cause them all to come out of their classrooms to look. The only thing that had not been explained was how the flames got there in the first place.

"The fires were in the bathroom and outside of it. There's no way anything from the labs could have reached that far. It looked like an explosion happened in the bathroom, and blackish, purplish flames came out," Dave was here as well. They were the only people around this part of the school at this hour. The other teachers had gone to either their homes or to their sleeping quarters, but he was accustomed to staying late to have discussions with Dr Reymond.

Out of everyone who worked here, they had known each other the longest. The principal of the school trusted him most.

Second to him was the secretary, who had proven to be worthy of knowing all the doctor and his school's secrets after working with him for many years. She and Dave were the only ones who knew all the history.

"But what caused it? The colour seems concerning," the secretary's name was Carla, and she was in her mid-forties. Her hair was blonde and reached her shoulders, and one could always find her wearing black glasses along with whatever outfit she chose. She was tall and had a voluptuous body that she often covered in large dress pants and big suit jackets. It was rare that she would ever be found in a skirt. That just was not her style.

"Indeed it is," Dr Reymond was terrified inside but trying his best to hide it. "How many stations came to the school to report on this during lunch?"

"About four, so not too many. I don't think the school's reputation will be harmed, but people are talking," Dave shook his head and then turned to Dr Reymond. "But they'll talk regardless," his face became serious. "What we need to do right now is find out what caused those flames and do something about it because if it has anything to do with you know what in that lab, then we're in big trouble,"

"I'm certain that it has everything to do with that but what I'd like to know is how it caused an issue in the bathroom of all places," Dr Reymond groaned softly. "The cameras had been tampered with last night, and now this. What if it wasn't a student retrieving an item from class? What if he came back for it?" He had been thinking of Alex Johnson earlier, but now his fear was taking over and forcing his mind to imagine the worst-case scenario.

"Cameras tampered with?" Carla was confused. "What are you talking about?"

Dave sighed. "Someone hacked into the security system last night, but we thought it was just a student,"

"What?" Carla's arms were folded as she asked this loudly. "You brushed something as serious as that off as just a student?"

"It made sense to come to that conclusion at the time but now . . ." the principal brushed a hand down his face. "Why would he come now of all times?"

"We should be checking to see if it's still there, not sitting in here asking about why he would do x,y and z." Carla's head whipped to the door momentarily before she faced the principal again. "Am I being insane, or are you guys just taking this too lightly?"

"I know it looks as if he might be behind this and that he's trying to get Dr Reymond's attention or sabotaging him, but I have a feeling that this isn't his doing," Dave sounded sure.

"Then who else would be behind all this?" Carla gestured to the TV screen.

"I don't know, but what happened with the fire today felt clumsy. If he was going to come back to rub something in Christopher's face or to make a statement, then he would do it better than that. Plus, why come back after all these years and attack a school bathroom? We've been tracking this guy for years and haven't found him. If he's still interested in Christopher, then when he shows his face again, he'll be clever about it," Dave said certainly.

Carla sighed. "Again, so who do you think could be behind this?"

"He said it felt clumsy . . ." Dr Reymond looked from Carla to Dave. "Maybe we were right about a student being behind this?" And now Alex Johnson was back in his head. *But he isn't mischievous . . .*

Carla was about to speak up again, but she paused to think. "Hmm . . . you think a student found it and ended up using it to do that?"

"I have no idea, but it makes more sense than James coming back just to start a fire in a bathroom," Dave shrugged slowly. "What do you say?" he directed the question towards the principal.

Dr Reymond did not like this. "A student tampering with something that dangerous," he saw flashes of the night he found his son as a pile of ashes in that glass chamber. The realization that what he and his partner had been working on for years was not something that would help humanity but destroy it had been soul-crushing, but he needed to see the dangers that came with tampering with the unknown for himself, so he could learn to stay away from it. "We need to find who found it and talk to them," he wanted to just tell the others who he suspected, but he had no evidence other than their conversation of yesterday. Was that enough?

"Yes, but first, we definitely need to hide it somewhere else or change the lock on the door. The only way they could have stumbled upon it would be if the lock broke, right? It's been years since we changed it," Dave brushed a hand through his hair. "We could be looking at a lawsuit here,"

"Wouldn't a kid have freaked out over finding it a bit more? The students have been quiet, and . . . what if the student still has it if they do? How else would those fires have appeared?" Carla scratched her head.

"I don't know. Maybe they do have it, or maybe it changed something in them," Reymond hummed softly with eyes on his lap. "When my son was lost, he didn't get taken away because it burned him to dust,"

Carla and Dave were silent.

"That happened because that thing changed his matter into dust when he held onto it. That's what it does. We had tried for years to get it to change certain aspects of the human body so that it could improve us, but we did not know just how unstable it truly was. And that was why that happened . . ." Reymond dreamed about it every night to this day. If only he had been a better father. "Perhaps someone found it, got curious, held onto it, and it changed something about them too. And that change brought about the fire,"

The office was even quieter now that Reymond had finished speaking.

Dave walked to the exit. "I'm going to check on it and then change the lock on the door. You two can discuss how we'll find out who got in and messed with it while I'm gone," and with that, he left the room.

DR REYMOND AND HIS allies were not the only people watching the news that night. No. Not in the slightest. Among the thousands of people within the same location as the school who tuned in was also a much more intimidating character.

"Yup, those definitely look like mine," a young girl said to his right. Her arms were folded. They were in a dark room which played the news on a gigantic screen behind a panel.

"Guess you're not so special, huh?" a boy towards her right said.

The girl stretched over him to punch him, and he made a brief noise of pain.

"Don't squabble in front of me. Remember the rules?" he said slowly from his seat.

"Right, sorry," they said at the same time.

He made a tsking sound and shook his head.

"So what do you think we should do? Think it's finally time to show the world what you've been hiding?" the boy asked.

"Mmm . . . not entirely," the man was quiet for a moment. "I just think that whoever made those flames needs to be put out. Them and the orb that he kept all these years. We can't have more people like you two out there, and we certainly can't have another space rock either. Otherwise, people simply won't be as impressed when I show you two to the world,"

"So what?" the girl said.

He looked away from the screen to stare at her.

She felt him touch her cheek gently.

He patted it and then pulled back while smirking at the screen. "You kids are going to school,"

JUN HELD HIS HANDS out for Alex to see that night. He was sitting at the edge of his bed while Alex stood in front of him, inspecting his palms.

"Hmm . . ." the younger boy hummed with a curled finger under his chin.

Jun found this pointless. "I highly doubt that you'd be able to see what's causing this with just your eyes,"

"I know, but I'm trying to pinpoint any visible changes that there might be about you," Alex suddenly held Jun's face and pushed his head back so he could look into the guy's eyes.

Jun found this weird. "I called you here to discuss what we should do about this. In fact, it was your idea. Why are you staring me down?"

"Because I don't have access to equipment that will let me see what's going on inside of you," Alex stopped what he was doing to fold his arms.

Jun was glad that his hands were off his body. *That sounded weird.* He shook it off. "All I can say is that the tingly heat I felt at my palms is gone now, so I guess that's a good sign?" and now he was staring at his own hands. "Maybe what happened in the bathroom earlier was just a temporary side effect," he could not be sure.

Alex was pacing. "I don't know. It felt pretty permanent to me," he stopped and pointed at Jun. "Maybe you just ran out of juice. Do you feel tired right now? Winded?"

Jun sighed. "No. The most I feel is worried that it'll come back and ruin everything," he saw himself being taken away to some research facility and the whole thing being broadcast on the news. News anchors had come to their school today because of his meltdown in the bathroom, so they would definitely show up if he got taken away. *And everyone back home would see.* He swallowed thickly at the thought of being perceived as an even bigger freak than the people he was being forced to go to school with.

"Whoa, your hands are sparking," Alex stepped back.

"What?" Jun saw purple sparks erupting from his hands for real. "Oh my God. Wh-what do I d-"

"What were you thinking of? You were good the whole time. What triggered this?" Alex was fascinated. "What's your power, though? Is it fire or electricity?"

"F-fire? I mean, when it comes right down to it, electricity is kind of like fire, too," Jun waved his hands to try to get it to stop.

"What do you think caused this? You were pretty quiet a while ago; were you focusing?" Alex was still keeping his distance in case things exploded.

"No, I was just thinking of what would happen if I got taken to a facility, and then you said you saw sparks. I don't know," Jun needed this to stop now.

Alex frowned. "And what were you thinking of when you let out that huge blast?"

Jun gave him an irritated look. "I was freaking out; wait," he paused, observed his hands and then took a deep breath.

Alex watched as the sparks started dying.

Jun thought of leaving this place and hanging out with his friends at the beach. Things felt much less heated after that. He breathed in deeply once more and then opened his eyes. The sparks were gone.

Alex was silent for all of ten seconds before squealing. "We made a breakthrough! The firepower activation relies on your emotions for now. Well, mainly anxiety? I don't know, but this is cool. It's like you're a superhero learning how to use his powers," he grinned at the guy he had managed to make friends with during his first week here.

Jun was not as excited as Alex. "No, I am *not* like a superhero," he folded his arms. "I'm a guy who got unlucky, and that's all there is to it,"

"Oh, come on. Don't be like that. Hey, we could use your powers for the science fair. Heck, maybe *you* could be the science fair project," Alex wriggled his brows.

Jun could not believe that he had proposed that. "No. Why would I want to be someone's science fair project? Don't be stupid, Alex. Plus, it wouldn't be fair to the other people in the contest. We didn't do anything for me to end up like this. I mean, apart from being somewhere we weren't supposed to be, but other than that, all I did was get zapped by some creepy glowing rock," he twisted up his face in confusion. "Again, where did that thing even come from?"

"I don't know, but it does make me curious. Hmm . . ." Alex tapped his chin as he moved closer to Jun.

Jun placed his hands in the pockets of his pyjama bottoms. It was around nine p.m. They had finished their homework before having this meeting. "Why was that thing there? Should we ask Dr Reymond?"

Alex sighed. "We can't. We'd get in trouble, remember? We weren't supposed to be there when we were,"

"Right, right." Jun rubbed a hand down his face. "Clearly, what we need to do is find a way for me to get rid of whatever that thing did to me, so nothing like what happened today ever happens again,"

Alex agreed. "Yeah, and along the way, maybe we can also try to figure out what that rock is? Maybe?" he asked carefully, shyly. He was tapping his forefingers together while smiling at Jun.

Jun's face was still. "Hey, it was in that freezer or whatever for one reason and one reason only: so no one would find it. So the minute we get rid of my mutation, we're just gonna pretend that we never saw anything down there, okay?"

Alex groaned. "Fine, but the staff might be onto us. I mean, people saw black flames, dude. They're gonna wanna investigate,"

Jun had not even considered that. "We did a good job at acting natural, but it would only be a matter of time before they figure out that we were probably the only students out of class at that time, so yeah. But as long as we have a good cover story, they won't think it's us, right?" he went to the seat at his desk and sat down.

Alex followed him to stand nearby. "Yeah, I guess so, but . . ." he was getting an off feeling about all this. "What if simply working on the way to get rid of your powers-"

"Mutation,"

"Man, you are no fun," Alex rolled his eyes. "Fine. What if getting rid of your 'mutation' won't be enough?" he pointed a thumb towards Jun's closed door. "That thing that we found next to the lab surely wasn't something from this world Jun. We don't have glowy, floating, zappy rocks," he shuddered. "As cool as it was, the fact that it exists and is at this school probably means trouble. Who is Dr Reymond hiding it from if he even knows it's there? And if he doesn't, whose is it? *What* is it? Are bad people after it? Your fire was on the news. What if the bad people saw and now they wanna come for you?" he sounded full-blown, panicked by the end.

Jun told him to breathe.

Alex tried, but it was hard to calm down. "I'd really like to take the time to just look into that rock, but at the same time . . . the fact that it's down there doesn't sit right with me," he gestured to Jun with a lazy arm. "And now you've been . . . mutated, so I don't know. For all we know, aliens could be after it,"

Jun picked up a pen from his desk and started clicking it over and over again. "I'd say you're being ridiculous, but we found a floating zappy rock, and it gave me the ability to shoot fire out of my palms, so at this point, anything is possible," he tossed the pen away, then looked into Alex's eyes. They were green. "Do you really think you'd be able to fix this?" he would say that he could get rid of the 'powers' himself, but he had no idea where to start. "You'd need a whole lot of equipment to look into this, won't you?"

Alex sighed. "Yeah, I would," he opened his arms. "But this school is a wonderland for such things, so that shouldn't be too hard, right?"

Jun felt a tad bit hopeless. He would just tell an adult, but he was sure that their grand solution would be to send him off to a lab somewhere. "We'll figure something out,"

"Exactly," Alex could see that this was getting Jun pretty down. *And he's like this because of me, so I owe it to him to help.* "Don't worry, man; I'll do whatever I can to get you back to normal so we can forget everything and focus on the science fair, okay?"

"The science fair . . . of course," Jun looked at the small clock on his desk.

Alex saw it too. "It's getting late, huh?"

Jun nodded, then got up to go to his bed. "Tomorrow, we can start trying to see if there's anything in any of the labs that can scan someone's body,"

"Like a CAT scan? I think we have that somewhere based on the brochures," Alex rubbed under his chin while walking to Jun's door.

"That and maybe something else? I think people would notice if we used that. Maybe we can make something?" Jun picked up his phone from his pillow and opened it. His old class group chat was buzzing, and he wanted to know why. *I usually feel a bit distanced from them regularly but now . . .* it was like he was on another planet. He really wasn't like them, was he? Even though he longed to be, and they welcomed him in. *They don't know about what's changed, and they never knew about who I was before either.*

"We can try, I guess. Yeah, we can try." Alex turned the knob. "Anyway, try to rest and stay calm, okay? It's all gonna work out, Jun. Put your trust in Dr Lex," he pointed to his own face before waving and leaving.

Jun waved after the door was closed and then sighed. He brushed a hand against the area at his left as he thought about how much had changed in just a few days. *Stay calm.* How could he when his life had been flipped over yesterday? *Whatever.*

He eventually got to bed and lay on his side, thinking about all the fun his old classmates must be having. *Meanwhile, I've become a mutant.* What was this? The X-men?

The faces of those girls in the hall suddenly filled his mind, and he also thought of the event on Friday that they wanted everybody to come to. Should he go? *It might be a good way to unwind, but I don't know if I'd be able to enjoy it.* He would have to think about it.

CHAPTER SEVEN

Jun's weird 'powers' hadn't acted up all day.

The bell rang for lunch, and he walked out of English class with hands in his pockets to head to the cafeteria. He and Alex were planning to meet there before they snuck off to look for some stuff to put together to scan his body. *I wanna think that it's miraculously gone, but I don't know. Things aren't usually that easy.* He was trying to stay calm like Alex had said and had been pretty much that way since relaxing himself last night, so that was probably why nothing had happened yet.

I don't know how we'll pull this off, though. Was there a way to reverse what happened, or were they going to end up running into a dead-end trying to figure this out? It was one thing for them to come up with an impressive science fair project but a completely different thing to undo the effects of a glowing rock that probably wasn't something of their planet. They were dealing with unexplored phenomena here. *Unexplored as far as we know, at least.* Even though he was upset about getting powers and worried about what it meant for him, somehow, the number one question that kept running through his mind had been 'why was that rock down there in the first place?'.

Jun had been looking at his feet as he walked up to the entrance of the cafeteria, and because of not looking where he was going, he ended up bumping into someone.

"Hey, watch it- oh, it's you,"

Jun rolled his eyes at the sound of Devon's voice. "You still go here?" he had not been seeing him around. *So much has happened, and it's only the first week.* It had been only a day since he last spoke to this guy anyway. But it felt like more since life itself had changed for him so much just yesterday.

Devon folded his arms. "Of course I do . . ." he eyed Jun.

Jun was not in the mood for whatever attempt at bullying him; this guy would try. What he had learned through living on both sides of high school was that all bullies were the same. If he didn't react to him or treat him like the fool he was, then Devon would eventually lose interest. *He can't be an idiot if he goes here, though.* Or maybe his parents were wealthy?

"What?" Jun asked after noticing that the guy was staring at him for uncomfortably long. They were still at the entrance. It was really wide, so their standing around did not mean that they were blocking the way, but Jun would still prefer if they moved to the side or something. *No, I'd prefer if he stopped staring.* What did this guy want? Jun needed to find Alex so they could get this over with.

"Do you have anything to do with the fire that happened yesterday?"

The hairs on Jun's neck stood up as he looked at Devon with wide eyes.

Devon's eyes were narrowed.

Jun cursed in his mind, then let his eyes return to normal. "What?" he asked as if Devon was asking him something stupid.

"Don't act like I'm being a weirdo," Devon told him. "You were looking for that nerd the other night for some reason, and then the next day, a fire happens?"

Jun wondered if he realised how ridiculous that sounded. "How on earth are those two things related in any way, shape or form?"

Devon scratched his head. "I-it made sense in my head. I mean, that was the only thing that was different about everything before the fire happened, so I have them written down as correlated. I-I just need more evidence to show how they're directly correlated, but I'm not an idiot for linking them,"

Jun actually found him pretty observant to link those two things, but he would not give Devon that validation. "Have you been trying to figure out what caused the fire or something?"

"Uh yeah. It's what everyone is talking about, and I like solving challenging mysteries, so I started working on this one," Devon admitted.

"Hmm . . . well, keep working on it 'cause me and Alex have absolutely nothing to do with whatever weird thing caused that fire," Jun patted his chest before walking further into the massive cafeteria.

"Hey, I saw the way your eyes popped out!" Devon cried behind him.

Jun walked faster so he would eventually become lost in the crowds of students.

Devon held onto the ends of his blazer sleeves before shaking his head and walking off. He knew there was something there. He just knew it. He was not crazy.

Jun found Alex sitting on the floor against a wall towards the back and sighed as he moved up to him.

Alex spotted Jun when he was a few feet away, so he waved. "Hey, you're here," he picked up a cup of pudding from his trey. "Want some? The food here is great, I tell ya."

Jun sighed and sat at his side. He looked at the chocolate pudding and decided to just have it. "We need to start looking for stuff quick, but we'll probably need to disable the security cameras in the labs first,"

"Oh yeah, the cameras. Shit." Alex watched as Jun ate his pudding. *I said he could have 'some', but I guess he interpreted that different than what I actually meant, but it's okay. No hard feelings.* He owed Jun, so he would let him do as he pleased. "You know, while hacking into them the day before yesterday and letting them play false footage, I kinda sorta noticed that there would be a way for the school's security to see that we did that, so um . . . the security team at this school probably knows about what we did but just not who we are," he said this slowly with guilt in his voice.

Jun stared at him quietly for all of ten seconds before groaning. "Okay, so definitely, if we snoop around again and hack into the cameras before we do so, then they'd notice a trend, right?"

"Yeah, but maybe we could erase the footage once we're done? That could work, right?" Alex tried to be optimistic.

Jun rested the back of his head on the wall before frowning at Alex. "Why on earth are you sitting here on the floor? There are literally empty seats right there," he pointed them out.

Alex gulped. "I'm not used to having my own seat at lunch,"

Jun blinked. "But there are seats available, so why not use them? You prefer the floor?"

Alex shrugged mutely.

Jun exhaled before looking forward.

There were a lot of students walking around, coming in to find a seat after getting their lunch and others sitting already.

Jun noticed someone in the distance who seemed to be walking right up to them, and he wondered who it was for a little. *Wait.* He made out the locks and complexion once she was close enough and gulped. *Chantalle.* Why was she approaching them now? He had felt like she was onto them since yesterday but now this kind of confirmed it. *And Devon is too. Shoot.* Maybe she would swerve soon.

She did not. She stopped walking right in front of the two of them and looked down at Jun.

Alex felt the presence of someone else before him, so he looked up. He turned to Jun, who the girl was staring at and then looked back up at her while gulping. The girls were really scary. "Uh, do you wanna talk to him or something?"

Chantalle shook her head. "What's going on?" she asked in a straightforward voice.

Jun started sweating. "What do you mean what's going on?" he decided to play clueless so she would go away. "We're having lunch,"

Alex nodded without a word, hoping she would go away now.

She stayed. "You know that that's not what I'm talking about," her arms folded.

Jun shrugged. "Well, I don't know what you're talking about then,"

Alex was so lost. "Did you do something to make her mad?" he whispered.

"No. She's just being weird," Jun looked away from her with the hopes that she would just leave.

But she didn't. Chantalle instead lowered herself so that she could be face to face with him and then spoke very softly. "I know that you caused the fire yesterday,"

Jun stared into her stoic eyes intently.

Alex felt caught. How would she know that?

Jun huffed. "If you think that I'm the reason for those black and purple flames, then you're crazy. How could I have possibly caused that? What? An experiment gone wrong?" he laughed to sell it and nudged Alex so the kid would laugh too.

"Ow- I mean. Ha ha ha. An experiment gone wrong. Ridiculous," Alex was even more scared because this girl seemed pretty sure of herself. *What do we do if she knows? Will she tell? Blackmail us? Ah!*

Chantalle seemed unamused. She looked slowly from left to right before meeting Jun's eyes again. "It hit you too, didn't it?"

Jun stopped the fake laughing once he heard this. "What?"

Alex was surprised by what she said as well. "Wh-what do you mean?" what did she know?

"You got zapped?"

Jun's face slowly went from confused to frightened. "I . . . you asked if it hit me 'too'. What does the 'too' mean?" he would not confirm anything until he knew for sure she could be trusted.

Chantalle stood straight again, then rolled her eyes. She then pointed to her chest. "Me. It zapped me before you," she was whispering.

Alex gasped, then turned to Jun.

Jun's eyes were as wide as his.

They both looked at Chantalle after this.

She did not share their stun, of course. "Come," she started walking towards the back cafeteria door next to them.

Jun did not know what to make of this, but all he knew was that he felt less alone.

Alex was the first of them to get up and run after her, curious to see what getting zapped by that thing meant for that girl. *And when did she get zapped?* Did other kids at this school get zapped as well? What was this? He was curious but also scared.

Jun got up slowly and then followed the two of them, wondering where things would go from here.

THEY WERE NOW UNDER a tree next to a concrete bench several feet away from the cafeteria.

"Okay, before we start discussing this more, I think that it's important that we all confirm that we're on the same page," Alex started as he and Jun faced the girl with the locks. He was scared of girls in general, so he obviously felt nervous around her but had to try to hide it because this was serious. *At least she's not a girl in a clique.* She seemed to be a loner. Girls who kept to themselves could be equally as terrifying as those who had a squad, but he felt a little safer around her than the girls of yesterday who had been speaking to Jun. *Even though she's kinda intimidating.* But he was too curious about this to let that stop him from finding out more.

Chantalle groaned. "Didn't we do that in the cafeteria? What? Do you think that me getting zapped could be a reference to anything *but* the glowy thingy in the back room of the first floor's chemistry lab?"

Alex gasped and staggered back before whipping his head in Jun's direction. "She *is* on the same page as us!"

Jun did not understand. "Wait, wait, wait, wait . . ." he waved his arms then pointed at her. "*You* got zapped by that thing too?"

Chantalle appeared wary of them. "Yes. I told you like five seconds ago. Why are you still asking?"

"But how? When? How did you get there? Y-you, don't look strong enough to move all the bags of steel that were blocking the door. Wh-what were you *doing* back there? What did it do to you? I-uh....!" Alex could barely comprehend this.

Chantalle shook her head and then looked around to ensure that no one was listening. She faced the guys after doing so, her arms folded. "Before you both came to this school, *I* happened to stumble upon that thing myself,"

"When? How did it happen?" Alex had his phone out, ready to take notes. "If you just happened to find it too, then doesn't that mean that other kids might have done the same thing?" he whistled. "Old man Dr Reymond's gotta find a better way to conceal his dangerous entities, am I right?" he laughed even though this was all frightening.

Chantalle rolled her eyes. "The way that I found it wasn't exactly just finding it by accident, though. So I guess I shouldn't have used the words 'stumble upon,'" she made quotation fingers.

"Wait, had you been looking for it? Did you know it was there?" Jun wanted to know exactly what happened.

"No. How would I know about some floating space rock being kept in the back of a lab?" Chantalle began to explain. "I'd gotten detention for smacking a guy during class 'cause he pulled on one of my locks, and the punishment the teacher gave me was to clean up the lab after we did a pretty messy experiment. I mean, the place is high-tech enough that it cleans itself, but just for punishment's sake, you know?" she could see that they were both hanging onto each of her words. "So I was there after classes had ended, by myself, cleaning up, and while I was doing that, I'd been listening to music," her eyes averted. "It was good music, so I kinda got into it and started dancing around, and in the process, some stuff fell out of my pocket, and one of them was a bead that I'd had in there, and it rolled all the way into the store room at the front of the class, and I went after it," she looked at them again. "You know how beads are. It rolled all the way to the back of the storeroom, which I noticed was way too wide to be normal, and the place it landed was in front of those bags of steel."

Jun was nodding slowly. "And then what? You just decided to look at what was behind the bags?"

"No. I picked up my bead and put it in my pocket after standing straight again, but in the process, I caught a glimpse of the silver door between two of the bags.

"Whoa . . ." Alex hit Jun. "Maybe if we'd been there during the day, we would've seen it too,"

"Or maybe I'm just super observant. It was really by chance that I caught it. I just happened to get a glimpse of the silver in the tight space between two big bags. The average person would *not* catch that. Trust me, if they could, then everyone in this school would have gotten zapped," Chantalle continued her story. "Anyway, I'm a scientist, so, obviously I got curious and started moving the bags, and then I saw this silver door, and it was fascinating as heck, so I tried to turn the handle to get in, but it was hard at first . . . until something cracked as I kept trying and it opened up and . . . there it was," she folded her lips and nodded slowly.

Jun brushed a hand over his head. "And then it just zapped you?"

"Was it behind that old curtain?" Alex asked while swaying a little with one arm folded and the other perched on top of it. He stroked his chin with his hand.

"Uh . . . no. It was just floating in the middle of the room, and I got super excited, so I approached and started observing; back then, I guess I had a bit less self-control, so I reached to grab it, and all hell broke loose after that. There was zapping and electricity, and the air around me felt like it was shaking, so of course, I got caught in the crossfire, and I ended up getting hurt and shaking, but I survived, and once I came to, I hightailed it out of there as soon as I could," Chantalle seemed relieved to have told someone.

"And this happened . . ." Jun said slowly.

"Last year," Chantalle moved one of her locks to the back of her ear. It was in a ponytail, but two strands hung at the left side of her face.

"With the way you were talking, it sounded like it might have happened a long time ago. Hmm . . ." Alex tapped his lips with a finger, then used the same finger to point at her. "And you got no side effects? Did anything happen? I mean, you knew that the fire was Jun's doing so-"

"I don't know what that thing was, but after it zapped me, I developed telekinetic abilities," Chantalle looked at her palm. "At first, it had been going haywire, and I nearly destroyed my own room, but after a while, I learned to control it better and not have it directly linked to my emotions like it was at first,"

Jun frowned just as Alex said, 'cool'. "You learned to control it? Do you use it often? How strong can it get?"

Chantalle placed her hands in her blazer pockets. "It can get pretty chaotic if I want it to, but I mainly just use it when I'm alone and too lazy to get up,"

"Wow. So you have powers, and you didn't tell anyone? Don't you want to get rid of them? Isn't it like . . . weird?" Alex wanted her to demonstrate.

"I was too scared that I'd be experimented on if I told people, so yeah, I kept it to myself," she sounded pretty calm about the whole thing. "And as for if I wanna get rid of them?" she locked eyes with Jun.

Jun felt kind of tingly when she did that, and he didn't know why. "Do you?"

She exhaled, then folded her arms and stared at the sky. "At first, I tried all sorts of things to reverse what happened, and of course, I did tests to find out exactly what changed in the process, but I wasn't able to get anything done in the end, so I've just decided to live with it. It isn't killing me, so as long as no one knows, things should be fine, right?"

"Hmm . . . right, right . . . wait, you did tests?" Alex asked.

Jun was interested in this too. "Did you find out what actually changed? How did you do it?" Maybe she could help them.

"I asked all the science teachers if I could use stuff in the labs for my 'science fair project'- even though I don't give a damn about that end-of-year activity- and they allowed me to, and I used everything I gathered to build a mini body scanner. It looked like a glue gun, but once I hovered it from my head to my toes, I was able to pull up what was happening in my body on my computer. I'm making it sound simple, but this thing took me months to create and was the most challenging piece of equipment I have ever put together," Chantalle sounded exhausted just talking about it.

"Wait, so like . . . does it scan your body on a cellular level? What body system does it display? Skeletal? Muscular? Organs? Nervous system?" Jun was very, *very* impressed by her. *I shouldn't be. Everyone here is a genius in their own right.* He looked down at Alex, who seemed to be in love. *Oh, now he's not afraid of girls.* He rolled his eyes even though this was kind of cute to him. *The day I admit that out loud is the day I will agree to die.*

"Everything but the skeletal system, but after doing my own blood tests and looking at how the systems I had access to were affected when I used my powers, I was able to pinpoint the one that got interfered with," Chantalle explained. "It's my nervous system. The brain obviously has a huge role to play in telekinesis, so it wasn't much of a surprise. But my muscles were also operating at a much higher level as well. I think that it overall improved my health too. I don't know. It's like . . ." she seemed to be trying to find the right words to use. "What it did was heighten my bodily functions so much that I became an enhanced human. But for some reason, my brain was the thing most improved to the point where I stumbled into the abnormal territory. Super territory. It looked to me as if maybe if I was zapped again, it might have done a bit too much, and I might have perished, but that's just a theory. I'm not sure. I don't know what it is, but it did change something in me. It heightened my bodily functions, but . . . I don't know. I would experiment on it by itself, but I'm too scared to go near that thing again,"

Alex had never met a girl so cool and smart. Did she have a boyfriend? *Wait, for what?* Was he actually interested in a girl? *More like her brain.* He tried to shake that off. "I wonder if you're right. A body functioning at optimum potential means a strong, firm heartbeat that pumps blood everywhere it needs to go, lungs that take in enough air to sustain all organs and a well-functioning excretory system. But if your heart pumps blood too fast and too hard, then your veins could burst open, and if your lungs took in too much air, then you could get hurt, so maybe you could be onto something in terms of being zapped again leading to your downfall. There's no way to tell for now, though,"

Jun was not sure about that theory. "So with you, your brain waves got a bit too enhanced, so now you have telekinesis, but with me, I can shoot fire. That can't be my brain in action, can it?"

"I don't know. We'd have to scan you too," Chantalle shrugged.

Alex was relieved. "Man, we were worried about how we'd be able to look into Jun and find out what happened so we could eventually stop it, but then you came along and now we don't even need to make our own thingy, so thank you," he wanted to hug her but was too afraid.

"You're welcome?" Chantalle seemed to feel awkward. "You guys can come to my room tonight to investigate Jun, but I don't know if there would be a way to reverse it, honestly,"

"Yeah, we figured," Jun felt less alone right now but also confused. "So that thing is just there, and none of us knows why it is,"

"I tried to look into why it might be there, but all I found was that this school used to be a research lab owned by our principal and a partner of his long-ago but all information about what they were researching here has been erased because it was too dangerous," Chantalle said.

"*All* you found? That's a lot! More than I found when I did my research," Alex was very interested. "A research lab? Maybe that thing was the dangerous stuff they were looking into,"

"But why would it be left in a chemistry lab where teenagers are all the time?" Jun scratched his head. So Dr Reymond did have something to do with this.

"When I turned the doorknob, the only reason it opened was that it broke, so the lock must have worn out after a while. It was probably concealed pretty well before, but it just happened to break recently. And I mean, I don't even know if we're allowed in the store room. I just ended up going there because something of mine fell. Since that happened to me, I don't think kids were ever given detention unsupervised again. Not that I think they know what happened, but it must have been wrong. Dr Reymond is strict on his policies pertaining to the labs," Chantalle said.

"Hmm . . ." Jun was not sure what to make of this. "So, where do we go from here?"

They were all quiet.

Alex spoke first. "We need to scan you, Jun. We do and uh . . . I think that we also need to investigate this rock from a distance. I think that I'll go pay it a visit tonight or something,"

"But you'd have to hack the security system, and it'd look suspicious. And let's not forget that it's dangerous. We don't need more mutants running around," Jun hissed.

"Okay, I'll check it out during the day and be sneaky about it or something. I don't know. There are no cameras around there," Alex shrugged.

"I do think that it would be wise to look into the rock itself, but I don't know . . ." Chantalle was looking into the distance.

Jun hummed to himself. "Dr Reymond used to have a partner?"

Chantalle nodded. "His name wasn't even mentioned in what I found, so something horrible must have happened while they worked together,"

Alex shuddered. "Who would have thought that this school had so much baggage?"

Jun rubbed a hand down his face. "I guess we can worry about that later. For now, we need to just focus on undoing whatever happened to me. I don't know if you wanna undo it too, Chantalle,"

"I'd prefer to not be a freak, so if that's the focus, then I'd like this telekinetic thingy out of my life for good," Chantalle looked towards the doors they had come from. "And I hope that that rock doesn't go too unstable and end up blowing up the school,"

"Yeah, me too. Dr Reymond was pretty careless to just leave it there. Did he forget? The room looks so old, and the lock broke. He probably thought it was concealed all this time when it hasn't been. What if someone else finds it? Do you guys think other kids here have powers?" Alex asked.

"I have no idea, but the bell's gonna ring soon, so we should head back in," Chantalle started walking, and the bell did ring when she did so.

Jun followed her with a shaking head. Alex was at his side. "This is all so insane,"

"Yeah, it is, but it's our reality," Chantalle shrugged.

Alex walked over to her side instead. "Hey, so uh . . . heard about that meet and greet thing happening tomorrow?"

"Yes, and I'm not interested,"

"Oh . . ." Alex felt deflated.

Jun saw this and tried not to laugh. "What are you? Some kind of loner?" he asked the girl.

"I could ask you the same question. When you first got here, you didn't even so much as look at anybody," Chantalle said as they stepped through the doors of the emptying cafeteria.

"Psh. I have friends, but they just don't go here," Jun told her.

"Well, same with me," Chantalle gave him a smart look.

Alex turned his head from Jun to Chantelle. "Am I the only one of us who doesn't have any friends at all?"

Chantalle brought her eyes to him.

Alex shuddered with happiness and fear all at once.

She seemed to be thinking before she ended up folding her arms and groaning a bit. "I'll come to the meet and greet with you," she grunted.

Alex's face lit up. "Really?"

"Yeah," she walked away after that.

Alex had never experienced something like that before. He turned to Jun. "I think she likes me,"

Jun felt kind of jealous. "Or feels sorry," he kept walking.

Alex followed him. "You can come too if you like,"

"Yeah, whatever," Jun thought of the girls who had requested that he attend. "I guess I should," he wondered how Chantalle would fair out hanging out with Alex all night. It would be interesting to watch, wouldn't it?

"I WENT AS FAR AS TO replace the whole door, so I think that for now at least, we won't have to worry about anyone coming across it by accident," Dave was in Dr Reymond's office that afternoon after lunch. By the time he had finished working on the silver door last night, Carla and Dr Reymond had retired for the night and had sent him a message saying they would continue their discussion another time. He had found that abrupt but decided that they had probably just wanted to try coming up with a solution to everything in the morning after resting their minds.

"Good, good . . ." the principal was looking at some new student applications that had come in this morning. He had been puzzled by them all day, actually. His school usually found students by scouting exceptionally gifted kids from other schools, so no one usually bothered applying. It was well known that this place was hard to get into and that it was only for the best of the bests, teens that the school board deemed worthy enough to attend. He considered these kids pretty bold for applying but so far, he found their application letters very, very . . . interesting.

Dave noticed how occupied he seemed but did not bother pointing it out. "So you never told me. Did you and Carla come up with a way to find out which students might have been behind the fire? I looked at the security footage of when it happened, but everything had been grainy. Whatever caused the fire must have interfered with the cameras 'cause I didn't see who might've gotten into the bathroom before it and who came out after. It's all corrupted, so I spent a lot of time repairing all of that this morning. That's why I didn't come in here to talk about this then," he took a seat.

Dr Reymond looked up from the applications. "I'd even forgotten that you could have looked at the footage to find out. Hmm . . . so the cameras got disabled?"

Dave nodded. "More like broken, but I fixed it up. That means that it wasn't just fire involved but probably also electricity and waves or something. Either way, it's all messed up, and things are gonna be a lot harder for us in terms of finding out who's behind this," he sat back. "But since the orb was in place when I went to change the door and the lock, we at least know that it's not in any student's possession, right?"

"Right . . ." Dr Reymond was staring at the pictures that came along with the applications.

And now Dave was curious. "What exactly are you looking at? You'd been so worried about all this yesterday, but now it seems as if something else has got your attention. Is all your paperwork suddenly interesting?"

Dr Reymond showed him the two headshots.

Dave raised an eyebrow. "Who are those kids?"

"People interested in coming to this school. These are some of the first applications I've ever gotten," he said. "They seemed to have had trying pasts but sound very willing to work hard and excel at STEM subjects."

Dave found this kind of odd. "Don't people usually wait to get recommended to go here?"

"That's been the case since we started this, but I never said anything that would lead people to think they couldn't apply," Dr Reymond smiled at him.

Dave was frowning. "So you're going to let them in? What are their grades like? Where are they from?"

"There are records of the two of them being in foster care during their early years of childhood, but then they got adopted by a wealthy man who had them under homeschooling for years until now. One of them would be a sophomore and the other a senior," he placed the headshots on his desk and hummed as he observed them.

"And their grades?" Dave was very curious about this. Those kids and their parents must have seen themselves as pretty darn brilliant to apply here without being scouted.

"They both perform well through their homeschooling program, but that doesn't really tell me if they're Reymond High material," the doctor laughed.

"So what? You look like you're already attached to these kids. Gonna just let them in because they asked, and their parents are rich, or are you gonna get Carla to send a letter saying that that's not how we roll around here?" Dave crossed one of his legs over the other.

Dr Reymond thought. "I think I'd like them to come in tomorrow if they can, do a series of tests that we'll grade and then by the end of the day, we'll get back to them. If they do well, then they'd be accepted, but if they do not, then they'd have to go back to homeschooling," yes, that was a good idea. It was also a great way for him to come up with other ways of letting brilliant children into his school. "And from then on, we'll put out that we'd accept applications but that a series of tests would have to be done in order to determine whether one can become a student at this school," he nodded surely.

Dave was impressed. "And you came up with that on the spot?"

"Right, I did," Dr Reymond chuckled, then picked up his water bottle from his desk. He took a sip and sat back. "And if they impress us and get accepted, then it would be perfect timing because they could stay for our school's little meet and greet gathering. The other students could get to know them the same day they get in,"

"You sound confident. What about them makes you think they're exceptional enough to pass any of the tests you have in mind?" Dave tilted his head, wondering what the doctor would say. "Is it a sixth sense of some sort?"

He laughed and then opened his arms. "I just feel as if there's something special about these two," he looked at their headshots again. "Aaron and Lisa . . ."

Dave noted the names before standing. "And about the kid who might have encountered the orb? I mean, they probably didn't have the orb when they started that fire since it was in place when I went to check on it, but you and I both know that the fire is linked to it,"

Dr Reymond wished he could just ignore that issue, but it was pretty important. "We'll just have to ask which students were absent from class when the fire happened," the same boy came to mind again. "If he's one of them, then I'd know for sure that he's behind this," he mumbled.

Dave did not hear the last part. "Right. That's the best way to go about this. Just ask the teachers," he walked to the door. "I'm guessing that would be a task for Carla?"

"Yes," Dr Reymond waved as he left.

CHAPTER EIGHT

"Okay, so according to this, everything seems normal with you except for your nervous system, so I guess it's just like with Chantalle. We made you think of things to freak you out and saw that the electrical signals from your brain are basically what's going haywire and causing fire to come out of your hands. That and electricity. This is just *so* cool," Alex kept having to use his handkerchief to wipe the sweat away from his forehead since he was so nervous about being in a girl's room at night!

Chantalle was sitting at her laptop while Jun sat on a stool next to her bed. Alex was in front of him with the scanner gun that they were using to investigate the changes made to Jun's body by the 'zap'. "So clearly, when people get hit by one of those lasers, it mainly interferes with that particular system. And of course, there's the heightened awareness and other enhancements that we've both experienced, but the nervous system is what's really been tampered with," she turned in her chair to face Jun and Alex. "But the question is . . . how do we reverse it?"

Jun clenched his fists after staring at his palms and then looked at his bicep. "I don't really feel all that enhanced anywhere else,"

"I think you are since I am, and we saw it through the scans, but I guess you'd only be able to feel it if you tried running or jumping. So during gym class," Chantalle winked.

"Ooo, what if you guys can fly too? Ever tried flying Chantalle?" Alex still could not get over the fact that she agreed to go on an outing after school with *him. It's like a date.* Was she interested or just felt sorry like Jun said? *I think he's jealous.* Or maybe she just wanted to be friends. *Even that's amazing in itself 'cause as far as I'm aware, I'm like the most unlikeable person on the planet.* What did Chantalle see in him? She seemed so cool and hot. Was he finally growing into his man body like his dad promised he would? *I haven't. I mean, I'm still covered in baby fat, for crying out loud.* And he was not sure it would ever go away. It ran in his family.

The girl shook her head. "I doubt that I can. If I could then, while my telekinesis was off the rails, I might have been flying all over the place too,"

Jun found the idea of that kind of terrifying but also amusing. "What if you can use your telekinesis on yourself?"

"Not sure if that's how it works, but I can try," she rolled her chair up to the two of them. "So what now? How do we go about doing this?"

Alex wiped his forehead and hoped that he wasn't grossing Chantalle out. "I don't know. For now, all we can do is keep investigating it closely and studying it because the only way to reverse it would be to first understand it," he looked at the clock on the wall, which read nine-thirty p.m. Chantalle's room was pretty neat to him. She had a bookshelf filled with fantasy novels and video games and a single poster of an anime character on the wall next to her bed. Her sheets were red while her pillow was black. The floor under his feet was covered in carpeting, but a lot of people's rooms were like that. *The main takeaway from this is she likes games!* He played video games, too but not as much as he read research papers.

Jun did not like the sound of that. "You're right, but it just means that we'd have to live with these mutations for a pretty long time until we can fix it. This stuff isn't going to be easy to 'understand' because it doesn't make sense. No one in the history of all mankind has ever had the ability to shoot fire out of their palms because a purple rock zapped them, so it's gonna be hard for a fourteen-year-old kid to figure out exactly how it works in order to get rid of it," he sighed at his unfortunate situation.

Chantalle was staring at him. "At least we're the only ones who know about it, and you've found out how to keep it under control. All you have to do until we figure this out is keep it hidden," she did not think that his downcast appearance was justified. "It's not the end of the world. Usually, in TV shows and movies, when this stuff happens, the person with powers ends up being hunted, but I got powers, and no one's been after me, so it's the same with you. It's all pretty normal apart from, you know, powers themselves,"

"I know, but it just doesn't sit right with me," Jun stared at his palm before rubbing it against his thigh. "But don't mind me. We'll get through this, right?"

Chantalle saw the corners of the smile he forced a while ago shaking. "It's not *that* bad, though," she laughed a little.

Alex giggled like a dope. "Your laugh is nice,"

"Thanks?" Chantalle raised an eyebrow at him.

Jun did not like that she laughed at him. "Well, for now, it's not horrible, but . . . hey, you're the one who said Dr Reymond had a partner. What if he comes back and tries to capture all of us to find out what they were working on in the past?"

Alex gasped. "I *did* say that the fact that that thing was down there in the first place may lead to trouble. Jun could be onto something," he pointed his finger at Chantalle.

"Guys, let's not speak stuff like that into the universe 'cause I'm sure that we all agree that dealing with this is hard enough. We don't need crazy scientists on the hunt for us on top of everything," Chantalle got up to sit at the edge of her bed.

"But it's not impossible," Jun turned his stool to face her. "So that would mean that I'm not crazy for reacting how I am,"

"Yeah, but your reaction was mainly towards having your powers. You only came up with a possible threat to make yourself look less like a drama queen for seeming so bummed out," Chantalle told him.

"Drama queen? I can shoot fire out of my hands! That's not only terrifying but freaky and-and weird and . . . this is not something that anyone would find appealing if they found out about it," Jun told her.

Chantalle nodded. "Okay yeah, I get it, but I just wanted you to relax a bit by saying that it's not as bad as it seems. And I mean, your powers go haywire when you freak out, so I think you should listen to me and try to look on the bright side,"

Alex kept looking from one to the other. He settled on Jun and nodded.

Jun rubbed his eyes with his thumb and fingers. "Okay, you're right. I need to relax,"

"Good . . ." Chantalle smiled at him just a little bit.

Alex hummed in thought. "Hey, guys?"

They both turned to him.

"Do you think that what powers someone gets depends on like . . . the state of their mind?" this just occurred to Alex, and to him, it was fascinating.

Jun frowned. "What? I don't know. Why would you ask?"

"Well, you guys didn't get the same powers, so I was trying to figure out why that was," Alex gestured to Chantalle. "She's cool and in control, so she got the power to control things with her mind, and you're . . ."

Jun narrowed his eyes. "I'm a hot head?"

"Ah, you're not a hot head. I was going to say that you're . . . well, you seem cool too but not because you *are* cool like Chantelle but because-" Alex heard her laughing, and it made him blush. "I-is my fly down?" he looked at his pants.

"No, no, you're good," Chantalle smirked at Jun.

Jun's face was pink too, but he seemed angry. "What? Why the laughter?"

"I think what Alex is trying to say is that you're cool because you're trying to be. I think you might be suppressing certain things about yourself so your powers ended up being fire. To show just how much you hold in," Chantalle wore a smart look as she stated her view on the matter.

Alex was so impressed. "Right. That's it. I know him better between the two of us, but you hit the nail right on-"

"That's not true okay?" Jun did not like what Chantalle said. "I'm not suppressing anything, and if I seem cool, it's because I am,"

"Really?" Chantalle did not believe him.

"Oh yeah, really," Jun said with an attitude.

Chantalle chuckled. "Okay,"

Jun did not like that brief response. "I'm literally just a guy who minds his business-"

"Why do you care so much about what I said if it isn't true?" Chantalle challenged.

Jun opened his mouth, but nothing came out.

Alex felt a lot of tension here. "It was just a theory on my part, so we don't know if it's real,"

"But if it is, then it might help with undoing what happened. I think you should take note of it just in case," Chantalle pointed to his pocket. "You've got your phone in there, right?"

"Oh uh yeah, yeah. Notes. Scientists need to take note of everything because it's important to keep a record," Alex sat in the seat Chantalle had been in as he typed into his phone.

Jun kept thinking of what Chantalle had said about him. *She doesn't even know me.* So he should just leave it alone, right?

"So," Chantalle started.

Jun looked at her.

"You guys are both pretty new here. How have you liked your first days so far?" she brought her legs up to her bed and crossed them.

"Uh- um I . . ." Alex wiped more sweat off his face. "It's been pretty cool aside from the whole . . ." he did not know what to call it.

"The school is okay. The classes are fast, but you adapt to them. I actually like them better this way 'cause at my old school, things seemed kind of slow," Jun was pulling his phone out of his pocket.

"I totally agree," Chantalle was staring in space.

Jun was scrolling through his phone.

"The neighbourhood I'm from is pretty poor, so I was lucky that I got the chance to come to this school on a full scholarship. It's a way better learning environment than where I'm from, so I'm grateful," Chantalle sounded like she was talking to herself.

Alex faced her. "Wow. That's pretty cool. Full scholarship?"

She snapped out of her trance and seemed a bit uncomfortable with what she said. "Oh yeah . . ."

"So the friends you have who don't go here are from your old school?" Jun asked while catching up on the messages from his best friend.

"Um . . . my best friend couldn't go to school since she had to take care of her mom but . . . Alex, what was your middle school like? You said you didn't have any friends," Chantalle did not want to talk about her past.

"Oh uh . . ." Alex felt put on the spot. "It was okay, I guess. Just . . . as you guys said, slow. Didn't have as many resources, and *sigh*, no one else cared so much about Maths and Science and Technology, so they found my enthusiasm totally weird and annoying, so I got beat up a lot," he played with his fingers and kept his eyes away from everyone while recounting this.

Jun held his phone down to look at him.

Chantalle shook her head. "The kids who bullied you were probably jealous of your brains,"

"I don't think so. They just found me annoying for sure," Alex chuckled uncomfortably.

"They must have been jealous of something. I'm sure of it. That's how bullies work. Maybe they were jealous because you were comfortable being yourself and expressing what you liked while they were forced to act a certain way in order to seem cool," Chantalle told him sincerely.

Alex faced her. "You think so?"

She nodded. "I know so. It happens all the time. Bullies are insecure,"

Jun felt a bit attacked by what she had just said. He suddenly remembered what he had been telling his best friend Carter about Alex on the night after his first day here. He awkwardly rubbed his arm. "Some of them are just jerks. Not everybody who's insecure is a bully,"

"That's true, but those who take it to a personal level tend to be spineless losers who won't look themselves in the mirror and try to improve," Chantalle sounded wise.

"Hmm, you're probably right. My dad told me that the way to make them stop harassing me was to try to be like them, but I was never interested in sports or trying to make girls like me," Alex felt better about himself as he spoke to Chantalle right now.

"Your dad deserves an L for giving that stupid advice. They were in the wrong, so they should change, not you," Chantalle was saying.

Jun watched as Alex's confidence rose just by listening to what Chantalle was telling him. She sounded so righteous. "Where is all of this coming from? Are you a Tedtalker or something?" he smirked.

Chantalle turned to him.

Jun found that she looked really nice at this angle. *Now that I think about it, we're two guys here in a girl's room at school. Is this even allowed?* No one stopped them from coming here, so he guessed it was? What happened behind closed doors at this school?

"I've just learned a lot about people through observation and interaction," Chantalle said simply.

Alex liked her a lot. "Have you ever been bullied?"

Chantalle laughed a bit. "Yeah. A lot. Where I grew up, kids didn't like that I showed interest in stuff like anime and video games or even that I topped all of our classes. I mean, some people found me cool and made it a competition when it came to doing well in school, but those kids were in *very* few numbers. Maybe only two of them were really interested in academics, and that was because they were as fortunate as I was to have good parents. Everyone else kind of came from broken homes. It was sad. So when they saw me excelling and showing interest in stuff that they didn't understand, they'd pick on me. I nearly got beat up by a gang of girls who hung out outside of my school once, but my best friend came to my rescue,"

Jun may not have liked how she talked about him, but he did feel pretty sorry for her. "At least you're here now where it's safer right?"

"I guess so," she turned to him. "What about you? Ever been bullied?"

Jun's mind took him to his middle school days, where every second of the day would feel like hell because of the constant harassment. He saw one particular instance where his pants had been pulled down in gym class, and everybody laughed. He had to shake his head to get those memories away from his mind. "Nope. I guess that makes me lucky, right?"

Chantalle wasn't an idiot. This guy had been having some intense flashbacks just now, wasn't he? *Hmm . . .*

"Yeah, you are lucky. I wish I was you," Alex laughed a bit before exhaling. "Man, it felt good to talk about this stuff with you guys," he played with his hands. "Especially you, Chantalle. You um . . . you're awesome, and I hope that you'll become a total badass scientist once you're done here. In fact, I know you will cause look!" he showed her the scanner she had created. "This thing is so fricken sophisticated! You're an icon!" he could drool.

Chantalle laughed at his excitement. "Thanks, but it took a really long time to make,"

"If it didn't take a year, then it wasn't that long," Jun got up from his seat. "Oh, by the way, guys,"

Chantalle and Alex were attentive.

"You remember the guy who was kinda crapping on you on our second day here, Alex?" Jun asked.

"Yeah?" Alex asked carefully.

"His name is Devon, and he kinda put together that you and I had something to do with the fire. He doesn't have any evidence, and I denied it when he brought it up to me, but he seems to think that we were behind it," Jun thought he might as well let them know.

"What?" Alex's eyes bulged. "That guy? How did he . . ."

"He just assumed, really. He said the only thing that changed at school when the fire happened was that we were working on something together at night, so he decided that it meant we had something to do with it," he shrugged.

Alex got up too and held his head. "Damn, he's observant."

"Devon . . . oh, the guy who got in because of that laser he made for his school science fair?" Chantalle asked,

The two guys were blank.

"Oh right, you're both new," Chantalle went on to explain. "He's this athletic kid who apparently has a high IQ that people only paid attention to when he nearly set his middle school on fire with this crazy laser he made. No one thought it would be dangerous since he was just a kid, and they never paid attention to how high his grades were, and people ended up playing around with it, and things went crazy. It was funny when I heard other people around school talking about it but was probably pretty scary to experience in person,"

"So *that's* how he got in? Wow," Alex had a bit of respect for him even though he was a jerk. "Well, he seems to be onto us, but if we don't give him any more evidence, we should be fine, right?"

"I guess so," Chantalle looked at the time. "Now hurry on out before someone suspects something,"

"Oh," Jun blushed as he went quickly to the door.

"What do you mean?" Alex was confused.

"I'm glad you don't understand," Chantalle smiled.

Alex was blushing too as he was dragged out. "O-okay, well bye. Sleep tight, Chantalle,"

"Bye Alex, bye Jun," Chantalle waved at them as they exited her space.

CHAPTER NINE

***

The girl that looked like a cheerleader to Jun was called Annalise.

She was stapling a flyer onto the school's notice board at lunchtime rather than eating with her friends in the cafeteria.

"Ah, I knew I'd find you here," a slick voice rang through her ears suddenly.

Annalise saw Devon approaching her from down the hall. They were not exactly friends, but because he was into sports and she was the leader of their school's cheerleading squad, he made sure to interact with her regularly.

The tall guy leaned against the notice board by his shoulder. They were on one of the upper floors of the building. "So, what you up to?" he caught what was on the neon green paper she had attached to the wall. "Oh, is this like a final announcement for the meet and greet later?"

Annalise had the rest of the flyers in one arm. She held them closer to her body with the stapler resting atop her stack. "Yup. I put most of them up around the school this morning, but I still had extras. A bit last minute, but just in case anyone still doesn't know about it, I'm just making sure they're informed. Even though I told people about the speaker," her aura was generally bubbly, and people often used that and how she fit the ideal beauty standard as a reason to pass judgements before knowing a thing about her. Oh, how surprised the students at her former school had been after hearing that Reymond High had scouted her. "You'll be coming later, right? I got Ryan and his band to agree to play us something. It'll be on the football field, but you can read that on this flyer," she pointed to the bright green piece of paper.

Devon had liked her since she joined the student body in the middle of freshman year. *And I'm pretty sure that she likes me.* She did not have to say a word. The chemistry was palpable in the way they interacted. "Of course, I'm coming, but uh . . ." he curled three of his fingers and held out his thumb and pointer finger to fit his chin in the space between them. A smug smile appeared on his face. "I don't have anyone to go with,"

Annalise heard the sounds of people leaving the principal's office at her back. "What about Ryan? He's your friend, and his band will be playing. And then there's Ansel, who told me he'd be coming since Ryan's playing," she held a hand to her mouth and giggled behind it. "Don't be silly, Devon. Plus, the point of the whole thing is to meet people so going alone won't be a problem. It's not a school dance . . ."

Devon's face dropped more and more as she continued speaking. Was she doing this on purpose?

"I'm sure that you two will fit right in once Monday comes by. You're up to speed, you're sharp, and you're both just as intelligent as the other students . . ." that was the principal's voice, Dr Reymond himself.

Devon saw him speaking to two people. A girl with black hair and a boy whose hair was the same colour. "Huh . . . those new students or what?"

Annalise turned around.

The two had large bags on their backs and small suitcases at their sides.

"I think so . . ." Annalise became excited. "They should come to the meet and greet!" she started walking towards them.

"Wh- hey, you can't just . . . ugh." Devon followed her with his hands in his football jersey. *So earlier this week, we got that Asian guy and now these kids?* He just hoped that they would not cause any trouble. *I know that he and the short kid have everything to do with the fire. I just need more proof.*

"So where are the rooms and stuff?" the black-haired boy sounded lazy and unenthusiastic. He was scratching the back of his head.

"Yes, I was getting to that- oh." Dr Reymond was surprised to see one of his students approach them. *Two actually.* Their football star was with the bright and bubbly Annalise. He may not have gotten involved with the kids of his school often, but he did make a point of knowing each of their names.

Annalise held out a flyer. "Welcome to Reymond High. Please, as an official welcome, come to our school's meet and greet on the football field later. We'd all be happy to see you there,"

They both seemed confused.

Dr Reymond was glad that she was being as friendly and welcoming as she always was. *They came in to start the testing even before the hour I told them to arrive.* At that time, the two teenagers had been with their guardians, but the man had left right after Dr Reymond, and some teachers had come to greet them. He had gotten to shake his hand and to look him in the eye, but that was all. It had been a strange encounter, to say the least, and although nothing about that man's hair or face or even his voice had seemed familiar, the eyes that sat in his skull and locked with the doctor's had sent him into a part of his mind he had not known existed. *A chilling experience, but I had no time to allow it to distract me.* So once the guardian had left, confident that his adopted children would be allowed into the school, Dr Reymond proceeded to guide them through the testing section of their acceptance process. *With the help of my trusty teaching staff, of course.* And boy, did these kids blow them all away. It had struck him as odd that they had seemed all set to move in with suitcases and backpacks strapped up even before they were officially told that they would be allowed to attend, but he supposed that that had just been an indication of how confident they and their parent were in their abilities.

"Ah yes. Remember what I'd been telling you two about a while ago? Sometimes our school has events, and this one is one of them. You should try to attend. It would be a great way to get to know the student body," Dr Reymond patted the boy's shoulder.

Aaron smirked after pulling the flyer away from the girl's grasp. He showed it to his sister for her reaction.

"To get to know who goes to this school . . ." Lisa held it herself.

"Yup. That's what a meet and greet are," Devon found them weird. *Are they twins?* The girl's skin was darker than the guy's. She was also pretty short, but girls tended to be a lot shorter than boys. "Hey, why are you spending so much time with them? When the rest of us got into this school, you were never around Dr R," this just occurred to him.

Aaron laughed. "We just came in and are already the big man's favourites," he nudged his sister.

"Don't touch me," she shoved the flyer into her brother's chest. *Adopted brother.* The two of them were far from being related by blood and how they came to be raised by the same man was quite a peculiar tale.

"Ah," Aaron frowned but held the paper in his hands.

"Oh no, it's not about picking favourites. These are just the first students in years that our institution didn't scout, so I cleared my schedule to ensure I had the time to see it and that things went smoothly with their entrance testing," Dr Reymond hoped that other students would not be upset like Devon seemed to be.

"What? You two didn't get scouted?" Devon was lost.

Lisa folded her arms. "Our guardian sent in our applications yesterday, and as soon as today, we were accepted after a series of tests,"

"Yup," Aaron placed an elbow on her shoulder.

Annalise was fascinated. "You two aren't only the first students to get in through applications but probably also the fastest to get in general,"

"Yeah, what was the rush about?" Devon turned to the old man.

Dr Reymond chuckled. "A week of school had already gone by, so I didn't want to waste time, and their parent was more than eager to accept my offer, so it all happened quickly," he was not sure if he could ever get the eyes out of his head. Had he seen them before?

"You agreed to do a bunch of tests today for tomorrow?" Devon did not get it.

Aaron smiled slyly. "Yeah. We got business to do here, so wasting time isn't an option,"

Devon found his expression a bit unnerving. "Okay?"

"And by that, he means topping every one of you people's classes, so watch out," Lisa was staring down the hall. "Now, where are the dorms?"

Dr Reymond was about to show them, but Carla came out of the office with something in hand.

"Doctor, just as you requested," she handed him a piece of paper and then went back.

"What's that?" Devon observed closely as the man's face changed to a frown.

"It's . . ." Dr Reymond trailed before pointing to Annalise and Devon. "Show them where the dorm rooms are. Devon, the empty room down the hall from yours is where Aaron will be staying while Lisa will occupy room QWA in the girl's section,"

"Okay. I'll show Lisa while Devon can show Aaron," Annalise caught onto the names quickly. "Come on," she hooked her arm in the new girl's and smiled while pulling her along.

Lisa was uncomfortable with the skin contact but said nothing. "There was a fire at your school a few days ago," she said as they walked.

"Oh yeah. It was pretty scary, but it got taken care of quickly, and no one got hurt, so I'm glad. Did you hear about it from the news?" Annalise was curious about her. She spoke in this strange monotone and seemed kind of stiff so far.

"Yes, and do you happen to know what might have caused it?"

Annalise shrugged. "Got no clue. It just happened, but hopefully, nothing like that will happen again,"

Lisa grew quiet after that.

Dr Reymond was looking at a list of all the students who had not been in class or had been late on the day of the fire. The list indicated who had been absent versus who was late pretty clearly, and only four students had been missing from class around the same time it happened. *But I think I know who the culprit really is.* Just as he feared, Alex's name was among the others.

CHAPTER TEN

The meet and greet had a pretty good turnout.

Pop music blasted from the stage in front of the bleachers, and all those who attended were scattered about the green dressed in clothing that for once was not synonymous with one another. It was nice since the students never got to express their individuality. For once, they were allowed to wear something that was truly theirs, and most of them went all out. Just having the chance to do that was enough to get them buzzing with enthusiasm, so adding upbeat music and tasty snacks made for a great atmosphere.

Chantalle stepped onto the perfectly cut grass in a simple blouse and denim jacket. She wore jeans on her legs, and dark sneakers covered her feet. *Wow.* She had never seen people so glad to be somewhere in her life. The way that students at Reymond High treated such occasions always brought her great amusement if she bothered to attend. It was entertaining to watch.

"Whoa, you're an early one, aren't you?" Alex appeared at her side, huffing and puffing.

Chantalle felt the skin on her cheeks heat up. "I-I . . . didn't expect to not have to wait for you. Did you run here?" Jun seemed not far behind.

Alex held his knees with his upper body bent over. He looked up. "We said seven-thirty, so I wanted to make sure that we were *exactly* on time," he held a thumb up. "Even though Jun was taking a while-"

"Don't blame me. You were the one going crazy with the cologne," Jun hit Alex on the top of his head.

Alex winced.

Chantalle shifted her genuine appearance of gladness to a teasing smirk. "You two look cute together,"

And now it was Jun's turn to blush. "What? Cute like a-a couple or-"

"You said it, not me," Chantalle took the first step into the crowds of students.

Alex finally caught his breath and saw his date walking away. "Hey, wait up,"

Jun followed him when he started walking. "So, uh . . ." he was pretty surprised by the way everyone around here cleaned up. They usually looked so prim and proper in their uniforms but now having the chance to dress down showed Jun that they were just regular teenagers. A lot of them had a better sense of style than he did. That made him kind of jealous, but he would keep that to himself.

"Do you come to these sorts of things often?" Alex was hoping they could discuss something other than their plight tonight. *I'll start my intensive research over the weekend.* That would need to be done after he finished his homework. *I don't want Jun and Chantalle to know this, but I'm kind of looking forward to diving deeper into all of this.* And it would certainly be a grand challenge to try figuring out how to undo the 'mutation'. *Jun thinks it can't be done by a teenager, but he underestimates me.* He was sure he could figure this out.

Jun had wanted to ask that. Walking among his schoolmates after school hours was awkward. His hope was that starting a conversation would be a suitable distraction from that.

Chantalle saw a lot of people laughing with drinks in hand. A few of them were dancing, and others were going crazy on the snacks. She did not know where they could all fit. "Not really. If I ever show my face at after-school events, it wouldn't be for long. And most of the time, I just won't turn up," she decided that getting some drinks should be first on the agenda. "You guys like blue punch?" she stopped walking.

Alex nearly tripped after stopping too.

Jun grunted and held the younger one in place. Why was he so nervous? "Blue punch . . ." he saw those girls he had labelled as cheerleaders chatting around the drinks table. They were with Devon, his friends and some kids he had never seen before. *That's not surprising.* Nearly all the kids here were foreign to him.

"Most of the punch I've seen has been red, so blue punch sounds new. Not that I've been to that many school parties to see loads of different punches, but uh . . . hey, how about I get you guys the drinks and we can uh . . . we can all hang out next to the stage?" that area wasn't too crowded from what Alex could see.

Jun spotted some teens standing and fooling around over there but not as many as there were where they stood. "You wanna get us to punch?"

"That's sweet, but I think we can all get our own drinks don't you think?" Chantalle was laughing softly. "You're treating this like you're on a date with the two of us,"

Jun placed his hands in his pockets. "Why are you obsessed with the idea that I'm in some kind of relationship with him?"

She raised her left brow. "A while ago, I implied that he was in a relationship with both of us,"

"I know, but you keep-"

"Wow, all of you made it," Annalise's voice came from the table of drinks.

Alex concealed his body behind Jun. That girl reminded him too much of the ones from his old school.

Jun became baffled once she closed the distance between herself and them.

Chantalle presumed she was speaking to Jun. Why wasn't he saying anything? *Looks like he's stammering.* Did he receive a personal invitation from her?

"Uh yeah, I came with uh . . . Alex and this here is Chantalle." Jun liked what Annalise was wearing. It was a loose white dress that stopped over her knees and sandals with straps that wrapped around her unblemished legs. A royal blue cardigan completed the ensemble and gave the outfit this sixties hippy energy. She even wore a flower crown. He'd pinned her as more of a rocker chick based on the colouring at the ends of her hair, but her style screamed girly and delicate. Jun was sure that whatever she wore would suit her. She was one of those kinds of girls.

Chantalle stretched her lips into a tight smile as she raised a single hand in greeting.

Alex waved promptly but remained behind Jun.

Jun wished he'd quit playing the role of 'socially awkward nerd', but that was likely impossible. *It'd be cruel of me to ask him to drop his entire personality, right?*

Annalise was not at all bothered by Alex's shyness. The girl was just glad that so many contrasting individuals came out. "I met Alex earlier this week, but I don't think I've ever met you, Chantalle . . . although we might have shared a class together," her head tipped to the right in thought.

Chantalle folded her arms while her expression stayed unchanged. "Think we might have been partners for robotics in freshman year,"

Annalise snapped her fingers. "That was it,"

"Partners?" Alex straightened his crouched form.

"So, you two are well acquainted, huh?" Jun would have never guessed.

"Clearly not since she didn't remember," Chantalle laughed lightly, but it came off as awkward.

"I remember clearly now. I just needed you to jog my memory, and you did that," Annalise sounded happy to be reminded. "That was a fun year, wasn't it? We made so many cool stuff,"

"This school is small," Alex stood between Chantalle and Jun. His curiosity aided in peeling away his shyness.

"Well, it prides itself on being for the best of the best. Guess that's a small portion," Chantalle smiled tightly at Annalise. "Yes, it was fun working with you,"

Annalise held hands at her back. "Hope we can make robots again some time," she caught the drinks table while surveying the surroundings. Her goal had been to have the whole student body come out to have a good time in honour of the first week of a new school year, and so far, it seemed as if that was going to happen. The football field was packed. "Were you guys heading for some drinks?" she pointed.

"Actually, yeah. Blue punch looks cool. I wanted to know how it tastes," Alex saw that Devon guy with his friends over there. He stepped back. "Although . . ."

"Who are they?" Chantalle pointed out the black-haired kids with Devon and his pals. One was a guy she would say was about her and Jun's age, and the other was a girl. She seemed younger, but Chantalle could not be sure. "Freshmen?" the only unfamiliar people she had seen all week were the newbies who came for their first year. *Them and Jun but I think I've seen all of them with how my classes are arranged.* And those two did not look like any new kids she had spotted.

"Who?" Annalise saw what had her eye. "Oh, them?" she turned a smile to the three. It was so nice that Jun managed to make friends despite being new. "They just came in today. Their names are Lisa and Aaron, and they're totally cool. Aaron's such a charmer, and Lisa's . . . she's nice. Me and Devon kinda got paired with them, so we've been introducing them to the student body," her eyes sparkled when an idea popped into her head. "Wanna meet them too?"

"Uhh . . ." the three of them stammered at once.

Chantalle stopped to clear her throat. "We wouldn't want to overwhelm them," Annalise may have been a social butterfly, but Chantalle usually preferred staying in her own corner unless her situation demanded that she be social.

"Yeah, and they look like they've found their crowd, so maybe we'll just . . ." Jun was not big on approaching new people either. Those kids looked kind of creepy to him anyway. *Maybe it's the black hair.* Was that offensive? He could not describe it, but there was something off. And that off feeling was causing a tingle at his fingertips.

"Oh, the guy looks like he's tryna get your attention," Alex pointed.

Aaron had a cup raised and was pointing the finger at it. He really was calling Annalise.

"Guess that's your cue," Chantalle knew that Annalise was a sweet girl but being around her was exhausting. Her personality just clashed with her own, but Chantalle would prefer to keep that observation to herself. *It's like I have to match her energy, or I'm not doing enough.* She blew out a sigh.

Annalise saw the boy moving towards her. "Looks like he wants to say hi to you guys," she smiled at them while he came closer.

Aaron was now right at her side, laughing at a joke that had apparently been told at the table of drinks. "Anna, I was just asking if you've ever had this combination. Check it. Punch and beer in one glass. Just the scent will tell you how great it is," he sneered.

Annalise's eyes popped. "Punch and beer? Who brought beer?" she seemed nervous. "There are teachers around, you know,"

"Relax, no one's gonna . . ." Aaron wrapped an arm around her and pulled her closer to his side.

While Chantalle and Alex just seemed misplaced and uncomfortable, Jun felt significantly bothered by Aaron's presence.

Chantalle's forehead was suddenly a few degrees hotter, and the centre started aching. She rubbed it and tried shaking off the pain while trying to come up with a way to tell Annalise that they were heading to a different spot. "Hey, Annalise, I think-"

Aaron only noticed them now. His eye twitched when he did, and though it struck him as odd, he hardly paid it any mind. "Oh, were you chatting it up with some friends, Anna?" he held his chest. "My sincerest apologies if I interrupted a valued discussion," his eye kept twitching. *What the hell?* He and Lisa had a meeting in his room after unpacking and settling in. Their plan to find the fire user was not much of a plan. All they could do was ask who they could about what they saw on the day the fire was set and try to narrow down the suspects until they caught the right person. After that, they would have to eliminate them discreetly, but that whole thing would come after they found the other orb. That would be a challenge, but they were willing to do what they had to to get their job done.

"No, no, it's okay. I was just talking about introducing you to them," Annalise made a gesture to the three. "Aaron, meet Jun, Alex and Chantalle. Jun and Alex are new too. Chantalle's been here a while."

"Sweet. You heard my name from her," Aaron's eye twitch persisted. What was up with that?

Jun frowned at the guy's sly smirk, but he was not sure why it bothered him.

Aaron turned his gaze to Jun.

Jun's eyes locked.

Aaron's face slowly turned from slyly amused to cautiously confused.

Jun was full-on, glaring at this guy.

Chantalle's head still hurt, but she ignored it to hold Jun's shoulder. "Jun,"

Alex did not get it. "Why are you looking at him like that?"

Aaron could not pull his gaze away.

"Everything okay?" Annalise had never seen a stare-off quite so intense. What was going on with these two?

Jun used every fibre in his being to rip himself away from Aaron, and when he did, a faint spark of electricity erupted between their eyes and left thin threads of smoke in its wake. He held his eyes. "Aw . . ." what was that?

Aaron saw it and the gears in his brain started turning. Did he . . . just find who they were looking for?

Annalise could smell the smoke. "What . . ."

Chantalle was dumbfounded, but one thing was clear. They needed to get Jun away from this scene. "We have to go, so it was nice meeting you, Aaron, but yeah," she grabbed Jun's forearm and dragged him away.

Alex was left like a lost animal. "Uh, bye!" he ran after his friends. "Wait up, guys!"

"Sorry about that. He must be having a hard night," Annalise could have sworn she had seen sparks just now. What was that? *Jun* . . . What was going on?

Aaron told her there was no need to apologize. "Guess it's true that most of the world's greatest discoveries happen by accident," he laughed to himself, then walked over to the punch table.

CHAPTER ELEVEN

Jun was led to the back of the bleachers.

"Care to explain what happened back there? Are your powers going haywire again? I thought you had them under control. Is this place stressing you out?" Chantalle ensured that no one was back here before accepting it as their place of hiding. But she kept her voice low just in case. They never knew who could be listening.

Jun's hands were held in hers. The action sent a rush down his body. "I'm fine," he removed his hands. "I just . . . I don't know. That guy just . . ." Aaron's eyes floated through his mind. "It was like he was some kinda trigger or something," he placed his palm on his forehead. "I feel normal now, but that was crazy,"

"Yeah, why were you glaring at him that way? Was it because he was getting too handsy with Annalise?" Alex folded his arms. "It's just how some guys are. They like touching girls,"

Chantalle smacked him. "And that can be pretty rude if consent isn't involved,"

"Ah. What?" Alex's hands were resting at the back of his head. Did he make her angry? "No, I didn't mean it like that. I meant it more like . . ." replaying what he had said made it pretty clear why she seemed disgusted. "I meant to say some guys are really comfortable with girls and-and not just girls. People! People in general!"

Chantalle knew that Alex meant no harm. "Whatever," her head was no longer in pain. "It's strange,"

"What is? The fact that having a stare-off with that Aaron set me off? I know. I don't know what it is about him, but something feels wrong," Jun's body had felt it more than his mind.

"Not just that, but once he came onto the scene, my head started aching for some reason," she thought back to that encounter. "Hmm . . ."

Alex's fingers brushed the base of his chin. "So, you got a headache, and Jun started glaring at the guy before his powers-"

"Mutation," Jun grumbled.

Alex found him tiresome. "Fine. His 'mutation' made sparks start up?"

"Yeah . . ." Chantalle looked through the back of the bleachers, but all she saw was the stage. It would be hard to see anyone from back here. "What did Annalise say? They're new, and they just came in today?"

Jun and Alex nodded together.

Chantalle grew quiet as she thought.

Alex was not sure what the relation was. "Do you guys think that, Aaron," he looked them both in the eye. "Might be like the two of you?"

Jun groaned. "I was wondering about that, but how would that be? He'd have to have gone to the school to stumble upon that weird thing in the lab, and when Chantalle and I first met, we didn't react to each other the way that we reacted to Aaron just now,"

"True," Chantalle directed a finger at him. "But it's kind of strange that he caused the two of us to react. My powers are all about my mind, and my head started aching, and with Jun, his fire and smoke erupted. It's gotta mean something, right?"

Both guys hummed at the same time.

They heard giggling from the other side, and a boy and girl emerged, moving sloppily to the area under the seats.

"Are they-oh," Alex was not prepared for the heated lip action that followed.

"I think whoever spiked the punch mighta have gone overboard," Jun was surprised. He definitely shouldn't have labelled the students here the way that he had upon entering. Just because they were classified as nerds didn't mean they couldn't get down. This was the most he had seen people act dirty in the flesh. "Is this allowed?"

"I think we should give them some room," Chantalle grabbed the boys and brought them out to the front again.

"Wait, but what do we do about . . ." Alex had to speak over the music.

Jun could see Aaron having a ball with Devon and his friends. What were they talking about? *He's good at fitting in.* Jun had kept to himself since coming here, so it was no surprise that he was not as popular. His pride had been the reason for that but seeing Aaron get along with who he was beginning to view as the 'cool kids'- *Not Devon. I meant Annalise-* was making him slightly envious. Rather than judging everyone, he should have tried getting to know people. Now he was an afterthought to the pretty girl.

Chantalle exhaled. "I'd say to investigate, but I don't know. That guy rubs me the wrong way,"

"Yeah, me too," Jun had hands in his pockets.

Alex couldn't sense anything negative about him. He had seemed friendly and nice. If he was a jerk, then he might have picked on him. "I wonder why you guys don't like 'im," he was looking for the sister that Annalise had mentioned. "Did his sister leave?"

Chantalle had been trying to spot her too. "Maybe? She's not at the drinks table anymore,"

"Okay, we look creepy," Jun was turning his back. "Let's get something to eat or talk about anything else other than those new kids," he didn't want people calling them freaks for staring.

It was as if his words summoned a server because right as they left his mouth, a pretty girl holding a tray of cabobs appeared before them. "Have a bite. They're good," she said brightly.

Chantalle knew her as someone close to Annalise. "Thank you," she picked one up.

"Don't mind if I do," Alex was eager to try.

She left after Jun held one for himself.

They bit, chewed, and swallowed all at once.

Alex was very satisfied. "Do you like it, Chantalle?" the incident of earlier distracted him from what was of most importance, the satisfaction of his date.

"It's okay," Chantalle went in for another bite.

Alex was mesmerized.

Jun had to laugh. Alex was way too easy. "Guys wanna dance when we're done with these?" A lot of people were dancing, but plenty of others were just standing around and talking too.

Chantalle shrugged. "Okay. Can you dance, though, cool guy?" her voice was sardonic, and a giggle came after her question.

Jun would never understand why she took such pleasure in poking fun at him. "I wouldn't say I'm a *bad* dancer,"

"You look like one of those guys who'd be scared to move in front of too many people," Chantalle's stick was empty.

Alex snorted. "Are ya stiff?"

Jun brushed off their ridicule. "I don't need to go crazy to have a good time,"

"I do. Hold this," Alex handed him the empty stick and ran towards the dancing teens.

"What is he- oh!" Chantalle clapped when the short guy began moving his body to the music. He was not an expert, but it was obvious he was enjoying himself. "That's it! I like that!" she clapped and laughed.

Other kids started looking and smiling.

Jun was embarrassed on Alex's behalf. "Dude, cut it out!" Alex would be a laughing stock next week. Why was the guy acting like a total idiot?

Chantalle was cheering him on, and surprisingly, the other students clapped too. She led a chant that went 'go, Alex, go Alex'. It matched the beat.

Jun had no words. Everyone was okay with this? They were applauding Alex's weirdness?

"Look at him go!" Annalise said in the distance.

Jun had never seen such a thing. Why were they so encouraging?

When Alex tired himself, he struck a pose, and people cheered.

Chantalle clapped over her head and found herself at his side. She wrapped an arm around him and kissed his cheek.

Jun's mouth hung. Alex's round face glowed a rosy red.

"That's my date!" Chantalle was laughing.

Jun just did not know what to think.

"The guy with the black hair?" Lisa emerged from the sidelines where she had hidden for her own sanity. Living underground her whole life did not prepare her for the countless noises and fast-paced lights that came with life on the surface. Saying no would have been easy when the pink-haired girl invited her and her brother to this event, but it was too much of a good way of finding potential suspects to ignore. And it seemed they were right for jumping at the opportunity.

"Yeah, he's just standing all confused. I think he's friends with the kid who was just dancing," Aaron was the only person at the table of drinks apart from his sister. The other students were making a game out of having dance-offs before the stage.

"So that's our fire starter. How easy was that?" Lisa was glad. Hopefully, this trip will not be for long.

ALEX HAD CREATED A program to help him find a solution to Jun and Chantalle's mutation.

Almost every hair on his head stood out of place, and the sun had only risen halfway, but here he was up at his desk. "Gotta make the best with the time I have," he never saw Saturdays as a chance to lie around and do nothing in the past, and this school seemed to agree with his beliefs. All of his teachers had assigned loads of homework to occupy him over the weekend. *Hence my odd working hours.* He yawned.

Chantalle's gadget aided him greatly in creating this simulator. He could see the results of their scans on his screen. "Tampered nervous system," the butt of his pen was rammed between his upper and lower rows of teeth.

How could he undo it? Was there a way? That orb had some crazy effects on his friends that he could barely explain with normal human logic. *I can explain what happened, but I don't know how it did.* What force was this? The only way to find a solution was to figure out the reason behind the events, right? *But if I'm clever enough, I should be able to solve the problem without knowing the specifics behind what caused it.*

He paid close attention to the scan results on his screen. They had all concluded that the best course of action, for now, would be to understand their mutation, but Alex wasn't getting much from these images other than what they had concluded before.

The guy flung his head back with his knees to his chest. "I know I can do it, but I'm working with almost nothing here," he brought his face forward once more and went over all that he knew about this.

Zap, emotions, nerves, electricity . . . He remembered the sparks and smoke of last night. *Accompanied by Chantalle's headache.* What really happened back there? *Got no clue, but I can still add it to my notes.*

He typed the information into his phone as he pondered. "They don't act up around other people, so what made that guy so special?" his theory of last night had been that Aaron was somehow like Jun and Chantalle, but there was absolutely no evidence to prove that. *Unless...*

Alex placed his feet on the ground and sat straighter. *Dr Reymond is hiding an orb in the school's lab, and Chantalle said he used to have a partner that no one knew anything about.* Would he be reaching too far if he assumed that the ex-partner of their principal might be associated with what happened with Aaron last night? *Me and Jun were pretty scared of him showing up, but what if he already has through the new kids?*

His paranoia was taking over full force when a knock came on his door.

"This early?" Alex's brain told him that it was Dr Reymond's partner himself coming to capture him and his first friends. *Oh no! Why was he so unlucky? Couldn't he just enjoy this? I should probably calm down.*

He took a deep breath with a hand on his doorknob before swinging it open. "Good mor- Dr Reymond?" Who could have predicted this?

The principal of their school was standing outside his door in casual attire. A T-shirt and jeans, to be specific. "Alex, my boy, may I come in?"

Alex was not okay with this at all. "Sure," he made room for the old man to enter.

Dr Reymond spotted his computer. "Starting homework early?"

Alex shrieked internally and ran towards the device. He shut it. "Trying to, but it's hard to when the sun's hardly up," he laughed. "So, what brings you here, Doctor? And how'd you know I'd be up?"

"Took a chance, actually. I have an event to attend later this morning that may become a whole day affair. They want me as a judge on some sort of science game show-"

"The Brainlympics??" Alex admired him even more. "They want you on that Doctor, sir?" he nearly forgot his manners.

"So, you've heard about it. Of course," Dr Reymond chuckled. "Listen, Alex, there's been something I've been meaning to speak to you about,"

Alex tried to hide his nerves by assuming a casual pose. "And what might that be, Doctor?" *Crap! He knows about us! We're soooo busted!* Should he lie when it was brought up or try to work his way around being punished? *Forget punishments. Jun and Chantalle will be shipped off to a lab in Indonesia or somewhere.*

Dr Reymond watched him closely. "You requested the use of one of the Chemistry labs on your first day,"

Alex was sure that his forehead had gone blue. His paranoia was often proven ridiculous, but right now, it looked like he was dead on. *Shit.*

"I denied you access, but on that night, my head of security noticed that the security footage had been tampered with. Also, following this, a fire erupted at school at the same time you were missing from class," Dr Reymond did not use an accusatory tone. Alex appeared guilty already. *He's behind this.* "Tell me, did you disobey my word on that day?"

I don't wanna be expelled. He was almost crying. "Dr Reymond I . . ." What was the best course of action? "Yes," he looked at his feet.

The doctor was growing frightful. The only good thing about this was that he had found the culprit. "And?"

Alex could hardly swallow. "A-and what?"

"What did you do when you went in there? Did you . . . see anything?"

Alex saw the floating purple entity that zapped Jun. It came to his mind quickly. "I used it to work on my science fair project," he did not have to give full details, right?

"My question was," the man stepped closer. "Did you see anything down there when you went?"

The orb technically had not been in the lab. "In the lab?"

He nodded.

Alex shook his head while maintaining eye contact. He was a bad liar, but he was good at cutting down the truth.

"Hmm . . . and the fire?"

"Our science fair project malfunctioned while we'd been trying to take a look at it in the bathroom," the words sped off his tongue.

Dr Reymond blinked.

Alex was frozen in a wincing expression.

"Our?"

Oh crap! Why did he give him that? "I uh . . . me and the same guy I'd been complaining about on the first day. He came back, and now we're partners again,"

"I see," Dr Reymond was not sure what to make of this. Was that it? The boys created something dangerous in the lab that caused a fire the next day? *Sounds too good to be true.* He was not sure. "And that's it?"

Alex nodded.

"Well, alright," Dr Reymond walked to the open door and stepped out.

Alex was not sure what that meant. Did he successfully fool him? *That sounds bad.*

"You have detention for disobeying that rule. Know that much," Dr Reymond was closing the door slowly. Only his eye was visible through the crack. "And I'll be watching closely," the door was shut.

Alex started panting after he left. *Jeez!* That was intense. For now, he got the principal off their trail, but the man-made it clear that he'd be looking. *So that means he probably didn't fully believe me.*

The guy stood straighter and took a moment to just breathe. This was getting wild.

CHAPTER TWELVE

He flashed off the excess water from his hands and then used the remaining droplets to cool down his face.

As he closed his eyes and allowed the cooling sensation to take over, he saw instances from his past. Glimpses that he had tried for years to forget. His son's ashes, his dearest friend cut all ties and his wife did the same not too long after.

They came one after the other, and each lasted a single second. In between each memory was an image of a rock glitching with purple energy. The noise made his pulse erratic and alarmingly quick, but that was not happening in real-time. He was only looking back at how his body had reacted after slamming the rock with the hopes of destroying it, only to be sent flying across his lab, breaking his back in the process.

Terror had eclipsed him when the cracks left by his action glowed with purple and made the enigma all the more agitated. Sometimes, the sounds that accompanied its glitches and bursts of energy would play through his mind randomly. He had been so terrified that it might destroy everything he owned that he had just stayed curled up on the ground, crying, wondering if it would be so bad to meet his end by the hand of the very same thing that killed his son.

He started gasping for air once the flashbacks ended. Looking at his reflection caused him to see his distress first-hand. His eyes, they were less tortured than they had been in the past, but he was sure that they would never be the same. He had lost too much. It was true that he had managed to do good through this school and other research projects, but the shadows of his past would always follow him.

Dr Reymond wanted to avert his eyes and get on with the rest of his day, but he was stuck. Sometimes, his trauma would bring forth this behaviour in him, but he knew how to handle it.

For a split second, his eyes changed to the eyes of James, his old partner, and that jolted him out of his stupor.

Christopher groaned before opening his pipe to dampen his face with water again. Today marked the beginning of the second week for his students. *I don't know why things have been more prominent on my mind, but it needs to stop.* Perhaps it had something to do with the scare of last week? That was likely.

Seeing the eyes of his partner in his hallucination made him think of his new students. Not them specifically but their parent. Was that who the man had reminded him of?

He shut off the water and frowned at his sink. *Eyes. . .* Imagining that man's eyes alongside his partner have allowed him to see that they were strikingly similar. Grey and hungry. While Christopher had loved science and discoveries because of the wonder it brought him, James had always had this anger about him when he worked. *I knew him well.* The other man had been dealt a bad hand in life. Being born to a broken family, to parents who did not want him. *Constantly surrounded by people who expected him to fail.* That was why the other man had reached the heights that he had. *To show them all.* And, of course, with Christopher's encouragement, he had seen the appeal of improving humanity. After all, humans with better health, body and minds were less likely to bring harm to their offspring. *So, no one else would have to go through what he did.* Christopher had hoped that that was a thought on his partner's mind, but he supposed that when he truly thought about it, he didn't know as much about James as he believed. *Human beings only show ten per cent of their true selves to others. The rest is kept within the walls of our minds.*

The man dried his hands and started getting dressed. *Quite strange that their parent would have the same eyes as him.* He would prefer to not think about this now, but it was on his mind. *How strange it would be if the very man that my closest companions and I have been tracking down for years had turned up at my doorstep only for me to not notice.*

He paused while fixing his bowtie, staring at his reflection again. Could that be the case? *But that would also have to mean that Aaron and Lisa were his adopted children.* Was he being ridiculous? *I'm thinking hypothetically.* If somehow that *was* his old partner, then why would he want to enrol his children in Christopher's school? *And why wear a disguise?* Maybe part of why he could not track down James was because he had changed his face. *Hmm . . .* an intense frown formed as he continued to ponder. Should he be concerned?

His mouth felt dry. If that really was James, then . . . *What does that mean?* What could possibly possess his old friend to send his children to Christopher's school while disguised as someone else? *It . . . doesn't make sense.* This belief was only coming about because of what happened last week and his flashbacks of earlier.

The principal shook off his thoughts to complete his suit and went over some reasons why his thoughts a while ago made no sense. *There are many people with grey tortured eyes around.* Imagining it was making him convinced that they really did belong to his partner, but he just tried to ignore his mind. He had read that an ill mind often added its own input to situations to justify its paranoid beliefs. That was likely the case with him and the adoptive parent of his students.

After thoroughly convincing himself to let it go, he picked up his briefcase next to his bed and walked to his door. *I have enough things to worry about.* His conversation with Alex Johnson had struck him as vague. There was more going on that the boy was not saying, and he would get to the bottom of it soon. *I should ask to see the science fair experiment that went wrong and caused the fire.* Would the boy show it to him?

We'll see. He walked out of his room door to face the day.

GOT THIRTY MINUTES. Aaron concluded this after checking his watch.

He and Lisa were in his room that same morning having a discussion about their mission. Both were dressed in uniform but were likely the only students still within the dorms. The rest had already reported to the school building. Classes had not started, but students preferred to be present at the building early just to lessen the risks of lateness.

Lisa had a small laptop resting in the palm of her hand. She was standing before her brother while peering at the screen. The guy was seated on his bed. "So, according to what I gathered from the school's database over the weekend, the alleged fire starter is a junior who- as we know- recently started attending Reymond High. His room is on the same floor as this one, and his schedule reads as follows," she proceeded to call out the classes listed before her and the times the guy had to attend them. "Name: Jun Sato. Age: Sixteen. Birth date: January first."

"Ha. New Year's day," Aaron pointed out.

"Yes," Lisa pressed something on her keyboard. "And because it would only be wise to do so, we thought to gather information on the people who had been at his side when the two of you had that reaction," she pulled up the information on the boy and girl who had also been introduced to her brother. "Chantalle Brown and Alex

Johnson. Johnson's a freshman who got scouted because his IQ is out of this world. Wow, nearly two hundred,"

Aaron whistled low. He was playing through the settings on his phone. "So, what's that? One ninety-eight?"

"Precisely. He beat us both without even being modified, but that's not the point. According to this, he's fourteen and turns fifteen in June . . . He has had a clean record but wait, what's this?" Lisa scrolled down. "He has detention?" she had hacked into the school's system last night to have access to all of this. They had agreed to do a deeper dive into these kids since Friday night, but the firewalls on this school's software were nothing to sneeze at. She was gifted with computers thanks to her enhancements, but even she had had difficulty breaking in. She'd only succeeded this morning, hence their meeting now.

"Detention for what? The weird dancing he pulled on the football field on Friday night?" Aaron chuckled. He and Lisa had not had a good view since they'd stayed on the sidelines for their short meeting, but someone had shown him a video. "It wasn't that bad. The kid's got moves. He's definitely a better dancer than you are. You just don't have the rhythm, you know? But it's nothing to be ashamed of. Not everyone can be a dance machine like me," he was older than Lisa by two months but acted like those months were years. He did everything that his elder brothers did to their little sisters. Teasing, bugging, bothering, all of it. She was especially fun to pick at because she was so stiff and strange. He had noticed that she wasn't typical since the day they had met, and she refused to touch him. *Feels like ages ago.* They had both been five at the time but were taken from completely different places. Neither of them had known a word of English. *But that wasn't the only thing we had to learn after stepping off that elevator.* He still remembered how fascinated he had felt upon viewing the techy silver underground world for the first time. Wonder and fear had never mixed so well.

Lisa ignored him. "According to this report, his detention was given for disobeying the 'don't use the labs outside of classes' rule,"

"Oh yeah. That rule . . ." Aaron frowned. "Why would he disobey that rule if he's a goody-two-shoes?"

"Not sure. Maybe his quest for knowledge got the better of him? The detention was given on Saturday, though. He must have used the lab then," Lisa hummed in thought. "But I digress," she went to the last person. "Chantalle Brown, a golden pupil at her old school, the hope of her community? Wow. So much pressure. Has had straight A's since elementary school. IQ of 145, which is the standard around here, turns seventeen in April and is a junior," she held her laptop lower.

Aaron straightened himself as he watched her place the device on his bedside table. "Okay, so that's the whole gang, but the person of main interest is Jun Sato,"

"Right," Lisa nodded. "But we'll have to get to him later. For now, our top priority should be seizing that rock. It can't exist while Father is yet to reveal his own discovery to the world. There can't be two of them at once, and there can't be more enhanced people. Otherwise, Dr Reymond could get some credit for Father's work," they were quite aware of their adopted father's past and what had led him to use them for his experiments.

"Yeah, and he doesn't deserve any credit since he bailed after things got tough," Aaron huffed. "Father thought he'd destroyed the prototype. Why do you think he kept it around? Think that Jun guy got enhanced because Dr Reymond wanted to continue experimenting? I doubt that, but I just wanna get the ball rolling,"

"That's definitely not the case. He was against the use of humans for lab work. A coward fearful of taking risks," Lisa shook her head. "Like we speculated, the most likely cause of Sato's enhancements was accidentally stumbling upon the prototype. What Reymond failed to destroy," she tapped her chin. "The question is, though, how did he stumble across it, and where did it happen?" she walked back and forth. "Reymond must have hidden it poorly if a student was able to find it. It should be easy for us to locate it if that's the case,"

"Unless he moved it since," Aaron brushed a hand through his hair. It stopped just over his shoulders. "But it'd be good to find out where all of this happened,"

Lisa nodded. "I would suggest simply approaching the Sato boy to ask directly about things, but I doubt he would be compliant. You said he and his friends ran away after the sparks arose during your encounter,"

Aaron pointed at her. "Yeah, I did say that, and now that you're bringing that up, maybe his friends might know about his enhancements. They didn't seem as freaked out about the whole thing as Annalise. She hasn't asked me about it since, but I know she saw the smoke and felt weird. But his pals just ran off with him,"

Lisa hummed in thought, standing still. "Perhaps they were with him when it happened?"

"Maybe . . ." Aaron pondered on it for longer. "They were with him . . . Chantalle Brown, Alex Johnson . . . wait," he locked eyes with his sister. "The lab,"

Lisa went back to her laptop to read about Alex after her brother stated this. "The lab that Alex got detention for using . . . Chemistry lab OW . . ." she looked right at Aaron. "What if students are prohibited from using these labs outside of school because Reymond is hiding something in them?"

"I mean, it's normal for schools to put a ban on using a potentially dangerous area without a teacher's supervision, but given this situation, I think we're allowed to make that assumption," Aaron moved his hand against his mouth a little. "Alex used the lab, found the prototype, brought it to his room to show his pals and Jun got enhanced,"

"That's possibly what happened, but we should still give that lab a visit. Let's say at lunch today? Do a thorough search? The security cameras are always running, but if I hack in before we go, we can get a lot done," Lisa proposed.

"Right. Good plan," Aaron rose to his feet and stretched. His back cracked in the process. "Damn. That's the kinda stretch to make a man wanna lie back in bed," he laughed as he wrapped an arm around his sister.

Lisa threw his arm off. "Don't touch me," she picked up her laptop and closed it. "Now, let's go. We're already late for class,"

"And on our first day. Tsk, tsk. Dad's gonna be disappointed," Aaron laughed on his way to the door. "So, what do we do about Annalise and what she saw?"

Lisa imagined the high-spirited girl and her pink hair. She felt uncomfortable just thinking about her. *Was rather kind to me, but I didn't appreciate her constant questioning.* She knew that Annalise had simply been trying to get to know her, but Lisa was not used to the people here. And because of that, interacting left her winded like she had competed in an Olympic sport. She'd prefer to let Aaron do the talking. *It's what he's best at.* She thought begrudgingly. "As long as she doesn't ask questions, we'll leave her," she walked through the door after he opened it.

CHAPTER THIRTEEN

"Yeah, so things have been fine, and everything is okay," Jun was on a call with his mom during the transition. He had his back to his locker while Chantalle and Alex stood at his side.

Chantalle could sense that Alex was uneasy. He kept using his fingers to pick at his bag straps. "You haven't answered my question. Made any headway in dealing with you know what?" she was very careful to not raise her voice while asking. Everyone in the hallway seemed caught up with their own business, but it did not hurt to be careful.

Jun was chewing his lip as he listened to his mother. She was not one to call during school hours, but her reason for checking in now was sufficient. *Said something about a daydream where I was in trouble?* Having strange dreams was not odd for his mom. She was superstitious and very old school, an overly cautious person. Jun would usually roll his eyes at her concern when she warned him to be careful following a dream of hers, but with the way things had been since he stepped foot in this school, he had reason to take heed of her word. For all he knew, her dreams of the past coming to fruition now may be the reason behind his current issues.

Alex snapped out of his thoughts after hearing Chantalle. "Oh, uh, about that-"

"Hey Johnson," a group of boys walked past him wearing smiles. "Gnarly dancing on Friday. You made the party come alive," they hyped him up on their way down the hall.

Alex had forgotten about that. "Haha. Right on," he said nervously with gang signs up.

Chantalle was glad he was getting praise, but she wished he would talk to her. "Alex. The whole weekend went by, and you didn't give any updates,"

Alex scratched his head. "Oh yeah uh . . . I haven't made much headway in working around everything, but I did take note of what happened with the new kids," he had not seen them for the day. Were they still here?

Chantalle rubbed her head as a ghost of that headache started up. "That was pretty weird, wasn't it?"

"So, you've been keeping safe and taking care of yourself?" Jun's mother had finished explaining her vivid daydream.

Jun saw the unstable rock and remembered his body convulsing on the floor with electricity just last week. The smoke of Friday night came to mind as well, and after that were the dreams he had been having since locking eyes with Aaron. Simply using words was not enough to explain them. *Just clashing of blue and purple forces but with heavy effects.* He had not told anyone about them, but he would wake up with his body sizzling like it had been burned. *But not by fire. By ice.* "Yeah, Mom. I've been okay, so there's no need to worry, but uh, when you say that in your dream something was after me, what exactly do you mean?" he turned away from his friends as he whispered.

"It was. I wanna say that we should hope they won't cause us any trouble, but that would be stupid," Alex continued to behave anxiously, pondering on their plight.

"Just that there was a threat looming over you that you were unaware of," Jun's mom responded. "But since you believe that you're safe, I'll try to relax," she laughed at herself. "The school can't possibly have people lurking at the corners to get you. It's the safest place you can be,"

Jun saw Aaron's eyes in his head but had to shake off the image. "Right,"

"I know," Chantalle said to Alex's statement. "If only there was a way to find out what their true intentions are and why they're here," she had not seen Aaron or the other girl since the meet and greet and was glad. "But I guess we should try to focus on undoing what happened with Jun and me before we investigate them, right?"

"Mmm . . . yeah. As long as they don't make themselves our business, then we can pretend they're not ours," Alex was sure that that was a bad idea, but he just wanted to end this conversation. *I need to scan the rock or get a sample of it to find a cure. There's no way I can rely just on Chantalle and Jun's scans to do this.* That had been made abundantly clear while he racked his brain during his research and was the reason for his unease now. Having the cause behind their mutations would speed up the process exponentially. *I wanna tell them that, but I'm pretty sure they'd be against it.* So, he would sneak into the lab again at lunch today to get what he wanted himself. *I'll try hacking into the security system in a different way.* He needed to be careful here. Dr Reymond had already given him detention for snooping around. If he was caught again, he might very well be expelled. *Would it hurt to just let Dr Reymond know what's up?* It was the old guy's fault for having that thing there in the first place. *What if he knows about Aaron?* What was it about Aaron? Alex was kind of curious to investigate him and his sister, but that would be unwise.

"I don't know if that's- hey," Chantalle watched Alex speed down the hall. "Where is he going?" what was going on with him? Was it because she kissed him on Friday? *It was on the cheek.* She rubbed her arm self-consciously before turning to Jun.

"Okay, bye, Mom. Yeah, love you," Jun hung up and sighed.

Chantalle found him to appear stressed as well. "What's up with you?"

"Nothing," he looked at her. "Do dreams have meaning?"

That question felt out of place. "Uh . . . they can represent what's at the back of our minds. Why do you ask?"

Jun scratched his head. "Nothing," he heard the bell ring. "We should get to class,"

"Yeah, we have Chemistry now," Chantalle placed her hands in her blazer pockets. "Alex is acting weird,"

"Ha. I think that's just how he is," Jun was still experiencing the effects of his nightmares. "I'd just ignore him if I were you. Not that I know him well enough to come to that conclusion. I've only known the kid a week, but it feels like a lifetime,"

"Right. I guess when people are in a crazy situation together, things feel longer," Chantalle spotted someone with pink ends walking past them. They stepped back. *Shit.*

"Chantalle, I was just looking for you," Annalise was holding a stack of papers in hand.

Jun now remembered that she had been there when that weird thing had happened. Was she going to ask about it? "Hey, uh, have you seen the new guy?" that was the worst question to ask, but his mother's dream made him paranoid. Keeping tabs on the most threatening person in his life right now was smart, right?

"Aaron? Yeah, he's been around with Devon. The one I've been trying to find since the day started is his sister Lisa. She strikes me as the shy type, but I'm sure that with enough positive interactions, she'll come out of her shell," Annalise handed Chantalle a flyer. "We're having cheerleading tryouts tomorrow. We need all the help we can get since we'll be competing at the cheer-offs next month,"

Jun's eyes widened as he watched Chantalle take the flyer. "You? Cheerleading?" he could not imagine it. The thought was kind of funny.

Chantalle nudged him with an elbow after hearing him snicker. "Thanks, but I don't know if I'd wanna try out. Cheerleading's not-"

"Wait, did you say that no one knows where Aaron's sister is?" Jun's body went numb. She had come here with Aaron, so there was a high chance that she could bring him harm as well. *It's only been a week, and this place has already driven me insane.*

"Yeah, but like I said, shy. But we'll work on her,"

"Or maybe some people should just be left in their shells? It's not the worst thing in the world for someone to be reserved, you know," Chantalle folded the paper.

"I guess so, but I just want her to feel welcome," Annalise hurried off. "See you guys later,"

Jun waved. "Huh, wonder why she didn't seem confused about the smoke and sparks from Friday,"

"We should be happy she isn't questioning it," Chantalle was walking once again. "And Aaron's sister . . . I know that Alex said we should try to ignore them, but they came here for a reason, and it's glaring that they're like you and me,"

"I know," Jun's stomach became knotted. "But we can talk about that later," he kept walking until they got to the lab.

Chantalle saw the girl who had been with Aaron on Friday night. *His sister.*

She was sitting up front at the other side of a lab table, away from the other students.

Jun saw her too. "Oh shit," she wouldn't do anything while here, right? Why *did* they come to this school? What was their relation to Dr Reymond and the rock? *His allegedly lost partner keeps coming to mind.* What if these kids were sent here to destroy the school? *I can't.* He needed to focus on this class. He could worry about all of this once the period was over and lunch commenced.

———— ❧ ————

RING!

"I know that it'd be weird for a freshman to throw a dorm party, but with how you rocked the school on Friday, I think it could be a hit. You know, if you decide to come," a kid named Grayson was talking Alex's ear off after English class.

Alex had no time to chat. He dashed out of the classroom after gathering his stuff and went straight for the bathrooms.

"Where you going?" Grayson called. He disappeared so fast.

Alex did not hear him.

He ignored the students washing up and using the urinals in the boy's room to head straight for one of the stalls.

Alex thanked the heavens that this toilet was clean before closing the lid and sitting atop it. *Okay, let's get into that system.* His fingers danced across his keyboard once he opened his laptop, and his teeth pressed deeply into his bottom lip. If he wasn't careful, he could be caught again and kicked out of his dream school. He had not been able to acknowledge it, but he knew that he had become popular. *Someone was inviting me to their party!* That would never happen at his old school. *And yet here I am, risking it all for Jun and Chantalle.* Had Chantalle kissed him on Friday night?

His cheeks heated at the memory. *And Jun said she only felt sorry.* Jun was jealous. He was sure of it. *Okay, man, stay focused.* A job needed to be done, and he needed to do it. *I gotta find something to put it in 'cause if I touch that thing, it might go completely haywire-wait for a minute.* He paused.

Alex let all the sounds from outside die down as he sat stiffly, brows furrowed by what his computer screen was telling him.

The teen peered closer at his device and tried to make sense of what was before him. *Is . . . someone else hacked into the system?* It could be someone from the staff doing some maintenance, but the end it was coming from said otherwise.

He had to reflect on this for a while. Who could be hacking into the security system at the exact same time that he was? *This calls for some more investigation.* While he had been hacking for the betterment of his friends, an outside body doing the same could mean the demise of everyone.

Once again, his fingers went wild across the keys as he dove into this mystery. *Hope I don't find anything too terrifying.* What if they were all in danger?

Alex noticed that the cameras within and just outside Chemistry lab OW were what was tampered with. The footage available was not what should be on display. *Hmm . . .* he rectified the issue but was confused to see that the incorrect footage was not different from what was actually there. *So . . .*

The lab was empty since all students had left for lunch. *Okay, someone hacked in and changed the footage a few seconds ago but for no reason?* Maybe they'd been flexing their hacking skills- "Hold on," his brows furrowed as two bodies came quickly through the locked door. It shut behind them, and they seemed to start conversing.

Alex blinked in stun and confusion. Was it normal for students to just switch the security footage to snoop around the labs without supervision? The people on his screen were in uniform, so they definitely went here. *And here I thought I was a renegade.* He scratched his chin. *What if they're about to do something messy?* From the looks of it, these people were a boy and a girl. *I shouldn't jump to conclusions, but . . .*

He would just pack up and deal with this later, but something caught his attention about this girl and boy.

Black hair . . . he gulped as it clicked. *The new guys.* Alex did *not* like where this was going.

After they finished speaking with each other, he saw them separate to different sides of the classroom. *Are they . . . are they looking for something?* That was definitely what was happening. What they were looking for? He had no idea.

He tapped a finger against the side of his keyboard as possibilities ran across his mind. *They're in lab OW.* The very same lab where he and Jun had found that creepy rock. *I wanna say I'm jumping to conclusions, but I'm not.* These kids showed up out of nowhere, and one of them made Jun and Chantalle's powers go a little wild on Friday. The obvious conclusion to draw here was that they had something to do with Dr Reymond, that rock and possibly his partner. *And now they're in the lab.* Was he thinking on the right wavelength? Were they looking for the rock? *But why?* Maybe they were sent by the government to retrieve it. What if Dr Reymond was the bad guy here? What if he stole that thing from the CIA? *I could be onto something.* Or maybe they were the ones in the wrong and were going to use that purple thing for no good. *There might be tons of those rocks, and Dr Reymond is the guardian of that one, and if those kids get their hands on all the others, they'll use it to destroy life as we know it!*

Alex was hyperventilating. *Calm down. Calm down.* He covered his mouth with his hands but, in doing so, threw off the balance of his laptop.

He caught it before it could fall and tried to restore his composure. *I don't know for sure what's going on, but I have a feeling that Dr Reymond is keeping that thing hidden for a good reason.* And why would he be the bad guy? He opened a school for teen prodigies. The guy was a saint. *Unless it's all a cover-up.* He planted his eyes on the stall door for ten seconds straight. *No, I need to focus.*

Alex got back to his screen but- *Where'd they go?* They had been there a second ago. Did he miss something? *I shouldn't have spent so much time panicking. Ughghgh!*

His eyes darted all over the screen until they landed on the door to the store room. He gulped. That place had no cameras and was also where- *Damn, they're clever.* Had they found the rock? Was it too late? What should he do?

The boy was glued to his spot in quiet panic for a moment. *No. I can't just sit here.* They could be up to no good, and that thing was dangerous. *I also need it for my research.*

So, he swallowed his fear and hopped off the toilet. *If they're anything like Chantalle and Jun, then they'd be more than capable of beating my ass if I get too close to figuring out their plan.* Was he being silly for thinking along that wavelength? *I'm not! This is serious.*

He ran out of the stall and went speeding through the exit.

Alex was panting as he ran past the cafeteria but stopped when someone stepped out and called to him.

"Alex!"

He turned on his heel four feet down the hallway. "Oh, Chantalle. I-"

"What has been up with you all day?" She sounded both worried and angry.

"I just uh . . . wait!" he ran up to her and grabbed her hand.

Chantalle was being dragged down the hall. "Wow. So, you don't give me an explanation but decide to yank me to where ever instead? What is going on?" she had concluded that he was hiding something but did not know what. "You know, if you've encountered a stumbling block in your investigation, you can just say so. I can help you to find a way around this-"

"And I'd appreciate your help, but you need to help me with something else," he stopped running for a second to explain at rapid speed. "The new kids are in the store room. I was gonna hack into the security system to get to the rock to use it to investigate, but while I was online, I saw them in the lab, and I just know that they're after the thingy 'cause why else would they be in there? I don't know how they found it, but this is bad, and I'm worried, and I think we should stop them," he kept pulling her after rattling this off.

Chantalle's eyes were wide. "Wait, what?"

Alex tampered with the door through his laptop once they were next to the lab and ran in with her. He closed it while panting, then shut his device. "See? The store room is wide open. They're in there," he whimpered in fear at her side.

Chantalle was still making sense of this. "They're in there?" she whispered.

Alex nodded. "I saw them, and we probably don't have time so let's go!" he ran right to the door but ran back like a mouse. "What if they kill me?" he hissed.

Chantalle shook her head and then held his hand. "Let's just take a look, okay? They don't need to see us," the noise from the door might have already given them away, but they could still try to be discrete.

Alex nodded his agreement.

The two of them walked on quiet feet towards the open door.

Chantalle was the first to peep in.

Alex followed slowly. "Shit," he whispered.

She covered his mouth.

The new kids were right at the back of the room and seemed to have discovered the hidden door. That Aaron guy was unstacking the bags of steel.

Chantalle tried to listen in.

". . . but I'd expect no more from him. Father did say he was too trusting in his younger days," the girl was saying.

Aaron got one bag down. He stretched to pick up another and moved it faster than he did the first. "It might have been easy to find, but the door might be hard to break down,"

"That won't be a problem for you and me,"

"It might be since we don't want to leave too much evidence," Aaron was able to move the other bags in little time.

"Excellent," Lisa stepped towards it.

Aaron dusted his hands off.

"Should we do something?" Alex whispered.

Chantalle was pretty uncomfortable. What had they been talking about? Had their father sent them after that rock? "We should but . . ."

"Shh," Lisa said. "Did you hear that?"

Alex moved his head out of the door frame.

Chantalle did the same, and they both breathed heavily with backs to the wall.

Alex held her arm. "We should run," he mouthed.

Chantalle shook her head. "You brought me here to stop them,"

"I know, but-" Alex stiffened by who came into their view.

It was Aaron. He walked right out the store room door to stand within their line of sight.

His sister came in slowly after but kept to his back.

Chantalle cursed in her mind.

Alex could not speak.

The older guy released a single laugh before folding his arms.

Chantalle was not sure of how to approach this. Her headache was coming back, but she would ignore it to deal with this. "The labs are off-limits outside of class time," she said.

Alex nodded silently, not sure what to do.

Aaron was quiet for a second. "I'm aware," he looked over his shoulder at his sister. "I think we might have been right," as soon as the words left his mouth, his eye began to twitch. *Wait.* Jun Sato was not here . . .

"It appears so," Lisa stated. Her hands were becoming tingly. *Odd.*

Chantalle did not know what they meant by that. *The headache's back.* It was not as severe as last time but was still bothersome.

Aaron opened his arms. "If it's so against the rules to be here, then what are you two doing? The doors were locked before you came. Did you open them just to come to get us? Noticed we were missing from the lunch tables?" he asked snidely. "You're both too kind,"

Chantalle knew what game he was playing. "We saw you two coming over here while on duty," she sent Alex a look so he would catch on. "Right, Alex?"

Alex was completely blank. "Duty?"

Chantalle could scream. "Yes. You know, since we're hall monitors?"

Alex gasped. Chantalle was so smart. He snapped his fingers and then nodded, pointing at her. "Yes, yes, hall monitors. We were assigned to keep an eye out for students being in places they shouldn't, and we just so happened to find you two scurrying into the lab, so there you have it," he was not really good at lying, so his words may have come off as forced. *But hopefully, they can't tell.* The Aaron guy looked suspicious of him, but his sister's eyes were elsewhere. *Think she's looking at Chantalle.*

"Exactly, and hall monitors get access to classrooms so we can check up on things," Chantalle thought at the moment. "Hence we're here," she gestured to their surroundings.

"Yeah," Alex added uselessly.

Aaron and Lisa exchanged glances.

Lisa cleared her throat, finally revealing her full body. She stepped to her brother's left with folded arms. "If you're allowed to be here because you're supposed 'hall monitors,' why were you hiding from us? Why not just call us out as soon as you caught us in the back?"

Alex flinched. *Shit.* Of course, they would try to challenge them. *Chantalle's still brilliant in my eyes, but there's no way she can counter that.*

"We were . . . trying to find out what you two were up to back there before revealing ourselves. Yup. So, we could know what punishment would be most suitable," Chantalle nudged Alex to get him to agree.

"Yeah!" Alex said with too much enthusiasm.

Lisa raised an eyebrow. "Surely you don't expect us to believe you,"

Chantalle and Alex were mute.

Alex was hoping she would have a comeback for that. "We do," he pointed at the girl. She was about his height.

Chantalle gave a stiff nod. "Because it's true," her voice squeaked. She may have been better at lying on the spot than Alex, but she still was not the best at it.

Aaron watched them silently with his sister for all five seconds before barking a laugh. He bent over.

Lisa ignored her brother's hysterics. "Alright, enough games. It's obvious that we all need to have a little chat," she tried to ward off the discomfort in her palms.

Aaron composed himself with a swipe at his teardrops. "Right, right we do," his eye twitch was still prominent. *Not as bad as last time, though.* "Listen, what we do in there," he pointed to the store room. "Is none of your business,"

Lisa's face showed her agreement.

Alex's saliva was like an iron ball. "What *were* you doing in there?"

"The background is complicated, so it would be best if you didn't get involved," Lisa wanted to know which of them was causing this. She tried flashing the graininess off her hands, but that did nothing. This was quite hard to ignore. *And shouldn't be ignored.* "Of course, it may be a little late to say that seeing you're already a part of this . . ." was Aaron experiencing what she was?

"Oh yeah. You *are* already a part of this. Hmm . . ." Aaron eyed them both.

Alex averted his own eyes when Aaron's made contact with his. "What makes you say that?"

Chantalle felt it ridiculous to keep trying to hide. "Look, we only got involved by accident, okay? We'd rather mind our business, but that's not how things work sometimes,"

Oh, we're being honest now. Alex pointed at her. "What she said,"

"As we speak, we're trying to find a way to undo what happened," Chantalle expressed.

"Undo what happened . . . and what exactly *did* happen?" Lisa asked softly.

Chantalle was getting a predatory vibe from the two of them. "Me and Jun got zapped by that thing, and now we're freaks,"

Aaron and Lisa's eyes widened simultaneously. They looked at each other, then the girl. "And then there were two of them," Aaron stated.

Lisa grabbed Chantalle's hand to inspect, but a spark arose, and she had to pull away.

Alex had been frightened. There was smoke vanishing before their eyes.

"I don't get it," Aaron rubbed his chin. "When you and I interact, nothing happens, but whenever we come in contact with them, there's all this drama,"

Alex heard a noise from the back. He peeped into the open storeroom door to have a look but saw nothing of concern. *Maybe one of the bags tumbled.* He tuned back in.

"It's the strangest thing," Lisa reached for the hand again, and this time the sparks were less.

"Um . . ." Chantalle had never been observed with such focus. "I told you two what's going on with us, so now you have to give us some details," she pulled her hand back.

Lisa was fascinated. "Seems the initial shock is only that. An initial shock," her palms were not as uncomfortable. "The second time I went in, the reaction was much less intense,"

"So, I see," Aaron placed hands on his hips. "You want details?"

Chantalle nodded.

Alex heard another noise. Did he imagine things? It was like something banging on metal. Something small and light is being thrown at a force. Like nuts and bolts in a tornado. *Why can't they hear it?* The others were probably too caught up.

"Just know that the thing that you guys got enhanced by is a knock-off of what enhanced the two of us," Aaron said.

"And we need to get rid of that knock-off because Dr Reymond had a hand in its creation. The true model shall be the only one in existence. That's how our father will get all the praise he deserves for working so tirelessly all by himself for years and years after being abandoned by his so-called 'partner'" Lisa did not hide her disgust for their principal.

Chantalle was taken aback. "Knock off?"

"Yes. That's probably why it's causing glitches when we come close . . . do you glitch out with Sato?" Aaron was curious about the answer.

"Sato?" Chantalle was lost but also quite interested in this lore. "Wait, there's a more refined version of the thing in that room, and you guys got enhanced by it?"

"What is it?" Alex needed to know. This was too interesting.

"It will be revealed to the world in due time but now, what is of utmost importance is that we destroy that reject and all traces of its existence," Lisa looked Chantalle over. "Unfortunately, that also includes you and Sato-"

"Wait, what?" Chantalle stepped away from the wall and moved toward the teacher's desk. She gathered that they were referring to Jun as 'Sato'.

"You can't kill them. That's illegal. What? Did your father send you to kill people?" This just got ten times worse. Alex went over to Chantalle and stood in front of her with open arms.

Aaron laughed. "Cute," he faced them. "Sorry, but if there are just random enhanced people walking around, then it'd raise questions as to whether our father was really the one to discover the anomaly. Granted, he was, but in the past, Reymond had a hand in everything as well. We'd prefer to erase his involvement,"

Chantalle frowned. "Don't you think it'd raise even more questions if two students mysteriously died after you guys started going to school here? I'd think that that would put a stain on your father's image. Especially if he's going to be using the two of you to advertise this thingy or human enhancer or whatever it is. The truth would eventually come out. People aren't stupid,"

"Yeah. You're being way too drastic. In my eyes, it'd be better to just find a way to get rid of Jun and Chantalle's enhancements," Alex was quaking in his boots.

"Exactly," Chantalle had an overactive pulse, but she put up a front of defensiveness to hide that.

Lisa and Aaron were silent.

Lisa eventually exhaled. "We are not the ones with the final say, but we could pose this option to our father,"

"But I don't think he'd be okay with that. I mean, you guys still know about Dr Reymond's involvement and the prototype," Aaron folded his arms.

"Dr Reymond knows about all that too, and so would the people your father worked with in the past. Gonna kill them too?" Chantalle said with sweat down her back.

Aaron tapped his chin. "Hmm . . . you got the point, actually. If the evidence that you were ever enhanced is gone, and so is the prototype, then our old man can take the credit no problem," he chuckled. "It's just gonna suck filling him in on all this," he heard a clanking sound from the store room. *What was that?* Did one of the bags of steel tip over?

"Trust me, once you bring up the possibility of his reputation being tarnished, the guy's gonna agree that this is the best option 'cause detectives aren't easy to fool," Alex used his hand to wipe away the cold sweats on his forehead. "So yeah,"

Lisa glanced at the open storage room. "Glad we had this discussion, but if you're unable to erase the effects, we might have a problem,"

Aaron pointed her way. "What you're dealing with is the prototype, but from what we know about this, once one is enhanced, there's no going back,"

Chantalle gulped. "Alex is already-"

"I just wanna know exactly what the purpose of this enhancer stuff is? Is it just to flex, or is your dad planning on distributing enhancement juice to the whole world?" Alex raised a brow of scepticism. So far, the motives here did not sound evil- *apart from wanting to kill Jun and steal all the credit- huh. Maybe it is evil.* He re-evaluated his thoughts. *Well, it doesn't sound completely heinous, but I just want a better idea in order to understand.*

"That sounds like anarchy waiting to happen," Chantalle imagined people lifting objects with their minds and throwing things around. Some people were shooting fire all over, and others were blowing up buildings. "Is that really the plan?"

"With my brother and I, we only developed these abilities because of all the testing performed on us. The completed project simply improves health, reflexes and brain capabilities. It basically ensures that one is functioning at their optimum performance levels," Lisa's tone was robotic.

"Testing?" Chantalle was sure that these two had been abused. *They were. Who uses kids for testing?* Whoever their father was was totally out of his mind.

"Indeed," said Lisa. "When the product is introduced, the option of the overly functional nervous system won't be a problem,"

"Cool but also whoa . . . what are your powers?" Alex was itching to know.

"You're just-" the clanking noises reached an all-time high before Aaron could speak.

"What was that?" Alex asked as everyone rushed into the store room. He came in after and saw the steel door with dents on its outer part. It looked like something from inside had caused them. "Oh, shit,"

Aaron rushed to the door and froze the control panel. He broke it, and the door popped open, revealing a highly unstable entity bouncing off the walls of the room at high speed. Its rapid movements caused an electric force to send them flying back with electricity pulsing through their bodies.

They all cried out as the shocks continued coursing over their cells, but when it stopped, they each sat up one after the other to try to understand what was happening.

Aaron was on his feet first. "Shit," there was still a repelling force working against them. He was not sure if he could get close to the anomaly at this rate. "Lisa, it's repelling us!"

"Not only that, it's going completely haywire. Why is that? What's going on?" Chantalle was on her hands and knees. Her body still felt shaken up from the shocks, so it was hard to stand up.

Alex's body was still spazzing out. He stared at his palms and then at Aaron's body, struggling to get near the unstable component. "Wait, don't go any closer!" was his hair spikey? That had been a nasty shock. How was he not dead? *Have I been enhanced?* It did not feel that way.

Aaron stopped. "Why not?"

Lisa was on her feet as well. Everybody was talking over noises of the humming repulsion and the overactive rock that was practically a missile with the way it shot from place to place with intense speed. "You and I are likely the cause behind its increased instability," she stepped further and further away.

Chantalle was fearful that the bell would ring and the next class scheduled to use this lab would catch all this drama. Their flying backwards had caused some things to be knocked off the shelves they had hit. Her back still hurt from the impact. "Oh yeah. Maybe it's reacting with the enhancements in you two," she said.

"Yeah. Or all of you together," Alex told Aaron and Lisa to leave the room as fast as they could, but Lisa was already out.

Aaron groaned but ran off. He shut the door on his way out.

Chantalle observed as the intense bouncing stopped, and the rock just floated directly out the door with its field of electricity contained around it. "Wow . . ."

Alex told her to stay back as he took careful steps towards it.

Chantalle would hate for him to get hurt. "Be careful,"

"I will, I will," Alex's body was still buzzing from the shock and fall. He would need to rest for a while to shake this off. "It looks . . ."

The orb's electric shocks were so extreme that they made sounds as they spurted around it. The humming remained.

Alex wiped the sweat from his forehead as he looked closely. "It's definitely messed up,"

Chantalle's arms were folded. Somehow, she was fully recovered from the fall earlier. "And what does that mean? It'll be easier to break?"

Alex was startled when the bell rang. "No. There are more cracks, but its energy is so powerful that it shows even when it hasn't been interfered with," he would touch, but he knew how much of a no-no that would be.

"Okay, whatever. Find a way to get it back inside so we can leave. The stupid door is broken, so this is gonna look so suspicious but-Alex!" Chantalle couldn't believe that he was just standing around.

They could get caught any minute now. *It doesn't even make sense to leave.* Whatever class was coming in must have started entering already.

Alex turned around. "I uh . . ." he looked to the scattered bags of steel. "Go on out without me. I don't want you to get in trouble,"

"What are you saying?" Chantalle did not like his tone.

Alex stooped to open one of the bags and removed the steel gingerly.

Chantalle kept listening for noises of students filing in. *Nothing.* Was there supposed to be a class here, or were they in luck?

He placed the steel from one bag into another and did a poor job at zipping it closed. Once the other bag was empty, he lifted it and used its open portion to swallow the rock!

Chantalle held hands at the sides of her head. This boy was insane. "What are you doing?!" she hissed.

Alex zipped the bag before looking at her. "Taking it away for experimenting. You heard them. We *need* to find a way to heal you and Jun. And investigating this thing is the best chance we got at getting anywhere with that."

"Alex, you're crazy. Put that thing back," Chantalle pointed to the door.

"No. I promise that once I'm done closely examining it and finding out how it works that I'll bring it back." Alex was surprised that it was not giving trouble within the bag.

Chantalle just . . . *He's not gonna listen, is he?* "Okay, just hurry up and get out."

Alex ran past her to the door.

Chantalle closed the door with her mind and stacked back the bags the same way. She ran to meet Alex outside the store room and was relieved to see that there really weren't any students there.

"Why did you take so long in there?" Aaron asked.

Alex started being dragged all over the room, hitting walls and bouncing around.

"Get out of here!" Chantalle held him in place with her mind, but he looked banged up.

"What do you- is he carrying it in that bag?" Lisa pointed. "Bring it here! We need to destroy it!"

"No, but it's the only thing we can use to-ah-to-to undo Jun and Chantalle's enhancements." Alex was floating close to the ceiling. He could feel the force of the rock wanting to break away from Chantalle's hold, but she was strong.

Chantalle was on her knees with her hands extended. "This is . . . hard for me too. . ." she was grunting and struggling. "You guys need to get out of here!"

Aaron did some quick thinking. "Fine. But when you're through, you *need* to bring it to us so we can destroy it,"

"But it's right there," Lisa pointed to the boy floating high up.

"Yeah, but when we get near, it starts going haywire, so before we can even get our hands on it, we need to figure out a way to get it to stay still," Aaron said. "Not much we can do when it goes this crazy whenever we're close, am I right?"

"Are you guys sure this thing can even be broken?" Alex's body was in a world of pain. He'd hit his shoulder while flying around a while ago. He hoped it wasn't broken . . .

"Hello! Can you people stop having a casual conversation and get out?" Chantalle's head was bursting from the pain.

Lisa groaned. "Okay fine. But we'll be checking in on you at this point next week. If you've made no progress, we'll do what we have to," she marched towards a desk with her laptop on it and used it to open the door so she and Aaron could leave.

Alex felt the force of the rock die in his arms. "Thank God,"

Chantalle brought him to the ground and then rested her hands in front of her to pant. "You're insane,"

"Hey, I just want to make sure that you and Jun don't die," he noted that Lisa had shut the door behind her. "Now come one. Let's get out of here," he tried to extend his free hand, but it hurt to do so.

Chantalle saw the way he flinched. "You took a nasty fall in the store room, and that rock was tossing you around like a ragdoll a while ago. Are you okay?"

"Yeah, I just need some rest, I think," Alex helped her up regardless. "We have class, but . . ." he brought the bag to the table and opened it to look at the floating rock.

Chantalle gulped. "It's all cracked up. I wonder if it can really be destroyed,"

"What do you think will happen if they can't destroy it?"

"Well, their dad didn't have a problem using them for experiments, so I doubt he cares at all about their safety. Sounds like a mad man. He might just kill them both," Chantalle said.

Alex gulped. "This is like the superhero movies,"

"It is but in real life, so it's just scary," she checked her watch. "We should go,"

"Yeah. Dr Reymond found out about me because I was late to class once, so if he finds the evidence of the broken door, he'll probably be able to tell that I stole this while late for class," Alex closed the bag after sighing. "I have detention," he might as well share this.

Chantalle's eyes widened. "Dr Reymond found out?"

"Not about everything. More like he found out that me and Jun broke into the lab and that we caused the fire, but I covered it up,"

Chantalle did not like this. "Why didn't you tell us?"

"There's been a lot on my mind. Sorry," he shook his head. "I hope he doesn't look into my lateness this time around," he was moving to the door.

Chantalle was right behind him. Things seemed to be getting worse and worse. "Well, we'll just have to keep as low a profile as possible,"

Alex sighed. "Yeah, I guess so," Aaron had frozen the control panel using his eyes. Did he have frost vision instead of laser vision? That was pretty neat. *And they want me to make progress in a week, or they'll come after us.* The stakes here were getting pretty high, but he was sure they would figure this out. *Yeah. And the only reason Lisa and Aaron are so threatening is 'cause of their dad.* How did the man and Dr Reymond end up having a falling out anyway? It sounded like Lisa and Aaron had been taught to hate their principal. *I wonder.* Oh, the questions he would ask if this wasn't a secret.

CHAPTER
FOURTEEN

Before Reymond High had been founded, the name given to the million-dollar structure that he and his partner had worked hard to build together was 'Hypernova Research Partners: Home of Life-Changing Discoveries'. The abbreviation HRP had been common in those days, but currently, not even that was used when referring to the old laboratory.

But James had no time to lament on that. It did annoy him that everything they worked for had been erased by his partner, but he was not one to stay fixated on past tragedies. No. If he ever brought up events of years prior, it would be to encourage himself to do better in his present life. A firm believer of the saying 'the past is a place of reference, not of residence' was he.

The man exhaled with eyes planted on the cylindrical tube containing the floating, blue orb. It rotated like a planet in its chamber and was a sight to behold. *People who let their fear stop them from venturing further will never do great.* He placed a palm on the improved version of what had brought forth the demise of Christopher's beloved son.

Not a day went by that James wouldn't think of it. He would never forget how a simple bad decision had shaken their worlds forever. *I'm better for it.* He could not say the same for his partner, for it had been years since they interacted. *His school is held in high regard, so I take that to mean he's done well for himself.* But was that really Reymonnd's passion?

James took a step back from the glass and remembered the day they had found it. Everything had started on that fateful day. *Star gazing during a meteor shower only to have one land before us.* They'd been studying astrophysics at university back then. Ambitious boys, they had been. *My ambition has not died.* He could recall exactly what happened when it landed on the roof of their dormitory.

A few students had come to find out what the noise meant and had been intrigued at the sight of a fallen meteor. James had felt a hum in his hands after picking it up, but no one had believed him. The hum was too faint to detect easily, but Christopher had suggested that they show a professor.

The man had examined it and concluded that it was a useless rock but had told them that if they wanted, they could keep it around. Christopher and James had been roommates back then, so they placed it on their dresser.

James had known that what they were dealing with was far more than what people presumed, so that same night, he'd started investigating. Christopher had been intrigued, so he had stayed by his side the entire time.

It had taken guts, but through getting nowhere several times while testing, James had decided to take the risk of breaking the rock in half. Oh, the world that had opened up to them once it was broken.

Inside was where its true beauty was held. Tiny crystals ranging from blue to white to purple and green were what made up the supposed 'meteor', and he and Christopher had only been able to see them because of the rich orange from his desk lamp. *Things went up from there.* They'd agreed to keep it secret while they performed various tests on their discovery, and it was during those tests that they realised its ability to improve human anatomy. *Testing with a cut on my finger is what led us there.* To this day, the skin on his left hand is still difficult to penetrate.

More and more secret testing sent them in circles since things were never straightforward, but they had vowed to conduct more research after university. And so came the birth of their research facility and the hundreds of scientists who agreed to work with them. All the world knew was that they were working on something groundbreaking and to look out for them in the future. People had been on the edge of their seats, watching closely as they toiled for years in silence but then . . .

Daniel's ashes came to mind. *To dabble with the unknown is to risk losing all that's precious to you.* His head lowered, and he placed a hand over his left eye. *I truly am sorry, but* . . . the glowing orb caught his attention. *It would be ludicrous to take its risks as its only worth.* Far too much could be done with this to just throw it down the drain. *And he knows that.*

He remembered Aaron and Lisa's confused faces when he first brought them into his underground lab. He had taught them the saying. And they agreed it is better to take risks than to ignore the potential.

He walked up to his large computer screen. They should have sent a report by now. He wondered if they had gotten anywhere in their mission. *The old lab is far from here.* When the children were ready to return home, they would have to take the submarine he left them to return. The machinery was quick, but Alaska was still far off from California.

James took a seat and started typing. *It's well into the night, but they've never been early bed goers.* He may have adopted the girl and boy for testing during his research, but he had learned plenty about them over the years, and they'd actually formed a relationship. *I feared I may have lost them quite a few times, but my past failure taught me to avoid such a mishap.*

His screen showed that Lisa's facetime was ringing. It had only been a few days, but checking in was important.

After the second ring, Lisa and Aaron appeared on his screen. "Father," they said together.

"Kids," he sat back. "How are you two?"

"Quite well, Father, quite well," was Lisa's response.

"We were just about to call you," said Aaron. "Lonely in that underground hell without us?" he was as cheeky as ever.

James shook his head. "Have you found the fire starter or the orb?" he cut right to the chase.

"Yes," they said together.

Well, that was some great news. "Already? Wow. It didn't take long, did it?" he rolled his seat closer to the control panel. "How did you find them? Who are they, and how did they acquire such power? Was it really the prototype? Where is it? How was it able to do such a thing?" the word 'unpredictable' came to mind. *I suppose it hasn't changed in all these years.*

"Slow down. We're getting to that," Aaron said. They were both in pyjamas sitting on a bed.

"Apparently, whenever we get in contact with the other enhanced people, there's some sort of reaction that takes place. It appears to weaken the more we interact, but we haven't done so enough to draw that conclusion," Lisa stated.

"People?" Dr Foster's brows creased.

"Oh yeah, uh, it's not only the fire starter who's been enhanced but also this girl who can move things with her mind. Telekinesis. This place is crazy," Aaron chuckled.

James blinked. "Two people have been interfered with?"

His children nodded.

James placed two fingers on his eyebrow.

"He looks stressed," Aaron whispered to Lisa.

"So, I see," she replied.

James looked at them. "There must be more," he held his chin. "Look at this. His neglect to destroy it has somehow led to a crisis at his precious high school,"

"I doubt that there's more, though. There would have been more accidents if that was the case. And we haven't reacted with other people," Lisa said.

James continued to frown. "Okay, but have you retrieved the orb? Did you destroy it?"

Aaron scratched his head. "Its instability is really proving to be a problem 'cause whenever we get close, it starts going haywire and jumping all over the place. I don't know what'll happen if our powers got in contact with it,"

"Why is it like that? If both are made from material from the same rock, then why would they react so badly when in contact with their energy?" Lisa's arms folded. Aaron was holding the phone.

The scientist started to ponder. "I noticed that the waves produced by each crystal's energy took different forms, but because they had the same effect, I never spent time investigating them. Well . . . ah yes. One of our earliest tests did reveal that many of their energies repelled. That's why we used individual crystals to develop our creation,"

"Whoa . . . you coulda said that from the start Gramps," Aaron shook his head but received a pinch from Lisa. "Ow," he frowned. "Do you happen to remember which colours repelled?"

"Does he need to say?" Lisa gave a dull expression.

"Oh boy," James did not like this. "It needs to be destroyed, so you two should try to do so as soon as possible. And as for the other enhanced students . . . we need to stage an accident,"

"Yeah, about that," Aaron started. "We had a little chitchat with the girl with the telekinesis, and she and their sidekick said that it'd look pretty suspicious if they just died right after me and Lisa showed up. And I mean, you need us to demonstrate the power of your discovery so that it may ring some bells in people's heads. Let's not forget that we are going to your old partner's school. Most people may not know that you two ever worked together, but there are folks out there who do and would be able to connect the dots,"

James groaned at his logic. "But we can*not* have evidence of Reymond's involvement. I know how humans are. The second he sees me thriving, he and everyone else who left after things went south would want to get their credit," he slapped his chest. "And even though I was the one who didn't give in, they would get their piece of the praise. I don't want that. It's been me all by myself from day one, and when I thought I'd found companions, they too gave up on me. I deserve all the praise, and I *will* find a way to get it. I am the genius, I am the go-getter, and I am the...."

"Father, relax," Lisa said gently.

James noticed his heavy breathing. This happened a lot . . .

The teenagers watched him take deep breaths to compose himself.

James set his elbows before the panel and clasped his hands at his lips. "What do you propose we do?"

"Their sidekick said that he's working on erasing the enhancements, so right now, he's in possession of the orb. We gave them a week to get somewhere. If their enhancements are gone, then there'll be no evidence. And, of course, once they're through using the orb, we'll find a way to get rid of it. Once that's done, we're good," Aaron seemed confident.

James sighed heavily. "You want me to put the future of my research in the hands of a teenager?"

"His IQ is higher than most scientists," Lisa pointed out.

James groaned. "It would make more sense if you brought them here to have me undo their enhancements, but I'm not sure how effective removing their powers would be . . . there was the fire, so if they wanted, they could report that one of them had been responsible for it and that was already on the news so . . . ah," he held the sides of his head. "I want them all gone,"

Aaron tilted his head. "Who?"

"Reymond, the children and even the whole school, but that would be a stretch," he sat back with folded arms.

Aaron and Lisa exchanged concerned glances.

"The plan was to stage an accident. It won't be suspicious if it's done well," said Dr Foster. "Don't you kids have field trips? Organize a bus crash where only the children of concern are done away with,"

"Huh . . . *do* we have field trips?" Aaron turned to his sister.

"I heard the bubbly girl speaking about a trip to a different school for 'cheer offs', but that's for cheerleaders and the school mascot," Lisa said. "It takes place in two months,"

"Perfect," James was hellbent on getting rid of those kids. "You keep mentioning a sidekick. They should be annihilated too. And Reymond, but I'll find a way to deal with him,"

Aaron's face showed concern. "I don't know how much that will-"

"Report back to me in a week's time. I expect you to have a cohesive plan by then," he said. "I must go now. I have to put together my treat for my old partner and former friend," he ended the call and got up to head out of his main research area. *Reymond . . .* He had been the one to walk away, but in his mind, Reymond had given up on him first. *You will pay for what you did to me.* Pictures of their good times growing up floated in his head before they were replaced by his partner bent over.

The last image was of Reymond in shambles. In front of him was that God-forsaken school, flames around it. *Turning everything we worked for into that.* He ground his teeth but found room to smile as the thought of Reymond's school burning persisted. *You will feel my wrath.*

He stepped into the bright hallway after that.

"HE'S GONNA FIND OUT this is here, and we're all gonna get expelled," Jun sat on Alex's bed that night, looking in incredulity at the floating piece of hell.

Chantalle was sitting on the floor, admiring but also watching closely in fear. This thing . . . "I wonder why it keeps having that reaction to Aaron and Lisa,"

"I'm just trying to figure out what it is," Alex had sensors hooked up to the entity, which had been placed strategically by Chantalle using her telekinesis. It came in handy several times today.

Jun sat closer to the edge of the bed. He just couldn't believe that while he had been awkwardly sitting by himself outside the cafeteria that these two had nearly died at the hand of this thing. *And it doesn't even have hands.* Alex had listed the changes he'd noticed about it after the new kids had come in contact. He could hear the hum and see the electric field as well. This was scary. "Whatever it is can't be part of our world. It must have fallen from the sky or-or come out of space or something. I wanna call it a rock, but I'm not even sure if its material is close. It just looks rock-like from the outside,"

"It would be interesting to get a feel of its texture. That might help in understanding what it is," Chantalle could not take her eyes away. "I wonder if, with time, it'll have less of a strong reaction to them,"

"I wonder, too," Alex was sitting at his desk and trying to make sense of what his laptop screen was telling him. This program was similar to the one he'd created for Jun and Chantalle but had been modified to give him an idea of the energy created by the rock. So far, all he could see was that it was synonymous with electricity, but each strike was hundreds of levels over the power of what they were used to. *So, is it just electrical energy?* In Physics, they would come up with a collective term for this. It was like electricity but leagues ahead of it in terms of power.

"Are you guys thinking about the 'initial reaction' theory that Aaron's sister came up with?" Jun had been given a clear run down of their interaction with the new kids.

"Yeah. I'm trying to figure out if as they come close more frequently if it would go less and less crazy, but I don't know," Alex said. "Is them being in the same building causing it to hum and react this way? What is in them?" he was trying to think of it in terms he understood. "What aggravates electricity? Conducts it? Metal . . . what makes it stronger? Coils uhh . . ." he scratched his head.

"We're not here to discuss that. You're supposed to be figuring out what it did to interfere with our nervous system in the first place. Then from there, you find a way to undo that," Chantalle encouraged him to stay focused.

"Right, right," Alex did not like not understanding things. That was why his mind kept wandering. His fingers typed across the keyboard. "Nerves, electricity . . ." he opened the program on Jun. "Might need to make another one so we can make a simulation," he moved the shoulder he had hurt today and pain shot through his body.

Jun would help Alex in a second, but right now, he was just captivated by the space rock. *I'm calling it. This fell from space.* "I wonder if aliens are looking for it,"

"Shit," Chantalle chewed her lip. "I read a comic about that once but don't you think they would have shown up by now? Dr Reymond has had this thing for years,"

"True," he moved his palm against his chin. "Hey uh," his phone buzzed after he started. Jun retrieved it. His friends were texting him. *So much has been on my mind that I haven't been keeping in touch.* It would be a shame if they dropped him because of that . . .

Chantalle had expected a question, but Jun was glued to his phone. "Hey, uh what?" she wrapped her arms around her knees.

They were up to her chest. The hour was about eleven p.m, and they were all in pyjamas.

"Hold on," Jun was doing damage control. His pals were making jokes about him, replacing them with a super nerd friend group. *Which is exactly the case, except I'm not replacing them.* He quickly typed that he would never dream of calling anyone here his friends and that they were all being morons for suggesting that. He sent a skull emoji to drive home that this was a joke.

Chantalle got up and sat next to him.

"Hey," Jun held his phone away. "Privacy, please?"

"Super nerds? Is that what I saw?" Chantalle raised an eyebrow. "Who are you texting?"

"None of your business," he put his phone away. *She's sitting so close.* He scooted to the left. "Why aren't you interested in cheerleading?"

Was that what he'd wanted to ask? "Because it's not my thing,"

Jun smiled. "Then what is your thing? Manga? Anime? Comics?"

"Yeah. And the science, of course," Chantalle looked to Alex. "And Alex," she whispered.

Jun's insides dropped. He gulped. "What does that mean?" he asked just as soft.

Chantalle seemed surprised. "You heard that?"

He was being creepy, wasn't he? "I wasn't supposed to?"

Chantalle just shook her head.

Jun rubbed the back of his neck. "I know I teased you earlier, but . . . I think it'd be cool if you tried cheerleading,"

Chantalle laughed. "As if. Why would you say something like that? Do I just fit the peppy, blonde white girl cheerleading archetype?"

He observed her locks, dark brown skin and jaded appearance. "No, but you could look at it like High School Musical. Fight the status quo. Woo!" he raised two fists but immediately regretted it. *That was cringe as hell.*

Chantalle laughed at him. "Since when are *you*, Mr Challenge-The-Norm? Last time I checked, you were the type who would do anything to fit in,"

Jun hated that she saw him that way. "You've only known me for a week,"

"True," Chantalle admired how Alex whispered possibilities to himself and scribbled notes onto paper. *His shoulder still hurts. He keeps wincing.* They should have gone to the nurse after he hit it.

Jun frowned at Alex. *What is it about him?* "You should try out. If not in the name of challenging the norm, then in the name of college applications. People like a well-rounded student. If you can flex a perfect GPA *and* sporty extracurriculars, then you'd be all set,"

Chantalle did *not* know where this was coming from. "Do you have some kind of sick fantasy of me doing cheer routines that you're trying to satisfy?"

Jun was mortified! "Nooo! What? I just thought it would be nice if . . . never mind," he went back to his phone. *What does she take me for?* Did he seem weird to her? A tornado of anxious questions started in his head.

Chantalle did not mean to scare him. She was just joking around. "I like your point,"

Jun put his phone down. "What do you mean?"

"Extra-curricular and college? That's not something I'd considered when she asked," Chantalle said.

Jun felt flushed. "So, you're gonna try out?"

"Did you just remember that she brought it up? Is that why we're talking about this now?"

He shrugged. "Yeah,"

"Hmm . . ." she tapped her chin. "I'll think about it,"

"Ah, come on. Everyone knows that means no," Jun laughed.

Chantalle laughed too. "We should focus on the problem at hand. If we don't fix our little 'mutations' by next week, Aaron and Lisa just might cut our necks without warning," she went to Alex's side. "If you want, I can take over. Your shoulder looks like it hurts,"

Alex rolled his chair to face her. "Ah, it's not that bad. Just a bit of an ache but nothing to- ah-ah-ah- sneeze at," his shoulder had sent a shock of pain through his arm a while ago.

Jun got up too. "Didn't you all get hit with a shockwave in the store room? Alex, you said you all got hit. That's how Chantalle and I got our mutations," he came slowly to Chantalle's side. "Aren't you worried that something might have happened to you too?"

"Hmm . . ." Chantalle had thought of that. "Maybe we should do a scan," she went to the door. "I'm gonna get my gadget- I should really come up with a name for it but hold on," she was gone in a second.

"I don't think anything happened to me. After you'd gotten hit, your eyes went all purple, and your fingers were tingly, but with me, I didn't experience any changes," Alex whimpered and held his shoulder. "Except for whatever's going on with this injury, but that has nothing to do with getting hit," he had tears in his eyes.

"I hope you're right then," Jun did not know what they would do if more of them ended up mutating. *Or getting 'enhanced,' as the new kids apparently put it.*

"I think I am," Alex faced his computer again. "Now let me keep-"

The orb glitched, and they both squeaked like scared girls.

Jun had a hand on his mouth.

It didn't look any more intimidating than it had when they brought it here, but that noise had been pretty concerning.

Alex cleared his throat. "I should get some glass to conceal it, shouldn't I?"

"I don't know how much that'll help," Jun hated this. "Dude, Dr Reymond came to your room on Saturday, and he's clearly hiding this thing," he pointed to the rock. "Don't you think he'll notice it's missing?" Chantalle had told him about that too.

"I'm gonna put it back tomorrow," Alex mumbled.

"Really? Have you gotten anywhere with it today? What would be the point of stealing it in the first place if you put it back before you get anywhere?" Jun folded his arms. The orb was giving him flashbacks to when he first got zapped. *What if it zaps Alex again?*

"I'm making progress *slowly,* okay? It's a process," Alex's leg shook under his desk. "And Dr R is way too busy to keep tabs on this regularly. If he does, then he probably only checks up on it every week or so,"

Jun narrowed his eyes. "Not after he got worried one of his students found it. The guy maybe has hidden cameras in its room,"

Alex made a yikes face. "I . . . doubt that would make sense. This thing has got some crazy energy. The cameras could get disabled at any point. Plus, he wouldn't wanna risk people finding footage of a floating glowy rock if they ever went into the security room," he was just trying to make things sound better than they were.

Jun groaned. "You need to save what you picked up on your software, then put this thing back tomorrow morning,"

"That was the plan from the absolute start, Sato," Alex snickered. "That's what they call you, you know. Sato. Aaron and Lisa are pretty weird," he held his bum shoulder.

Jun sat on the bed. "I don't know if we can trust them,"

Alex hummed. "They didn't seem like the lying type when we met them, but-"

Chantalle came back in. "Okay, let's do this quick,"

The results of Alex's scan revealed that nothing had been altered.

"Thank God," Jun rubbed hands of relief on his face.

Alex was smug. "See? I know my body, man. If something had happened, I would be able to tell. You can call it my superpower,"

Chantalle rested the gadget next to the laptop. "It's not a superpower to have literal normal senses. Most people can tell when something changes in them,"

Alex did not like that she busted his bubble. "Well yeah, but . . ."

Jun gestured to the laptop. "What have you figured out so far apart from that it's like electricity?"

"Uhh . . ." Alex scratched his head. "All I can infer is that it's some out of this powerful world electro-energy and that it jump-started your nervous systems that way,"

Chantalle folded her arms. "Okay, so what's the opposite of jump start?"

The trio was quiet.

"Sit stop?" Alex laughed at his joke.

"Our lives may be on the line," Jun rolled his eyes.

"I don't think they'd go back on their word. We gave them valid reasons why their plan made no sense," Alex stated. "But I get that we should be quick about this. Uh . . ." he snapped his fingers. "I mean, maybe an equally powerful zap might get things to normal again. We don't know,"

"You want us to make it zap us again?" Chantalle seemed horrified. "It already did, and nothing happened,"

Alex shrugged, but it hurt. "That was more of a shockwave. I'm talking about another direct zap," he licked his lips. "We're dealing with something completely unknown. That could very well be the way to solve this,"

"Or it could kill us," Jun did not like how close it was. *Just floating in the middle of the room.* A chill went down his spine. "Maybe we can try using normal electricity if we're going with that,"

"I do *not* think that any of those things are the way to go. I know none of this makes sense, but we still need to be practical guys,"

Chantalle was sure that they were just saying anything. "Shouldn't we look for something to relax our nervous systems?"

The boys hummed in thought.

"That could be an idea. Yeah. Maybe even a drug could help, but I'm sure the actual solution would be way more complicated than that," Alex sighed. "But trial and error,"

"Yeah," Jun sat back as silence fell among them.

Chantalle gathered her hands. "Let's call it a night,"

Alex started closing his software. "Yeah, I guess we should,"

Jun and Chantalle left after saying goodbye and packing away the anomaly. Chantalle had done the honours.

Alex set his laptop on his desk and settled into bed right after they left.

He struggled with finding a comfortable position to sleep in for two hours until his need for rest overpowered, and he fell either way.

That was what he thought anyway. The real reason why sleeping came naturally in spite of his pain was due to the absence of it. His fractured shoulder had healed all on its own during the course of his thrashing and turning. But Alex had not realised this.

"SHIT," DAVE BACKED out of the empty room with an open mouth.

It was gone. He did not know where it went, but it was not here, and this was not good.

"What will Reymond say?" he whispered.

He had just been working on finding James when an idea to bulk up the door's security came to mind. What he did not cater for was that the door would be tampered with and the entity missing.

It's glaring who would've done this. What was that boy up to, and why did it involve something so dangerous? *I need to tell Christopher.*

CHAPTER FIFTEEN

"I'm pretty sure nothing happened. I don't think it was the same as one of them getting zapped," Aaron spoke to Lisa in the hall the next morning before school. They were next to his locker.

Lisa had brought up the possibility of further enhancements occurring from the shockwave of yesterday. She did not feel any different, and her brother had not reported any abnormalities, but they could not say the same for the others. "We don't know. The prototype is unstable. We're lucky it didn't kill us,"

Aaron sighed at her paranoia. *Or I guess you could call it responsibility.* She had been pretty uptight since they were kids. Always preparing, considering and thinking ahead. *Guess it levels out how chill I can be, but I know it stresses her out.* Her thoughts and suspicions mainly stayed in her head, so sometimes they became excessive, overheating her mind. *And that's why she's got fire.* And his cool attitude was the reason his eyes could shoot ice. *I wonder what Sato's brain is like.* "Yeah, but we don't have time to think about that," he was whispering. "We need to start acting on Father's plan,"

Lisa nodded. "I'll try to convince them to join the cheerleading squad, and we'll join as well. We'll work on things from there. We have a month,"

"Boys do cheerleading?" Aaron raised an eyebrow.

Lisa shrugged.

Aaron scratched his jaw. "Hmm . . . I guess anything is possible, but how do we convince them without seeming like total weirdos?

They already know that we're after them," planning to annihilate someone, in theory, was one thing, but the actual execution would surely be intimidating. *And then he's gonna take down Reymond.* Aaron wondered how their dad would do that. Was he thinking straight?

"Maybe we can get the happy girl to help? She knows them well, so they won't be confused if she approaches them," Lisa rubbed her fingers against each other on the one hand. She knew all about how cheerleading and cheerleaders operated and what they wore and did, and it did *not* sound like her thing. *But this is what Father wants so . .*
.

"Happy girl," Aaron laughed softly. "Her name is- Annalise!" he saw her walking past them with her friends.

"Oh, hi Aaron, hi Lisa," Annalise and her girls stopped. "How are you two doing?"

Aaron always had a smile of charm on his face when engaging with others. He had lived in isolation his whole life, but that did not stop him from being Mr Congeniality. The media had helped immensely. "We're doing great, but we heard about your cheerleading tryouts on Friday and were wondering if uh . . . we could both join in on the fun?" he gathered his hands.

Annalise blinked as her friends squealed. "As in you too?" she grinned.

Aaron could see them fangirling. "Yeah. Is it weird for a guy too," The girls screamed.

Lisa's eyes bulged. "Why?"

"We would be so, so, *so* happy to have you both," Annalise turned to Lisa with Chantalle's words of yesterday in her mind. Not everyone needed to get out of their shell. "Are you sure you'd be comfortable with this, Lisa?" she showed concern, not wanting the new girl to feel out of place if this was not something she would enjoy.

Lisa shrunk at the compassion. Her eyes wandered to the side. "It sounds exciting,"

Annalise tilted her head. "Are you sure?"

Lisa's cheeks heated. "Why are you questioning me?"

Annalise felt her friends and Aaron turn to her. "Just to make sure you're not forcing yourself into something you won't like. Anyone can do anything, but not everyone *wants* to do everything, you know?" she tried a friendly smile.

Lisa hummed. "Well, I want to do this,"

"Why? 'Cause cheering sounds fun? It is," one of Annalise's friends said.

Lisa did not like having all their attention.

Aaron found this amusing. *She's such an awkward bean.* "Yes. Cheering sounds hella fun to her," he wrapped an arm around his sister.

Lisa removed it. "Exactly,"

Annalise was glad. "I hope you have a good time then," she was about to leave.

"Wait," Lisa held her arm but pulled away instantly. Touching was weird.

Annalise perked up.

"How many people are you expecting?" Lisa was trying to find a way to rope in their subjects of concern. *Things will be tricky when it's time for execution, but for now, we must start with the basics.*

"The sign-up sheet doesn't say much, but we're hoping that as the week goes on that the numbers will sky-rocket," Annalise had sounded happy at first, but now her mood dimmed. "The kids here aren't the type to like physical activity, so that's part of why but we're working to change that. It's important to move around once in a while, you know? It stimulates the brain. Sitting and experimenting are great, but I've always been told that it's good to be well-rounded. Everyone should have a balance of arts, sports and academics,"

Chantalle popped into her head again. "If they want to," she really did not want to come off as pushy. She had not considered that until interacting with Chantalle again.

Aaron nodded. "Nice, nice . . ."

Lisa did not like their odds. "My brother here was just saying that it would be nice if more people that he knew would sign up. Like-"

"Devon?" said a girl with brown hair.

Annalise smiled as her friends laughed at the thought. "He said he'll be coming but only as a water boy,"

"But we all know that he just wants to see cute girls," a different girl spoke and made everyone laugh.

"He and his friends,"

Aaron had a good laugh. "Classic Devon,"

Lisa rolled her eyes. Her brother got comfortable way too easily. *It's been a grand total of four days, but I'll leave him.* She was sort of envious, actually. "Not him. We were just discussing um . . . the group you introduced him to on Friday," she wanted her brother to catch on and help her. She played with her fingers while speaking. This was exhausting.

Aaron caught her drift. "Yeah, they should join. They seem like the perfect candidates for a cheer squad. We got totally fit cute girl with the neat sense of style, the lanky guy and their sidekick,"

Annalise seemed intrigued. "That would be awesome, but I already approached Chantalle, and she wasn't interested," she pouted.

No. "Approach her and the rest again. She might change her mind," Lisa rushed.

Annalise was surprised. Would Lisa feel more comfortable if they were there? Had she formed a bond with them? *That would be so cute.* Annalise had not seen them interacting, though. *Probably happened while I wasn't around.* She smiled gently. "Okay, well, I'll do that. Maybe you guys can help me to convince them,"

"Uhh, we'd rather not," Aaron patted Lisa's head.

Lisa threw his hand off.

Right. She's shy. Annalise nodded her understanding. "Okay, well, I'll tell you what they say if anything changes," she smiled and waved at them both before leaving.

Aaron laughed. "We're making progress quickly," he folded his arms.

"We don't know if that will lead anywhere, but we can hope," Lisa had not thought anything of their mission at first, but after interacting with the other enhances, she had started thinking. How would that go down? *Killing them.* It would look like an accident, but she and Aaron would both know what actually happened.

DR REYMOND HAD NOTICED the orb back in place this morning when Dave had brought him to have a look but based on the state of the door and the disruption of the stacked bags before it, he could tell that it had indeed been stolen and then placed back. *Now it resides in my office.* It floated in one of his drawers as he thought, but a new location was in the works.

The man kept his hands clasped at his desk as he waited. This situation was serious, so it made no sense to treat it as anything less. They had the evidence to know who was behind this, so now was the time to get right down to the bottom of the issue.

Alex Johnson entered the office that morning. His face was sweaty, and his lips were trembling, but by all means, he tried to hide how he truly felt. *Crap.* Jun had been right. Dr Reymond found out, and now he would be expelled! They had called him from class on the speaker a while ago, and the only thing he could think of when it happened was packing his bags and leaving his dream school. *Nooo!* Maybe he could deny everything. *Yeah, I mean I put it back as soon as the sun rose so . . .* he was foolish to think the world-renowned scientist would not find out.

"Have a seat," Dave stood behind Reymond's cheer, arms folded.

Carla locked the door after leading him in. She would not be joining them.

Alex sat after gulping. "Yes, sir?"

Dr Reymond's face was solemn. "Why don't I let . . . you tell me why you're here,"

Alex's fingers scratched his seat.

The principal was waiting.

Alex wiped at his sweat. "For late attendance?" he had not been late today, but it was worth a shot. *At least my shoulder's better.* That was the only good thing about this.

Dave rolled his eyes. "What's going on, kid?" he asked it flat out.

Alex was prepared to lie. "What do you mean what's going o-"

"We know about your involvement with this," Dr Reymond pulled his drawer open and retrieved the orb.

Alex's eyes bulged. It was contained in a glass box which was cracked at certain points. *Damn. Does its instability increase with time?* How was he sure they were not all in danger?

"Your lack of reaction is telling," Dave pointed out.

Alex snapped out of his fascination. "What? I mean-" he pointed and screamed. "What is that thing?"

Dr Reymond rolled his eyes. "You know what it is, Alex. And we know that you know and that somehow you still want to be involved with it even after the fire it caused,"

Alex chewed his lip.

Dr Reymond shifted it to the side. He could feel its energy shaking the glass. *Not good.* Why was it behaving like that? *I'll find out right now.* "Why did you lie when I asked if you'd come across anything while using lab OW? What is the point in this secrecy? I'd like to think that if a kid saw something so intimidating that the first thing they'd worry about was their safety. But instead, you've been using it to do who knows what behind everyone's backs. Don't you know how dangerous this could be?" he was genuinely concerned.

Alex gulped. Did it even make sense to lie at this point? His eyes stung as he thought of his fate. *He's not asking about Jun, so that's good.* But they had to come up with a cure. He was the main person in charge of that. If he left due to expulsion, then . . .

Dave could see the gloss in his eyes. Was this kid about to cry? "Listen, we just want answers. This isn't a comic book or a movie. This is real life, and it's serious. Your life could have been at risk. Why did you take this, and why didn't you just leave it alone after finding it? How did it cause the fire? From what we know, it's been safely hidden in that back room for *years*. It hasn't caused a single problem until now. *What* did you do?"

Dr Reymond gathered his hands on his desk.

Alex made a whimpering noise. "I-I didn't . . . I didn't tell you because I . . . I didn't want to get expelled! This is my dream school. It wasn't my fault I found it. It was an accident, but then it- and I- and you said- but it's too late to turn back now. I'm sorry, but we're in too deep,"

This frightened the principal. "What do you mean we're in too deep?"

Dave frowned.

Alex had chosen his words poorly. *He hasn't mentioned expelling me, but I'm still scared.* "It's complicated,"

"If it's complicated, then you need to tell us. Whatever it is, we can help. Wouldn't you prefer having adults who have a better understanding of this by your side?" Dave did not like this.

Alex held tightly to his seat, scratching the material with his fingers. They had a point.

Dr Reymond gathered that they were scaring him. "Listen, Alex," his voice was softer.

The boy looked right at him.

"You're not going to get in trouble. Not you or anyone else involved. We just want to understand this and help as much as we can," he wanted this boy to trust him. It was always sad when kids kept problems to themselves for fear of punishment. They were supposed to trust the adults around them. Not fear them.

Alex thought. "Are you sure?"

Dave nodded. "Yes. We promise. We want to help and understand what's going on,"

"Promise you won't tell anyone either? The state of people's lives is on the line," said Alex.

Dr Reymond sighed. "Yes. We just want to help,"

Alex heard a crack from the box.

Dr Reymond glanced at it too but left it where it was. He may have to conduct some tests. "Please, share with us what's been happening,"

The freshman saw Jun's convulsing body, the shockwave of yesterday and the new kids all flash through his mind in a split second. It ended with a purple strike of lightning through his mind.

JUN HAD HEARD ALEX'S name call on the grand speaker about fifteen minutes ago.

"And that's how you work it out. Now in the case where . . ." his chemistry teacher was explaining something upfront.

Jun was anxious. *Does she feel it too?* He turned to Chantalle.

Chantalle kept looking out the door. She faced Jun afterwards.

Yeah, she doesn't like this either. He tapped his pen against his notebook. The new girl was in their class.

She sat quietly up front with her notebook open for notes. Not at all concerned that Alex was called just now. Were they being paranoid?

Jun suddenly thought of something. *How come the rock isn't going haywire right now? Alex said once they get anywhere near it, it goes crazy.* Come to think of it, it had not seemed to lose control during class yesterday. Was it only a sometimes thing? Perhaps when her brother was around? *None of this makes any sense.* He just had to shake his head.

"Sorry to disturb your classes but would Aaron and Lisa Portman, please come to the principal's office?" the speaker cracked again.

Chantalle's eyes widened. What was going on? Alex was one thing but now . . .

Jun sat uncomfortably.

The class was staring at Lisa.

Lisa blinked at the speaker. What was this exactly?

"Go on. You shouldn't keep them waiting," said their teacher.

Lisa frowned before closing her book and packing her things. This was not good. She had heard them call the Johnson boy before. *Calling Aaron and myself right after can only mean one thing.* What did he tell Reymond?

Jun wiped the sweat from his face after she left the class. "We're in some deep shit," he whispered to Chantalle.

"I know," Chantalle whispered back. She faced him. "What if they expelled him?"

"If they did, it's because he ran his mouth," Jun said.

Someone in front of them turned around. "What are you guys talking about?" he spoke at the same volume. The lesson had continued.

Jun folded his lips. Were they talking too loud? "Nothing,"

The boy narrowed his eyes. "Do you guys sell drugs?"

The two blinked. "No," said Chantalle.

"Oh," he turned forward in disappointment.

"What is with these kids?" Jun would laugh, but their situation was too nerve-racking. If they called either him or Chantalle, then they knew they were screwed. *The question is, what would it mean?* Would they be transported to a Norwegian lab? *Maybe.* If that happened, it would definitely be on the news. And everyone back home would see . . .

AARON WAS PRETTY PISSED about this. Once he heard that kid's name on the speaker, he knew it was all over. *He looks like a blabbermouth.* They should have known. Reymond wasn't an idiot. He would find out eventually. *And I didn't exactly conceal the door very well.* He was standing in the office with his sister and Alex.

Alex's eyes were on his lap. He tapped his thumbs.

Dr Reymond was standing with his hands on the back of his chair. "You two . . ."

The siblings tried to hide their anxiety. What had this kid told the principal?

Dr Reymond appeared stressed. "Your father conducted experiments on you?" he had cold sweats on his brow.

He's dead. Thought Aaron. What was wrong with this idiot? Why did he . . .

They heard a noise from the glass box as the rock started hitting it.

"I said they're the reason it's out of control. Get it out of here," Alex pointed out.

Dave picked it up and ran straight out of the room. He gave it to Carla for holding, then returned, hoping no one would see. "This is serious. We've been trying to track down James for *years.* If you know where he is, we need you to tell us. He-he's dangerous, okay?"

"Why did he send you here?" Dr Reymond appeared sorry. These poor children. *I should have found him long ago. Curse me for being so slow.* He was so disappointed in himself. Because of his incompetence, these innocent kids . . .

Lisa was relieved he did not know. Otherwise, they would have some serious issues. *So how much is he aware of?* She was being as calm as she could.

Aaron, for once, was not laid back. "To go to school. That's it, and that's all,"

"But he experimented on you," Dave stepped forward. "It means he's still interested in the anomaly. Are you sure he didn't send you here to find it for further experimentation?" he did not trust them. These children had been raised by James their whole lives. James was not exactly a bad guy, but he had become corrupt. That was at least how it seemed. *Using children for experiments. Oh my God.*

"Yes, he did, but that doesn't mean it had anything to do with your orb. We only found out it existed after using the lab during lunch. We'd wanted some peace and quiet as I'm quite sensitive to loud noises, but when we entered, we heard it causing a ruckus, and then he came in with his friend, and that was how we learned of its existence," Lisa came up with that on the spot.

Dr Reymond was not sure. Her file *did* say she had sensory issues but still. It made no sense that James would just send his children here for no reason other than to get an education. *I met him and didn't even realise it.* He was a fool. "What if he bugged you or something? Maybe it's not just reacting because you have a different section of the meteor inside you but also because he wanted you two to destroy it with your cells. I can't imagine why he'd want it gone but . . . anyway, this is serious. We have four students with tampered nervous systems going to this school. We need to find a way to undo the damage,"

Dave agreed.

Aaron tried hard not to face-palm. "We're completely okay with-"

"He's brainwashed you. My goodness," Reymond felt sick to his stomach. These children . . . He could not believe James would stoop this low. "Has he completed a perfect model? He used you, so you must know where he has gotten in his experiments. Will he release it to the world?" things were blurry.

"Where is he?" Dave was sure they knew.

Aaron twitched with anger. "We don't know. When we travelled to and from home, we were never shown where we went. He's a private guy,"

"Or he just didn't want to risk having you tell anyone," said Dave.

Lisa and Aaron knew the lab was in Alaska, but there was no way they were letting that slip.

Dr Reymond placed an elbow on his desk. "First order of business is getting rid of these mutations, and the next will be finding James and putting a stop to all this,"

"We also need to destroy that thing. Its instability is concerning. If it's releasing shockwaves and electricity regularly, then the other students may be at risk," Dave told him. "Don't you agree?"

The principal nodded. "You're so correct, but I need it for experimenting. I need all of you to meet me this weekend to do so," he was busy this week.

Aaron shook his head. "But we don't-"

Lisa held his wrist. "We'll be there. We didn't know this was as serious as you're making it out to be. We thought we were helping our father,"

Aaron would snap at her, but he realised she was being smart. If they did not know they were in cahoots with their dad, then they'd leave them alone. *There's no way he can undo this anyway.* The enhancements could not be reversed. At least in the case of him and his sister.

"I would call the others here, but you three can tell them all about this. They need help too," Dr Reymond sent them away.

Alex got up quickly and then left just as fast.

He tried to walk down the hall to avoid any interaction with the siblings, but before he could move down the staircase, someone grabbed his arm. "Ah!"

Aaron turned him to face them. "Like running your mouth, do you?"

Lisa watched quietly.

Alex gulped. "He was pressing me. I couldn't . . . be glad I didn't tell him all about your dad's plans. I only told him that you two were enhanced so he could understand why the rock was going so crazy,"

Aaron was not happy with this. "If you could open your mouth a while ago, then you'll do it again," he spoke through his teeth. "You need to understand why these things are confidential," he pointed at the boy's chest. "Meet me at the back of the school at lunch. I'll show you why it's important to keep things to yourself," he went down the stairs after that.

Lisa followed him.

Alex was left with shaking hands. *That guy has ice vision.* He was toast.

THE DRAMA OF EARLIER had caught a few people's attention, but most had forgotten after classes went on normally. It was not common for their principal to call so many students into his office. Something big must have happened, right? Many had had questions at first, but now they had simmered down. It was the transition, and kids were just interested in getting their books and heading to their next class.

Most of them were anyway . . .

Devon was not giving up on this. He hid behind a line of lockers with eyes on that Alex kid. "He's acting nervous,"

"Dude, why are you stalking him?" asked Ryan. They had been talking about crashing the cheerleading tryouts when Devon suddenly got fixated on that freshman boy.

"Yeah, you're being weird. Just 'cause he got called to the office doesn't mean he did something wrong. Look at him. Kid's got nerd written across his forehead," Ansel shared a laugh with Ryan, and they high-fived.

Devon did not join them. He took this very seriously. "I'm not being weird," he looked at his friends. "First that fire that happened right after that new guy was asking where the little guy was, then new kids come in, and Annalise says some weird stuff happened when they met him and the new guy, and now he and the new kids got called on the speaker?" he held up three fingers. "It's gotta be a joke at this point. You can call me crazy, but I can tell clear as day that something's up,"

"Bro, Annalise said it herself that she might have just imagined that. How on earth would it be normal for smoke to just come out of nowhere after a stare-off?" they snickered.

Devon groaned. "It *isn't* normal. Something's up with those guys, and I wanna get to the bottom of it. If it's major enough for them to want to keep it so secret, then it's gotta be huge," he continued observing the nervous boy. "Dr Reymond must have found out. Wonder if he'll tell me if I asked,"

His friends found him odd.

"The others are here," Devon tried his best to listen in.

Jun was so glad they found Alex. "Dude, what happened in there?" he whispered.

"Did you get in trouble? Doesn't look like you're expelled. I'd imagine you'd cry down the whole building if that happened," Chantalle's arms were folded.

Alex gave them a look of fear.

Jun and Chantalle immediately grew concerned. "Alex . . . what happened?" Jun was getting a bad feeling in the pit of his stomach. It hurt.

Alex tried to gather his words. "It's not as . . . okay, it is bad. Dr Reymond knows, but-"

"You told him?" Jun hissed hysterically. His world shattered right at that moment. "Dude, why? Why? Why? What the heck, Alex?"

"Shush. He's not sending you guys to some weird island for testing. And after thinking about it, I realised that we were stupid to think he'd do that since that rock was his problem, to begin with. Couldn't he get arrested for child endangerment if this got out?" Alex thought about it. "Anyway, he knows, but he wants to help to undo the enhancements,"

"Mutation," Jin said through his teeth.

Alex rolled his eyes. "Right,"

Chantalle swayed and rubbed her neck. "So that's all? He knows?" she whispered.

Alex began trembling. "Uh-uh,"

"What else? What did he say to the new kids?" Jun was kind of relieved that the doctor wanted to help. *This is weird 'cause in the movies, people usually freak out when an adult finds out.* But this time, a sense of security washed over him. *I hope he wasn't lying.* If that guy for one second tried to ship them off, he would go ballistic. *I never asked for this.* He imagined explaining to his friends that he was in an underground lab in Russia. *Damn, what if the government finds out and uses us?* There was no way their parents would allow that. Dr Reymond would get sued. *And that's why he won't tell other people.* He hoped he could trust that man.

"It's not what he said to them but what they said to me," Alex whimpered. "Aaron wants to meet me at lunch to teach me a lesson about letting things spill," he barely got the words out. "I've been beaten up at school enough to know what that means. Only that, in this case, the guy who wants to beat on me is a superhero. He has ice vision. Doesn't sound as intimidating as laser vision, but it's still scary as heck. Guys, he's gonna kill me," he danced in terror.

"Relax, relax," Chantalle held his shoulders. "You need to try some deep breathing,"

Alex refused. "What am I gonna do?"

"Did you tell Dr R everything about them or just that they're mutated too?" Jun kept an eye out for people listening. No one seemed to care- *Is that Devon?*

Devon walked out of his sight immediately after. *Caught.* He only heard pieces of what they said since they spoke so softly. *Aaron wants to beat up the little guy?* He heard something about Dr Reymond knowing something and Aaron being a superhero. *I wanna say I heard wrong, but something's gotta be up.* He would be following them at lunch for sure.

Jun was not sure how he felt about this. Devon had already confronted him before. *Shit.* Did he hear anything?

"So that's all he knows. But I didn't rat out their dad's plans or anything. It's just that Dr R just knows for sure that his old partner did experiments on them. I understand why that'd piss him off, but I'm scared," Alex could not focus on any classes after that threat. He was terrified. "He's gonna kill me,"

"Just don't meet him then," Chantalle did not like seeing him this way.

"But he'll come after me eventually. You know how this works, Chantalle. Or maybe you don't," Alex hopped from one leg to the other. "The terms of our arrangement don't apply anymore. Reymond found out so they can kill us all they like. He seemed angry enough to just cut off my head. He can probably do that!"

"Shh." Jun looked for anyone who might have heard. "You need to chill," he whispered.

Alex could not. "A super-powered being is after me," he enunciated.

"He won't kill you for the same reasons we brought up earlier. It'd look too suspicious. Will he hurt you? Probably but we won't let him," Chantalle snatched Jun's wrist.

"What?" Jun did not understand, but he liked the skin contact.

"Jun, we have enhancements too," she couldn't believe she had to spell it out. "If we show up with Alex, he won't stand a chance. We gotta defend our own," Chantalle let him go.

Aw man. Jun rubbed his wrist. "Our own?"

"Our own?" Alex had never felt more included. "So, you guys are gonna beat him up instead? Yes! Fight the power!" this had never happened before. *I forgot that I have friends.* "You guys are awesome," he hugged them both.

"Wait, but what if he actually challenges us?" Jun pushed Alex away. "We don't know how to use our mutations that well. He's probably had more practice than we have. Heck, he's *definitely* had more practice than the two of us. Hasn't he been like that since he was a kid?" he became nervous. *I kinda wanted to punch the guy since the day we met, but he scares the shit out of me.* Could he fight and win? *Maybe in a fist fight.* He clenched his shaking fists. This would be his first face-off.

"I've been throwing things around with my mind for quite some time, so if you can't handle him, I'll do the honours," Chantalle patted his back. "Don't worry, Alex. No one's going to get to you. He needs to learn that if he messes with one of us, he messes with *all* of us,"

Alex had never been more in love. "You're so amazing," he started crying.

Jun scratched his cheek. "Alex, come on, man, not in the middle of the hall,"

"I can't help it. I'm so happy," Alex sniffed. "Aaron doesn't understand," he wiped away some tears.

Chantalle handed him her hankey. This was pretty awkward . . .

"If he was me, he'd give it up too. Dr Reymond had an unstable rock. He had questions. Of course, I was gonna answer them. It didn't make sense to lie at that point. I could have said that you two were the reason it was going crazy, but . . . okay, maybe I could have thought it through better," Alex wiped his eyes.

"You were under pressure. We get it," Chantalle wondered where they were. "There's no turning back now anyway. Reymond already knows,"

Jun gulped. "When is he gonna undo everything? Does he even know how to do that?"

Alex sighed. "He said we can try over the weekend. I don't know if he'd get anywhere, but he's way more experienced than I am, so at least you guys would have a better shot at becoming normal again, right?"

The bell rang as soon as they agreed.

"Okay, we need to head to class," Chantalle said her goodbyes and then walked away.

Jun went to his own class with Devon and Aaron on his mind. *He's gonna figure it out.* Dr Reymond may not tell the whole world since his reputation was on the line, but with Devon, he had nothing to lose. *Might even have something to gain.* Would someone pay Devon for releasing information on enhanced humans? *Mutated humans, and yes. I'm pretty sure they would. Heck, that rock could sell for a million if he auctioned it off.* They needed to be careful. *I'll tell the others soon.* His sense of normalcy was on the line.

CHAPTER SIXTEEN

A aron went to the back of the school first thing for lunch.
"You're being an idiot. I don't think intimidating him will
stop him from saying more. If anything, it would scare him into
doing the opposite. What if Reymond asks why he's afraid of you and
he tells him about this little . . . what are you planning? To beat him
up?" Lisa sat with her legs crossed on a stone bench. They were at a
back wall with the concrete ground spreading up to a green section
of trees. There was a wall beyond them. "And won't the cameras pick
you up?"

Aaron used his ice vision to freeze the surveillance camera from
the back while it pointed away from him. He used such intense ice
that it broke off right after. He smirked at his sister. She sat with her
lunch in her lap while he stood closer to the wall.

Lisa rolled her eyes. "I don't think this will help anything,"

"It will," he walked up to her. "If he knows that his life is at risk,
he'll be too afraid to say anything again,"

"I just told you what would likely happen. He'll be so scared
that he'll report you, and who knows what Reymond will do?" Lisa
frowned. "You're being an idiot,"

Aaron was doing this partially because he thought it would work
and partially because he wanted to use his powers on someone. They
had them but hardly got to use them. If he was a jerk for using ice
to intimidate a smaller kid, then he would take the label. *I cooled
off right after giving the threat, but I came all this way. Might as*

well commit. "You won't understand, Lisa. You hardly understand anything. You're like a robot, remember?"

This aggravated her intensely, but she kept quiet and looked away, pausing her eating.

Aaron forgot that that was off-limits. "Okay, I'm sorry. I didn't mean it. You're amazing and-ow!"

She sent fire at his trousers.

Aaron extinguished it with his eyes. "What the heck?"

Lisa seemed pleased. "Apology accepted,"

Aaron brushed off the snow and rolled his eyes. "You're such an asshole . . ."

"He's here," Lisa noticed the boy approaching. "And he's brought the posse,"

Aaron stood straighter with folded arms.

Jun led the way to the new kids. *Aaron.* His insides boiled, but he trembled at the same time. Chantalle and Alex had said that interacting with them more may lessen the effects of their reaction, but this was only the second time he was meeting with them. Would something crazy happen?

Aaron just had to shake his head. "Wow. Couldn't face me one on one like a man?" He folded his arms when they were against the wall. "Had to bring your bodyguard and girlfriend along?"

Alex was shaking all over. "You see Jun as my bodyguard?"

"I'm not his bodyguard, and she is *definitely* not his girlfriend," Jun stepped forward.

Lisa swung her legs while eating. The cafeteria served chicken nuggets and fries today. Not the healthiest option, but she appreciated the dry meal. It was easy to consume.

"Why'd you go so strong on the 'definitely'?" Chantalle tilted her head.

Jun's face grew warm. "Pshh. Because you would never . . ."

Alex seemed hurt.

"Uh . . ." Jun dismissed that. "Aaron, you're an assho-" a spark erupted between them, and smoke filled the air.

Aaron stepped away with a hand on his mouth. "Shit,"

Jun took ten steps to the left and waited to see what would happen.

Everyone was silent.

"This is ridiculous," Lisa muttered.

Looks like we're in the clear. Jun cleared his throat. "Aaron, you're a dick for threatening Alex," his voice sounded awkward while raised. Had he ever defended someone before? It didn't help that he was scared of this guy.

"Yeah. It's not his fault things came out. You should be happy. Now you don't have to live with the burden of fulfilling your dad's wishes or being superhuman . . . enhanced . . . I don't know what to call it but consider this a blessing. Dr Reymond is going to take that burden off your shoulders and probably work to have you taken away from your glaringly abusive father who used you for experiments!" Chantalle found it worse after saying it out loud. "Aren't you happy?"

Aaron made a face. "What? No," he held his chest with one hand and gestured to his sister with the other. "We like being this way, and we like helping our dad. We know what he went through. We wanna see him happy. And if being the proof that his work is valid will do that, then so be it,"

Jun groaned. "You're not responsible for making your parents happy. They gotta be responsible for that themselves. If your parents end up using you to bring themselves fulfilment, then that's messed up 'cause you're gonna be under a lot of pressure," he pointed.

Alex was nodding. "Yeah!" he didn't know what to say, but he was nervous and frightened.

Aaron's eyes were narrowed. "I'm starting to think that you ass cracks are thinking of ratting us out to the big guy. Gonna tell him why we're actually here? That we're here to destroy that thing so he won't ever be able to use it for credit?"

"If we did that, would it really affect you that much?" Chantalle tilted her head.

Aaron looked briefly at Lisa. "Yes. He'd try to keep us from doing what we're supposed to. He's obviously been keeping it around for that reason. And now that he knows our dad is really gonna use the other one for recognition, he'll have more reason to cling to it,"

Lisa was nodding.

Jun found this stupid. "I'm pretty sure Dr Reymond wants nothing to do with that thing. Why else would he lock it up in a chamber at the back of a lab?"

"When the money starts flowing, we'll see how he reacts," Aaron's eyes were glowing an icy blue that nearly seemed white. "I can see him switching up right now. Which is why we need to destroy it,"

Chantalle hated the way his eyes seemed. Would he attack? She stepped forward. "How are you so sure it *can* be destroyed?"

"Well, if not, then we need to bring it to our father," Lisa told them. "Once it's out of Reymond's possession, we'll be satisfied,"

"It *needs* to be destroyed. It's evidence," Aaron turned to her.

Lisa frowned at his eyes. "Are you really going to attack them?"

"Yes. Because they're talking funny now. They told Reymond about us, so it'd only be a matter of time until they say something else," Aaron looked at them with those cold eyes. The entire eyeball was consumed with the icy blue. "You can't, okay? All of you need to keep your mouths shut. And to be sure that you do that, I'm gonna- ah!"

Chantalle sent him ten feet in the air with her mind.

"Whoa!" Alex backed up. "Why did you . . ."

"He was gonna attack us!" Chantalle shouted in a panic.

Aaron's arms were flailing. He looked down and started zapping.

Chantalle got hit in the shoulder with a block of ice so intense it numbed her muscles. She broke her hold to grab it.

Aaron went falling to the ground but created a snow pillow with his eyes to land on. He rolled off it and hopped to his feet to continue shooting at them.

Chantalle got hit in the stomach this time. It was more forceful than the last blow, so it sent her right into the wall with the discomfort of that numbing, aching sensation taking over her whole body.

Jun was able to dodge some of his blasts, but he got caught in the leg despite being farther.

Alex staggered away after Aaron caught his knee. "Ah!"

Aaron laughed. They were pathetic. He stopped to turn to his sister. "Think they got the point?"

Lisa rolled her eyes. "You're being immature," she looked at her nails.

Jun did not appreciate the laughter. "Dude, what the heck? Did you give us frostbite?" he couldn't move his leg.

"Chantalle!" Alex went to her but got hit in the bum. "Ah!" he turned around with hands on his buttocks. "That hurts, man. Seriously!"

"I know. Nothing burns more than ice. Ever heard of freezer burn?" Aaron zapped Alex's chest.

Alex fell with a hand over it.

Jun growled, then shot vicious flames at Aaron.

Aaron saw it coming and used his ice to combat it. Water and smoke were left after the clash.

Jun looked at his palm. "Jeez . . ." that was intense.

Lisa was coughing. "If you keep up this way, you might burn down the whole school,"

Jun saw electricity sparking around them. "Cut it out, man. You've made your point. We weren't going to tell Reymond anything. We just want out of this,"

"Do you?" Aaron came up to him with those blue eyes.

Jun saw the sparks again, but Aaron kept advancing.

Aaron came right up to his face, and the reaction was insane.

Jun felt a force repelling them, but he fought it to send a blast of fire right at Aaron's stomach.

"Ah!" Aaron cried bloody murder! He backed up in agony but only tripped and fell to his back seconds after. His fist pounded the concrete as he lay.

"Aaron!" Lisa got up to watch over him. She knelt next to her brother and lifted his hand to see the wound. "This . . . this is bad,"

Aaron's stomach looked like crushed cherries. It was burned down to the muscle.

Jun's lips trembled as he looked from Aaron to his friends.

Alex could hardly move his legs. "It hurts . . . it hurts . . ." he grabbed his bum again to ease the pain, and surprisingly, it stopped hurting right after he did. *What?* He turned over to sit while staring at his hands.

"You bastard!" Aaron got up despite his agony. He had an arm around his bloody stomach. "I was just fooling around, and you decide to kill me?"

Lisa got up too. "You shouldn't move. We may be stronger than ordinary people, but we can still die,"

Aaron went up to the fool and punched him.

Jun felt that right to his core. He staggered back.

Aaron caught up and zapped his abdomen.

"Gah!" Jun held it, but Aaron zapped his arms. "Stop! It was an accident! You were getting too close, and you hurt my friends!" The ache was spreading all over as Aaron continued.

Lisa ended up cutting through his ice with her flames. "Relax!"

Aaron did not appreciate that. "I'm teaching him a lesson,"

"You're killing him," Lisa gestured to the boy whose arms were frozen.

Jun fell to his back with ice sticking his arms around his stomach.

"He tried to kill m-me . . ." Aaron could hardly stand.

"I know, and all of this is horrible because now we have to explain it to someone," Lisa tried to stop him from falling, but he collapsed to his side.

Aaron's eyes squinted as the burning, and sizzling sensation took over his entire body. This hurt like a mother and more. "You idiot!" he snapped at Sato.

Jun was in his own world of pain. He could not remove his arms from his torso. "You . . ."

ANNALISE WAS LOOKING for Chantalle in the cafeteria.

"They usually eat out there, but I don't see 'em," Ryan told her.

Annalise was standing before their table. She had just finished her lunch and wanted to use lunch break as a chance to ask them to join the cheer squad since Lisa wanted them to. "Hmm . . . do you think they're in a classroom?" she just realised something. "Where's Devon?"

Ansel swallowed his fries. "He went to the back of the school to look for them. I don't know why but he's stalking those guys,"

"Yeah. So as soon as he finished his lunch, he just picked up and left, weirdo,"

Annalise was just as lost as they were. "Okay . . . so they're at the back of the school?"

"It's what he says. He heard them talking about it. I don't know. The guy's been weird these days,"

Annalise hummed in thought. She turned to the exit. "Thanks, guys. I'll go there. Maybe I'll catch Devon on the way," she hurried off.

She *did* catch Devon while searching.

Devon was walking quietly along the side of the building.

"Hey!" she waved her arm.

Devon turned around. "Annalise?" he put his hands in his pockets. "What are you doing here?"

She jogged up to him.

Devon immediately blushed. Was she worried about him? *I wasn't with my friends. She probably wanted to check to see if I was okay.* "Did my friends tell you I'd be here?" he scratched his cheek with a smile. "I'm fine, so-"

"I was looking for Chantalle and the others," Annalise was panting. She wiped some sweat from her face. "Your friends told me that you said they were at the back of the school, so here I am," she noted the long way they'd have to walk to get there. "Well, almost," she nodded at him. "Why did they say they'd be eating behind the building, and how do you know? Your friends said you've been . . . stalking them?" she was confused by that.

Devon cursed his idiot friends in his mind. *She doesn't even care about me.* But he would still pursue her. They were meant to be. "I'm not stalking them. I'm being reasonable and checking up on them since they and the new kids clearly have something going on," he kept walking.

Annalise was at his side. "Why would you- oh, because they got called by the principal this morning?"

Devon's hands were back in his blazer. "Not just that," he pointed at her. "You said yourself that some weird shit went down when you introduced them. They're like . . . fire and ice,"

"Fire and ice?" Annalise wondered if he heard himself. "Because of the smoke?"

"Yeah. You saw smoke and sparks; there was fire after the new guy came in; what causes smoke when it gets in contact with fire? Ice," Devon had been thinking these thoughts all day.

Annalise was . . . "Devon, I'm pretty sure I just happened to see something that wasn't there. There's no fire or ice or . . ." she could hear frantic noises as they approached the back. "What's that?"

Devon knew that he had caught them. "Exactly what I was talking about. Come on," he grabbed her hand and dragged her to the back.

"Ah-ha!" Devon pointed at the people of interest. "I knew that-what?"

What he caught was the freshman kneeling next to Aaron with hands on his stomach, Aaron's sister kneeling at his other side, the girl with the locks standing next to them nervously and the new guy kneeling at Aaron's feet. It looked like they were all arguing. Not anymore, though.

They all turned to him.

Annalise never had. . . "What is going on with you guys?" she ran up to Aaron. "Are you okay?"

Aaron pushed Alex to sit up. He was all healed, but his uniform was a mess. There was blood and singed holes which exposed his belly. "I'm fine. We were just . . ." he looked to Sato. He had caused this, so he needed to come up with an excuse.

Jun's uniform was also messed up. The ice had melted due to Alex's sudden healing, but it had still ripped his clothes. Who would have thought freezer burn could be so intense? "Experimenting. Yeah, we were fooling around the lab, and something blew up, so now we're just . . . we look rough," he smiled awkwardly.

Devon wasn't an idiot, and he knew that Annalise was not one either. "Dude, the principal called almost everyone here into his office, and now you're all messed up? What the hell is going on with you guys?"

Chantalle and Jun exchanged glances. "Nothing," she walked up to them. "We've just been tampering with a lot of the lab equipment," she was still in awe at Alex's abilities. *He got enhanced.* But the rest of their powers had not been interfered with. This was making her head spin.

"Yes, and it seems we haven't learned our lesson because we've all been negatively impacted by a hazardous experiment we were just conducting out here," Lisa rose to her feet.

Annalise's brows furrowed. *Lisa seems comfortable with them.* Is that why she wanted them on the squad? Because they all liked doing crazy experiments together? *No, something else is going on, but it seems it's making them close.*

Devon saw sparks happen between the new guy and Aaron.

Jun backed away from Aaron immediately.

"I saw that," Devon pointed.

Chantalle needed to distract them. "Annalise, why are you here with Devon? Just walking around?" She smiled.

Lisa climbed to her feet.

Annalise looked at her briefly. "No, I just um . . . I wanted to ask you to join the squad again,"

Lisa had not wanted to be here for this. She did not want to seem suspicious. *As long as she doesn't mention-*

"And I'm not being pushy because Lisa over here actually wanted you to," Annalise smiled at the new girl.

Lisa's mouth hung.

Chantalle was bewildered. "Oh . . ." she turned slowly towards her. "Why exactly?"

Lisa's cheeks were warm. "Because . . ."

"We're joining the squad, and we wanted to see some familiar faces," Aaron stood up with his clothes in ruins. *I'll get you back, Sato.* He cursed the guy in his mind.

Devon made a face. "You guys joined the cheer squad?"

Jun was just as lost. "Why?"

Lisa held her hands behind her back. "For a sense of normalcy," she played the role of a child deprived of a regular childhood, looking at her feet innocently.

Chantalle remembered the fact that they had been tested their whole lives. *Even if they claim to support it, it can still mess someone up.*

Aaron caught on. He sighed. "Yeah," maybe they could trick them into joining if they acted sad enough.

Devon had no idea how they went from addressing the obvious weird stuff to cheerleading. "Wait but cheerleading's for girls,"

"Yeah," Jun added.

Chantalle gave him a glare. "Anyone can do anything," she found it strange that Lisa would do this, but maybe she and Aaron really did just want to do something normal with people they knew? *This isn't adding up.* "Well, I guess that . . ."

Jun smirked. "She'll join."

Chantalle blushed. "Yeah, sure," she became smug too. "But only if Jun and Alex are on board as well," she hooked her arm in Alex's after he stood.

"What?" Alex was lost.

Annalise was more than happy to hear this. "The whole squad, huh? Okay," she laughed. "Sure. I guess we'll see you guys at tryouts," she held Devon's hand. "Bye,"

Devon would complain, but she was holding onto him. He became smitten. "Bye," he said to the freaks.

They were left standing around in silence.

Alex stared at his palms. *So that's how my shoulder healed up.*

The bell rang.

Jun pointed to where the two had left. "We should-"

"Yeah, head to class," Aaron bumped his shoulder into his on purpose as he left. *Gotta get changed.* And he and Lisa also needed to tell their father about what Reymond knew. *No.* The man would flip. They would keep this secret as long as they could. *Once we get rid of them, and he gets rid of Reymond, it won't matter anyway.* He nodded to himself.

CHAPTER
SEVENTEEN

D r Reymond stopped reading files to massage his forehead. James' eyes, the unsteady entity, those kids and his past had filled his dreams since discovering the truth behind the students.

He sat back to exhale. Further experimentation had already begun on his part. He had started observing the orb closely since the night after things had been revealed. Not all the equipment and appliances from the HRP lab had been relinquished after he sought to build this school. Most of it was kept underground. That was also where the anomaly would be detained from now on. Dave had put together a massive chamber in only one night. In hindsight, the best option from the start would have been to keep it there. But too many demons lurked around the items, which reminded him of his past. *I also preferred having it close in case something happened.* His hand hovered over his lips.

Christopher wanted more than anything to do away with that thing forever but destroying it was out of the question for now. In the past, his efforts had only driven it to become more of a problem. Hence the issue is presented now. *I'm a fool.* His elbow was on the arm of his chair as he rubbed his forehead. Poking around at it, using the old software he and James had designed brought him great discomfort. That thing had ruined everything for him, but before he could finally put a plan in place to have it annihilated, he needed to investigate closer to understand what it did to those children.

Then there's James, who's on a rampage. It should not be as hard as it was for them to hunt him down. *I'm more than certain that he's hiding underground somewhere. Most likely not in the states.* But where? His adopted children stated that they knew nothing about his whereabouts. Dave seemed to not fully trust them, but Reymond was not so quick to paint children is deceptive.

He shifted his work files to take a look at the results of the tests conducted on the orb over the past few days. *It changes.* He got up with the papers to head to his back window.

The football field could be seen. Cheerleading tryouts were happening. He saw large groups of students lined up. Alex, Jun, Chantalle, Aaron and Lisa were among them, from what he knew. He had not exactly been in touch with them, but he did see the names on Annalise's signup sheet. *At least they can smile even in this time of uncertainty.* His heart bled the most for the children James adopted. They were so innocent that they simply believed that being part of their father's experiments was a good way to help him. *James, you sicko.* So much time had passed. If they were to meet again, would James be anything like the boy he had known?

His hand gripped the edge of the window. *Don't worry. I'll find a way to undo what's tainted you.* This was his mess. He was responsible for cleaning it. The biggest problem was how he would get rid of Aaron and Lisa's mutations if they came about from a different orb.

The man scratched the front of his head in exasperation. *This weekend.* All would be dealt with when he met all of them on Saturday to closely inspect and form solutions to the problem at hand. *I'll do what I must because I have to.*

"THANK GOD IT'S FRIDAY!"

Lisa took a step away from the person who hollered this. She wore shorts and a hoodie along with some sneakers for these cheerleading tryouts and was not happy about it.

A girl was doing cartwheels and flips to workout music on a blue mat placed at the centre of the field. Annalise and her cheer girls were sitting on the grass to watch, clapping along and smiling. They have behaved this way towards everyone so far. Lisa was sure that even the people with no athletic ability would get onto this silly squad. *They can't help but be inclusive.*

The girl on the mat ended with a split causing the cheerleaders to clap and scream.

Devon sat with them next to a water dispenser. *I saw what I saw on Tuesday.* He had his eyes on Jun and the new kids. He knew that if he came up to them with questions that they would deny it all, so his new tactic was to keep watch from far. *Something I'm damn good at, if I do say so myself.* How was that going for him so far? Not so well. If they ever whispered among each other, their voices would be too soft for him to pick up, and when they weren't whispering, they seemed normal. *I'll catch you, idiots. Don't you worry.* And when he did . . . *I don't know. Something crazy's going on with them, and I think it's got to do with fire and ice. Maybe I can expose them?* Were they mutants? Like in the X-men? Annalise was the only other person he spoke of this with, but she seemed hellbent on ignoring what was obvious. *All she cares about is Lisa.* Devon was starting to think she had a crush . . . *Nah.* He laughed to himself painfully. Annalise wasn't like that . . .

"That was incredible," Annalise was on her feet. "Now that you're done, you can go ahead and sit right over there," she gestured to the sidelines.

Aaron kept peeping at Sato and his squad. "I think we need to start planning how exactly we're gonna execute, you know what. Father said to report back to him in a week, i.e. next Monday."

"I know," Lisa said through her teeth. "It's just been bugging me that we're planning to keep him out of the know when it comes to Reymond discovering us."

"Psh. He won't be able to get rid of our enhancements. He may think he's smart, but he's just an old man. As long as we get rid of who we need to, things will be fine." Aaron spoke in her ear. He was aware of Devon keeping close watch over them. Even now, the guy was staring. *Only a matter of time till he approaches.* That was not of much concern.

"And what about the prototype's destruction?" asked Lisa while the next person waved their arms and kicked their legs to a song. Most people here had no rhythm. How was Annalise able to enjoy their half-assed performances?

"He only cares about annihilating everyone. We know that, so don't worry about it," Aaron saw Jun staring at him. "We'll talk tonight."

"Good idea," Lisa felt Jun's gaze. Another issue was the fact that 'the sidekick' had gotten enhanced too. *Healing.* That may pose a problem when staging an accident. *So much to consider.* Her head hurt.

"Jun, don't make it obvious you're staring," Alex pulled Jun's face towards his.

"Sorry. I'm just . . . I don't trust them, and I'm looking for reasons why you guys shouldn't either. They're always whispering, conspiring. You're telling me that doesn't look like people who want us dead?" he hissed.

"We're whispering right now." Chantalle felt out of place in these shorts and her oversized T-shirt. She could not remember the last time she partook in a sporting activity during school. Back in the day, the places the other students could find her were the library or at the back of the school building. Always reading books. To be outside with her legs exposed was pretty new. She didn't even know what she would do for her audition. *Tryout.* A breath left her lungs. *Lisa wanted me on board.* At first, she had thought that Lisa was interested in doing something fun while out of her abusive situation, but after some thinking, she began to wonder if there was some other motive. *We discussed why it would make no sense for them to kill us. And how would joining a cheer squad help with that?* Jun's paranoia was messing with her head. He had been talking her and Alex's ears off since the fight on Tuesday. He just didn't believe that Aaron and Lisa were no longer after them.

"Yeah, but it's not the same. We're the good guys," Jun's hand was to his chest. "They're the ones raised by an evil scientist who for all we know could be living in some underground facility somewhere,"

Alex crossed his eyes in annoyance. "Dude, Dr R is on this. We keep telling you we don't gotta worry anymore," the fight with Aaron had been scary; he would not deny that. Ever since it happened, though, there were no more threats. He kept reminding himself that over the weekend, Dr Reymond would look into things and that the scary scientist would be hunted and taken care of.

"You guys are too trusting," Jun held his chin. Someone else was going forward to display their skills. Why did he agree to do this? "We haven't gotten around to telling him about you, though, Alex,"

"I don't think we should," Alex mumbled.

Chantalle and Jun looked at him together. "Why?" they asked at the same time.

Alex shrugged. "What if I don't want to lose it?"

"What b-"

"Okay, shh," Chantalle nodded at Devon. "We can talk about this another time."

"Like a meeting in our room?" Alex asked.

"Like when we're not around people, so yeah," Chantalle scratched her head. "Although I've got a lot of work piling up."

"It's Friday," Jun locked eyes with Devon for a second. He managed to end the contact. They were all well aware of the close tabs he was keeping on them since finding the five of them in a questionable position at the back of the school.

"Fine. We'll talk in my room after we're done here," Chantalle saw Annalise coming forward after the last person went. *She's even bubblier than usual.*

"Okay, I know I said everyone would have to show us their talent to determine whether they get in or not but guys," she set a hand gently at the area beneath her neck.

Aaron and Lisa exchanged glances. Was she crying?

"So far, everyone's been so amazing. I think I'm just gonna let the rest of you in. Woo! Spirit!" Annalise hopped up and down as everyone cheered. A friend of hers came to her side.

"And by that, she means we need as many people as possible, so we will take anyone," this was the same girl with light brown skin and curly hair. She clapped once. "We're gonna do a quick practice before you guys head off, okay? Would that be fine? Just so everyone knows what we have in mind."

"Thank God," Alex nudged Jun. "I legit had nothing planned."

Jun smacked the back of his head before walking with everyone else to the safety mat.

Aaron tried his best to keep far from him. Things may have calmed down between himself and the others, but no matter the time that passed, he and Sato would always react.

Jun felt his glare. The hatred that seared his veins was unlike any other. It was so strange that he was equally as terrified.

Annalise and her friends started moving people to different positions they had in mind for the first section of their routine.

"I think the boys should be together," a different cheerleader said. "What do you think?"

Annalise tapped her chin with eyes on the three guys.

Devon's eyes narrowed. *The girls have been touching everyone so much. I bet Aaron, and the other guys can't wait for them to move 'em.* He should get on the field, shouldn't he?

"Okay," Annalise held Aaron and dragged him to the side, then went for Jun.

Aaron's brain snapped. "Uhh, no!"

Jun caught on right after. "Yeah- I mean no. Uh, you can uh- me and Alex can stick together but Aaron. Aaron he uh- he . . ."

Chantalle knew what they were trying to do. Why was Jun being so obvious? "Aaron and Lisa should stick together," she was standing directly behind Lisa. The shorter girls were up front, while the second row contained more average-height girls. Tall ones were to the back.

"What? That won't look uniformed," said the girl with the curls.

"I can stand around the end with him. We can have boys and girls at the end. Shorter girl next to a tall boy. I'll be the short girl on the left, and Sa- Jun can be to the right with a short girl," Lisa tried.

Devon stopped being jealous. *Humph.* This was interesting. He stood. "What's so bad about Jun being close to Aaron?" he came closer to the mat.

"It's not about what's so bad. It's about what's best for Lisa," Chantalle folded her arms.

"Exactly," Lisa looked briefly at Chantalle.

Chantalle tried a short smile when she did.

Lisa faced forward to avoid eye contact. "I like familiarity," she started walking to the left. "Or if not a boy and a girl on the ends, consider a short person and tall person. So Alex can stick by Jun at the other end since he and I are similar in height,"

Alex heard people giggling. "I am short," he placed hands on his hips. "And just like Lisa needs Aaron. I guess I need Jun," he bumped his hip against Jun.

Jun was mortified. "Yeah, yeah, yeah," he stepped away as more girls laughed.

Annalise sighed. "Well . . . we can try that for now, but if it doesn't look good, we'll think of something else," she instructed Aaron to go join Lisa.

Aaron gave Jun a nasty side-eye on his way to his sister.

Devon rolled his tongue around his mouth. *I'm not an idiot.* Contrary to what many believed. That right there was a clue.

Practice consisted of trying different formations and having the newbies listen to the music picked out. When they were done, everyone packed up their stuff to head to the dorms.

Alex held his bag on his shoulder while walking between Jun and Chantalle. "Okay, but uh . . . new problem. How on earth are we gonna keep you and Aaron away from each other for the whole routine? You guys think something will happen?"

Jun grunted. "I'd say to just leave the team, but it's a good way to keep an eye on those guys."

Chantalle rolled her eyes. "Targetting us would be stupid. We already said that, and they agreed."

"But did they confirm that their sicko father agreed?" Jun took a swig from his bottle of water angrily. "And although I do wanna keep a close watch, it's kinda suspicious that Lisa wanted us on board with them. Chantalle, you *gotta* see what I mean. Why did they even join in the first place?"

"To have fun like they never got to as kids? That's what I thought," Alex supplied.

"I do agree that it's weird, but something in me is also saying that Lisa . . . maybe wants me as a friend but is too shy to ask," Chantalle shrugged.

"What?" Jun had never heard anything more ridiculous. "Those freaks aren't here to make friends. They're here to...."

"Jun, you sound like a jerk right now. Come on. Yeah, Aaron tried to beat me up, but since then, there've been no upsets. And again, it'd make no sense to kill people after just joining a school. We told them that they'd get caught, they agreed, and their dad most likely did too," Alex scratched his head. "I think our main focus should be on trying to keep things secret from people. That is Devon. The guy's turned into a stalker," he was getting breathless as they walked up the grassy hill hundreds of feet from the dorms. *Aw man.* He was quite unfit.

"If we're lucky, Dr Reymond will actually get somewhere with us over the weekend, and that won't be a problem," Chantalle hummed in thought. "Although, it's still strange that Aaron and Lisa would just take this lying down after showing so much allegiance to their dad. They must have told him, right?"

"Of course. And now their dad is after all of us as we speak," Jun was so glad she said this. "I'm telling you guys, we're not safe,"

Alex knew he had a point. "Okay fine. I guess later we'll talk about all of that because there is a lot to talk about,"

"Yeah. Like why you don't want Reymond undoing what happened to you. Me and Jun are gonna tell him," Chantalle bumped Alex.

"Ah. No please . . ." Alex had felt the presence of someone behind him. He turned around to look but saw nothing. There was a tree and a bench some feet down, a trash can next to it. *Hmm . . .* He ran up to it and peeped, but no one was there.

Jun and Chantalle caught up. "What are you doing?" asked Jun.

"Sorry. I thought Devon may have been following and listening in." Alex started walking again. "But I guess it's just us,"

"Seems so," Jun adjusted his backpack. "Do we all agree that we're not in the clear in terms of the new kids?"

"Fine, but how do we confirm that? Spying? Like what Devon's been doing?" Chantalle said as they left the bench.

"Precisely," Jun was determined. "One of us should listen in on them in their room one night. Do they share a bed 'cause they're siblings?"

"What? Of course not. Dude, what are you saying?" Alex laughed at Jun with Chantalle.

The gang kept speculating on their way to the dorms, laughing now and then in the process.

Devon's head poked out of the trash beside the bench once they were far enough. He smirked as they disappeared from his view.

"SECURITY FOOTAGE FROM the compound and streets around the city suggests they appeared out of nowhere," Dave leaned against the entrance of the facility they put together for this new project. The orb floated behind an indestructible glass wall to the far right. Despite their efforts to clean up, things were still pretty cluttered. Dozens of desks were stacked in the corner with abandoned equipment on top of them. This floor was indeed part of the research lab in the past, so the room chosen was not the only one on it. There were others with more appliances that were no longer in use in other rooms. They just chose this one randomly.

"When you say 'out of nowhere, do you mean they suddenly became visible on footage or something else?" Reymond was trying to start up an old machine he had used in the past. His large expansive computer was not functional, so he and Dave had had to improvise to create something smaller. The result was a tricked-out desktop sitting on a high desk. He had an elevated platform at the centre of the room with a tube around it for scanning. *I hope they won't be too intimidated by everything.* Labs would always be scary to children. *This is why my heart goes out to Aaron and his sister.*

Dave scratched his head. "They didn't suddenly appear. It was more like . . . okay, last night I tracked down their trail extensively, and the last piece of footage I could find was at a marine centre. What I got was just them walking through to head onto the main street before taking a taxi to come here,"

Christopher paused his motions. "Marine centre?" he walked up to Dave.

Dave nodded. "My main assumption is that they used that place to get here. The question is why and how?"

"Maybe a portal they have set up over there? Or . . . do you think they came from underwater?" he suggested.

Something in Dave's mind clicked. "Like a submarine?"

"That's all I can come up with."

"Shit." Dave bit his thumbnail. "That's gotta be it," he hit the side of his head. "Should have thought of that sooner."

"So, what can we gather from this? That James is operating underground? That was definitely obvious. The question is underground of where?"

"A marine research centre wouldn't have underwater cameras, would it?"

"The researchers carry cameras on them when they dive. There are no cameras just strategically planted down there," Reymond said. "I'd suggest that he has some sort of network of tubes for his submarine to follow, but I doubt."

"Hey. We can still take a look," Dave snapped his fingers. "Unless you wanna fake some sort of parent-student meeting for him to come by so we can go see for ourselves how he gets here. And not only that. We can catch him once and for all,"

"That's an idea . . ." Dr Reymond was staring absently at the tube set up in the middle of the room. "I already said that in order to avoid the hassle that we communicate with parents online. We would have to fabricate some sort of emergency for him to not be suspicious. That one of his kids is sick or something."

"Hmm, lying. Would we have to get the kids on board? Would they lie to their father? I don't know. They claimed to be clueless about everything he was up to when we called them over, but for all we know, they could have reported everything to James, and as we speak, he's thinking of a way to get rid of us,"

Dr Reymond placed his palm on his face and wiped it down. "I did believe that they may be brainwashed, but I don't like thinking that kids are acting maliciously."

"They're *James'* kids. And if they are, it's not their fault. We need to do some deeper questioning. I even said to myself that they probably know where he is but were covering for him," Dave tapped his elbow with one finger.

"That might be so . . . I guess I'll have to interact with them more to find out. Gain their trust. Who knows what idea they have of me in their minds after spending time with James. The two of us did *not* leave off on good terms in the past," he sighed. "I'll talk to them today," he gave Dave his back. "Now go wait for them in front of the dorms like we discussed. And make sure no other students see where you're bringing them."

Dave said a quick 'sure' and then headed off.

". . . WHILE WE'RE ON our way back, I stick my head out the window, singe a hole in the tires, the bus loses control, stumbles towards the edge of the bridge and in the heat of everything they fall out by 'accident'?" Lisa restated a potential plan given by Aaron that same morning.

Aaron opened his arms. They were in his room. "You got it so right. Doesn't it sound foolproof?"

The girl groaned. "What are the chances that in the process of things getting out of control that the bus actually moves to the edge?" she placed an elbow in her lap and held her cheek, sitting at the edge of her brother's bed.

Aaron pocketed his hands. "I'll . . ." his eyes wandered. "Shoot ice in its way."

"That doesn't make sense," Lisa fell to her back. They had asked for more details about the trip from Annalise after practice yesterday. Part of what they found out was that they would be travelling in a bus and would need to cross a bridge over water to get there.

"I don't see you coming up with any ideas. We only have like a day and some to report back to the old man," said a cross Aaron.

Lisa massaged the side of her skull with closed eyes. "What if I blow up a tire and everyone has to get off the bus because of the fire? Or I start with the tire then let my flames swallow the whole bus, and they just happen to get burned?"

"Huh . . . you know that uh . . . makes sense," Aaron sat beside her. "But it sounds way too easy. And your fire is black and blue. That'd look insane."

Lisa opened her eyes. "I'll lessen the heat to make it orange."

"Right. I forgot we have crazy control of our powers," Aaron snorted. "Unlike the rejects who only got enhanced like what? A week ago?"

She sat up. "Do you think that Reymond might actually get somewhere today?" she looked at her watch. "What time are we supposed to meet his right hand outside the dorms?"

"Guess now would be a good time," Aaron stood. "He said eight a.m. specifically," they had gotten a visit from Reymond's lackey last night before bed. He assumed that he had done the same with the others.

"Let's go," Lisa was already on her way to the door.

"And I don't think he'll get anywhere. Enhancements can't be undone," Aaron opened the door and heard a different door down the hall doing the same.

Jun hid how much it shook him that Aaron just happened to be stepping out at the same time as him. *His sister is with him.* So they *did* sleep in the same room. *Come to think of it, this is the first time I'm seeing her here.* Wait, Aaron slept on the same floor as him? *Well, that's uncomfortable.*

Aaron pocketed his hands and nodded at Jun.

Jun nodded back, guessing that was a greeting.

Aaron rolled his eyes. "You go first."

"Oh- I mean. I was gonna do that anyway," They still needed to avoid getting close. He sped and walked down the hall while reaching for his phone. Now he was dialling Alex.

"Yo, yo, it's the A-man," Alex answered right away.

Jun had never cringed harder. "Why?"

"I was just trying something out. Sorry," Alex cleared his throat. "What's up?"

Jun walked past some kids in the hall and got strange looks from others in their dorm rooms. He was now on his way to the stairs. "Just calling to ask if you're already where they told the guy to meet us."

"I'm on my way. Are you?"

"Yes."

"Cool. So we might meet u- oh, there's Chantalle. Hi!"

Jun held his phone away from his ear. "Where exactly are you guys?"

"Outside the dorms."

"Okay, wait for me. I'll be there in a second," Jun hung up and then looked over his shoulder.

The siblings were only now coming down the flight of stairs.

Once they were all out of the hall, another door opened on their floor.

Devon moved his eyes from left to right before stepping out of his room. On his way down the hall, he met some of his friends.

"Hey, man, we got to practice in like an hour. Why are you only out of bed now?" asked Ryan.

Devon did not have time for this. "Because I . . ." where did they go? "Did you guys by any chance see the new kids walk by here?" he had been listening for their doors to open since he got up at five.

"Uh yeah. That Jun guy looked like he was in a hurry, and Aaron and his sister went right after him."

"Okay, cool. Where did they go?" Devon kept glancing down the hallway.

Ryan and Ansel exchanged looks. "Wait. Are you still stalking them? I thought that was just a phase-" Ansel seemed weary.

Devon growled. "I'm just gonna guess they left the dorms. Bye," he walked right past them and ran down the stairs, nearly bumping into some guys coming up. *I got my phone in my pocket and everything.* He would catch them doing something weird and show it to *Annalise first, then the two of us can figure out together what we'll do.* Because the truth was, Devon was not sure where he would go from here. Did he just want to prove to Annalise that something was really going on? *I guess so.* And he would quite enjoy rubbing it in Jun's face that he figured them out as well.

THE FIVE STUDENTS STEPPED into the underground world in awe.

Alex spotted a computer with a seat in front of it, tables stacked to one side and a big glass wall towards the other. "That's it," he walked right up to the glass wall which contained their problem.

It was just floating there with huge waves of energy surrounding it, still sparking like it had been when he last saw it. "Whoa . . ." the boy pressed a hand against the glass and felt a hum.

"The material will keep it at bay as long as it doesn't increase in instability," Dr Reymond appeared at his side.

Lisa came to his other. "It's not reacting with Aaron and me."

"Because of the glass," the man pounded a fist against it. "It's like a shield against external forces," he smiled.

Lisa looked quickly at her brother.

Aaron shrugged.

That's pretty impressive. Lisa thought of Dr Reymond's containment of the prototype. "Did you have this material lying around to keep it contained?"

Jun stepped slowly up to the tube in the middle of the room. A light shone from within it, causing him to gulp. *Damn.* If he didn't feel like a freak for having powers before, he certainly felt like one now. *Reymond's gonna make everything better.* He looked at his palms.

"So amazing," Chantalle was rubbing her hand on the glass structure while Dr Reymond continued conversing with Lisa and Alex.

"Did you guys just have all this around?" Aaron kept near the computer in order to keep far from Jun. No matter what they did, they would always react, it seemed. *Fire and ice.*

Dave walked slowly towards him. "In a sense, yes. This place used to be a research lab, after all," he locked eyes with the kid. "But you knew that," he tried to detect dishonesty in the boy's eyes.

Aaron didn't get this stare down. "No, I didn't," he called his sister.

Lisa stopped listening to their father's enemy to join her brother.

Chantalle looked at her. *How do we know for sure why she wanted me on the squad?* From here, Lisa just seemed innocent. *But there's most likely an ulterior motive.*

"We should start spying as soon as we're done here," Jun whispered.

Chantalle was not sure how well that would work.

"Let's get to business Doc," Dave called.

Dr Reymond had been telling Alex how they created the material. "Right," he moved over to his computer. "So, two of you got interfered with by that orb while two were from a different one created by James," he felt shame that he let that happen. "Am I correct?"

The kids lined up behind him, with Aaron a few feet from everyone.

Jun and Chantalle looked at Alex.

Alex held a shush finger to his lips.

Lisa crinkled her brow. "You developed healing powers," she pointed at the sidekick.

Dave frowned at the same time Dr Reymond did. "What?" they asked together.

Alex forgot that Aaron and Lisa knew his secret. "Uhh, I . . . no, I didn't."

Aaron laughed to himself. "If you didn't, we would all be dead from that time. Don't act like you don't remember."

"You're able to heal?" Dr Reymond stepped toward him in fascination. He held Alex's hand.

Alex pulled it away. "Yeah, but I like having that power. I could help people."

Aaron wanted to tell him that that was the same thing their dad thought of enhancements but held back.

"Why did you have to heal everyone so they wouldn't end up being dead?" asked Dave.

Lisa could strangle her brother. "A brief altercation behind the building. Hardly anything to be concerned about."

"Altercation over what?" Dr Reymond asked. "To see who was stronger?"

"You should be asking Aaron those questions," Jun just put that out there.

Aaron wanted him dead. "I just wanted to talk. You're the one who started blasting fire."

"Wasn't it Chantalle who sent you flying in the air first? And you didn't wanna talk. You made it clear that you wanted to beat me up," Alex folded his arms.

"You misinterpreted his words," Lisa mumbled.

"No, he didn't. You wanted to beat the crap out of him. Even gave a date and time for it . . ." Jun was pointing at the one he hated.

Chantalle shook her head as an argument between Jun, Alex and Aaron started.

Dave had no energy for all this.

Dr Reymond started waving his hands to get them to quiet themselves, and at the same time that he did, the orb hit the glass.

The room became dead silent as all heads moved in its direction.

The doctor went towards it to investigate. "Hmm . . ." he turned towards the kids. "Did it react with your emotions?"

"Heck, if I know. That thing doesn't abide by any rules," Aaron was already tired of being here. Reymond wasn't supposed to know about what happened. *These big-mouthed idiots.* Didn't they think he would try to find out why they were fighting and realise that he was mad that they ratted them out, revealing that he and Lisa were more than aware of their dad's plans? *They're all so stupid it hurts.* Killing them would not be difficult.

Reymond tapped the glass with a single finger and then got back to his computer to type something. "I'll just take note of that."

Chantalle stood next to Lisa. She was nervous about doing this but bumped her shoulder into the shorter girls anyway.

Lisa raised an eyebrow.

Chantalle smiled at her.

Lisa had never been more lost. *Is this an attempt at friendship?* She could not tell.

Chantalle faced forward again. *She looked confused.* Maybe she should ask directly once they were done here. Would she get an honest response?

"Okay. Now to do some scans," Dr Reymond joined his hands.

When everyone was scanned and the data was noted, Dr Reymond and Dave observed it together. The kids were on the other side of the lab.

"Should I have brought my own scans for reference?" Chantalle pondered.

"I'm pretty sure that whatever software he's operating is way more sophisticated than your little glue gun," Alex chuckled. "Not that your glue gun isn't cool 'cause it is."

Chantalle smacked him upside the head and then moved her eyes towards the brother and sister standing several feet from them. "I think I'm gonna get close to Lisa."

"Why? Because she allegedly wanted you on the team with her?" Jun glared at Aaron. That guy was definitely up to no good.

"No . . . yes and also to maybe try to find out the truth. If we become friends, she might open up to me about their 'true' intentions," Chantalle quotes. "You know since we're all paranoid."

"You think she's just gonna tell you if they have some major plan to get rid of us behind our backs?" Alex scratched his head. "Maybe if you get her drunk. Or she's dared to."

"Like at a slumber party? Pretty sure those guys have no problem with lying," Jun laughed to himself. "Friendship only works in the movies. We need to be as cold as they are."

"Aw, man, was that your attempt at some kind of pun? Because Aaron has ice vision?" Alex shuddered. "Dude, come on."

"Sounds like something you'd do, huh?" Jun shoved Alex.

Chantalle shook her head while those two started play fighting. "I don't know. You said they played dumb for Dr Reymond, but maybe part of them is innocent. If you were raised by a tyrant, you'd be messed up too, wouldn't you? Maybe interacting with a normal person would appeal to her more humane side, and she'll talk."

Jun could not see that working. "Fine. Have a sleepover with her then," he laughed.

"That's actually not a bad idea. I bet Annalise and her friends would be interested in that too," Chantalle smiled.

Jun had been joking. "Uh . . . okay, well, you'll try your My Little Pony Friendship is Magic bullshit while I do things the right way. Spying."

"I can see you getting caught and beat up already," Alex shook his head.

Jun folded his arms. "I'm good at stealth. How do you think I survived middle school?"

"Why would you need stealth to survive middle school?" Chantalle asked in confusion.

Jun felt their eyes on him. "Uhh . . . just . . ." something suddenly occurred to him. "Wait, these cheer-offs are for all schools to participate in?"

"Probably just the ones in our district; why?" Alex asked.

"Is it televised?" Jun was sweating.

Chantalle knew exactly why he seemed uneasy. "Yes, it is. And if your old friends weren't interested in watching cheer-offs before, they wouldn't be now. You'll be spared the embarrassment," she patted his shoulder.

"Huh?" Alex was a little confused. "Old friends?"

"From his old school. I think they're the reason he's so . . . him," Chantalle made a gesture around Jun.

Jun scowled. "That's not why I was asking."

"Yes, it was." Chantalle was not an idiot.

"Well . . . the district . . ." Jun's old school classified as being in this district, didn't it? He knew cheerleaders from where he studied before. They would be there. And would see him. Cheering. *Shit.* "Maybe I should be the mascot."

"What's the big deal? 'Cause, you're a boy? Me and Aaron are guys, and we'll be cheering too," Alex folded his arms. "And plus. You were killing it during practice," he tried to imitate Jun's moves.

Chantalle giggled girlishly. "I think between the two of you that you were the one making most of the killing."

"You were good too, I'd say," Alex blushed while speaking to her.

"I'm no dancer . . ." Chantalle said somewhat shyly.

Jun just blinked. Why did it seem that more and more Chantalle was becoming repelled by him?

The guy grunted and looked away.

He saw something at the door in the process.

Jun frowned. What . . . was that? He quickly walked towards it to take a look outside but saw nothing down the hall after doing so. *Hmm* . . . He did not like this place or the idea that he did not know what he saw. *That rock can't create monsters, right?* They didn't know that. As everyone kept saying, it was unpredictable.

CHAPTER
EIGHTEEN

Annalise and her friends were some of the main people on the cheer squad. There was no practice today, but they were trying to come up with ideas to make their routine memorable. That was why they used the football field on a Saturday under the supervision of the coach, who also booked it for football practice.

She just finished watching a video that her friend Hannah showed them for reference.

"I really think we should add that in. Just saying," Hannah stood in front of everyone on the bleachers.

The other girls were impressed. "Lisa should be at the top of that pyramid. She's small. What do you say, Anna?" said the girl to her right.

Annalise blushed. "I mean . . . if she's okay with it, we can try that. But I don't think she likes-"

"Annalise!"

They jumped when they heard shouting from across the field.

Annalise tried to find where the noise came from. "Who's voice is that?"

"Sounded like Devon," they were murmuring.

Devon dashed past his teammates like a mad man.

"Matthew! Where the hell have you been?" the coach snatched his arm.

Devon nearly fell. "Coach, I'm sorry, but I have something very, *very* important to tell Annalise. I'll be back, okay?" he yanked his arm away to run towards her.

Annalise blinked when the guy ran right up to the bottom of the bleachers, covered in sweat. "Dev-"

"You *need* to see this," Devon seemed beyond eager.

A moment later, the two of them stood behind the bleachers, with Annalise holding Devon's phone and trying to make out what was on screen.

"See that?" he stood in front of her to point. "I knew something was up. Remember what I was saying? With what happened at the Meet and Greet and then earlier this week when we found them doing 'experiments' which was obviously bullshit because there was no equipment yet Aaron's clothes were like that and-and Jun and Aaron can never . . ." Devon was breathless.

Annalise had to squint her eyes. "I see that they're in a room with the principal and security guy, but . . . what is that?" she tried to zoom in on something.

Devon appeared at her side. "That's the thing that's making them have powers. From what I heard, Dr R is-is trying to make them normal."

Annalise could barely see. "It just looks like glowing lights. You say this is underground?" none of what Devon was saying made sense, but at the same time, it kind of did since there was some weird stuff happening with those guys. But not enough for her to believe him just yet.

"Yes. The guy got them on an elevator, and he punched in a secret code, but I saw, so I followed. The code was-was five, five- there's more, but I had to wait like ten minutes to use the elevator again and then I was late, but I caught what I could, and that's the evidence, so what do we do now? You know that I'm right," Devon put his hands on his hips to smile.

Annalise tilted her head. "You think this glow is giving them powers?" she gave a confused expression. "I know things seem odd, but powers? Devon, this isn't a superhero comic-"

"So why was there smoke between those two that night you were with them like you told me and why-why . . . Annalise, you gotta believe me. I don't know where to go from here- actually, I do. That thing is dangerous. What if it kills everyone in school?" Devon paused. "Hmm . . . or what if it can give us all powers?" he smirked.

"Why would you- Devon, this is insane," she would dismiss it because it was too strange and unsettling.

"No, it's not. Come with me so you can see for yourself," Devon grabbed his phone and held her hand.

"Huh? Why would I . . ." Annalise yanked her arm away. "Look, I believe that something isn't right, but if it isn't then . . . maybe we should just leave it alone," she rubbed her arm.

Devon's mouth was agape. "What? And let those guys keep playing us for fools?" he folded his arms. "I need a better picture of it anyway. They should be done down there. It's like afternoon now. We should-"

"Picture for what?" Annalise's mind was painting bad things. "To tell the police? Trying to get Dr Reymond in trouble?" she bit her lip. "Do you think he's experimenting on them?"

Devon had not spun it that way. "I just said it sounded like he was trying to get whatever happened to stop. Shit. Why didn't I record a video?" he wasn't very bright, was he? Even if he was gifted. "Shit on me."

"Do you have proof that something happened other than what I saw that night and how we found them?"

"No, but . . ."

"We should ask Dr Reymond what's going on in case it's concerning."

"Uh, what? I'd get in trouble for following them. The security guy kept looking out for people on their backs."

"You were curious," Annalise did not know what to do. "Or we should just leave it like I said. I don't like messing with . . . I guess I'm a little intrigued but- what did it do to them?" she asked Devon.

"Gave them powers. All the signs point to that." Devon told her like this was obvious.

Annalise sighed. She got quiet.

Devon blinked. "What?"

"What was glowing?"

"Some kind of purple floating rock. It was kinda scary- I mean cool."

"Rock?" Annalise crinkled her brow. "And he was using it to help them?" she thought of Lisa and Chantalle.

"I-I don't know, but I doubt he'd conduct experiments. Like I said, it sounded like he was trying to help. Not that I heard much. They each went in a tube, and he- hmm. That was pretty sus."

Annalise did not like this. "I wanna turn a blind eye, but . . ."

"Maybe opening his computer can help us to know exactly what his intentions were. He was using one down there. He must have taken some notes. If his notes are messed up, then it means he's crazy, and we call the police," Devon had heard only faint words to mean that Dr Reymond wasn't the bad guy, but it did not hurt to check.

"Mmm, we'd have to go down there?"

He nodded.

"What if someone sees us?"

"They left. I'm sure. It's been hours," Devon was already walking away.

"Devon, but you can't-"

He walked backwards. "I need more evidence anyway. If you don't wanna come, you don't have to," he saluted and turned around.

Annalise tapped her feet in unease and then followed him.

The elevator Devon referred to was situated in a store room outside the school towards the back. He did see the code because he was able to punch it in so they could head down.

Annalise kept close to him while they walked the haunted halls. She did not know that they were so, but it sure did feel that way. Some doors that lined the walls were locked, and others were open and led to dark areas with clutter and junk filling their insides. From the looks of things, this used to be a lab. "Dr Reymond is a good man," she whispered.

"He is, so I don't think he's the reason those guys got messed up. Maybe somebody else did that to them."

Annalise looked up and saw rust on the walls. She gulped.

Devon took a look into one of the rooms and then assured her the coast was clear before entering.

Cautious steps led her in behind him. "Oh my God," Annalise's mouth hung open.

Devon stood in front of the glass as well. "It's even . . . weirder up close."

Annalise had to step back. She could almost feel this hum from that smarting, pulsing, shaky orb or whatever it was that floated behind the glass. "Will this be enough to contain it?"

"I don't know, but Reymond set it up," Devon held up his phone to take a picture. "This is like something out of a movie."

"A sci-fi movie where half the cast dies before the end," Annalise found it within herself to get closer and rest two fingers against the glass.

The hum was palpable.

"Is it hot?" Devon asked.

Annalise moved her hand. "Kind of," she kept staring. "What is that thing?"

The electricity around it pulsed so much that it would move from time to time.

"I don't know," Devon was in awe. "I didn't get a good look at it before. Whatever it is isn't safe."

"Right, so we should go," Annalise was not interested in digging into this any further.

Devon ran to Dr Reymond's computer. "Let's just see if he's okay first," he opened it, but it needed a password. "Okay, this is gonna be impossible."

Annalise nervously arrived at his side. "We should go."

"Hmmm . . ." Devon tried something, but it denied him access. "Know anything about hacking?"

Annalise shook her head because this was not a good idea. "Leave it alone ok-"

The rock made a noise that scared them both, and Devon's elbow crashed into the keyboard when he turned to face it in fright.

It remained stationary behind its glass, but the computer screen changed.

Devon frowned at it once he noticed. "What the hell? Is this some kind of code?"

Annalise tried to read it. "It looks like it, but . . . did you get the password or something?"

"I don't know. My arm just hit and . . . I guess I did," Devon was trying to close this, but there was no 'x' button. "Uh . . . see any x's? I don't want Reymond to come here and see I was messing around with his stuff."

Annalise was nervous. "We'll just have to leave it."

Devon used his eyes to scan the screen. "This is an x, but it's part of the code or whatever this is," he sighed. "Worth a shot."

"Wait, no-"

Devon hit the x in one of the brackets, and . . . nothing happened.

Annalise sighed with relief. "Okay, let's just leave this alone-"

They both heard a crash come from the area where the rock was and saw it rammed right into the wall behind it.

Devon got clumsily to his feet and ran to look. "Shit."

Annalise was at his side, frowning. "What on . . . is it stuck in there?" she saw the wall pulsing with electric energy. It spread to the ceiling. "Devon, what did you do?"

"I-I just pressed the x but maybe . . ." Devon went back to the computer to try to find some clue. "Uhh . . . the heading says 'layout' so- what if this is the code for this thing? Is it like a computer program then?"

Annalise gulped. "It's stuck in the wall and is making everything electric."

"J-just the wall and the ceiling," Devon tried to calm her down. "I'm sure nothing will-"

The lights in the room started blinking.

Annalise did not want to be here. "How do we stop it?"

"W-we'd have to get it out of the wall, but there's no way in."

Annalise shook her head. "Maybe if we do something to the layout, it'll help?"

Devon saw smoke coming from it. "What the hell even is that thing?"

"I don't know," Annalise said desperately. "Let's get Dr Reymond to fix this before . . ."

Just as quickly as things had gone crazy, they stopped.

Lights were back to normal, and there was no electricity creeping through the walls and ceiling. Even the hum behind the glass had vanished.

The two surveyed the room with just their eyes in silence.

Devon looked at her with his green peepers wide.

Annalise gave the same reaction. "Tell Dr Reymond what we did?"

He shook his head. "Let's go," He held her hand and brought her right out. The scary glowing rock was still very much stuck in the wall and glowing off and on where it kept itself.

"An electrician needs to come to look at things because it could have gone worse," one of the Physics teachers stood in Dr Reymond's office that afternoon after school on Monday.

Reymond sat at his desk with Dave and Carla before it. "None of the kids got hurt, right?" he asked.

The teacher shook his head. "Everyone was safe, but the surge was insane. It blew up our circuit diagram. The lights have been wonky all day. Since the weekend, actually."

"Comes and goes from what I've seen," said Dave. "Something weird happened on Saturday one time, something else weird on Sunday and now today."

"What do you think it is?" asked Carla.

"I'll take a look at things later," Dr Reymond assured the teacher. "As in tonight, hopefully. For now, just pack up and get some rest. The day's over, and it's been long," he seemed compassionate.

The teacher sighed on his way out.

Reymond sat back.

"On top of everything, now the lights are giving trouble," Dave had a good chuckle. "Over the weekend, the scans gave you everything you needed to know, and you've been using simulations on your laptop to try to find the best way to go about this, right? Got anything?"

"No. Not using what we have, that is," Dr Reymond was pondering over a desk of paperwork. "I have a strong feeling that to eliminate the problem, I'm going to need the meteor. There has to be something in there that can cancel the effects of the others. Like some kind of nulling entity, but James has it, and we still don't know where he is."

"You do know how he got here. I seriously think Dave and I should take a trip to the marine centre pretending to want to do some sightseeing underwater when really we go for a dive just to look for some kind of tubing system or something that can tell us where he went. It's probably hidden underwater," Carla suggested.

"You're right. Underground under water. We'd have to carry a contraption to help us find it. Something that can see through stuff. Like an x-ray machine. Is that possible to get?" Dave turned to Christopher for approval.

Dr Reymond nodded. "I can work on that when I have some time,"

"You never have time, so this might be a while. I just looked at your schedule for this week, and over the weekend, you have quite a few conferences to attend," Carla rubbed her forehead.

"I know, but whenever it gets done, it will get done. It's not like either of you could handle that kind of task."

Dave and Carla exchanged quick glances.

"Just bear with me," Dr Reymond sat back. "Now, would you have to break into his lab to find the meteor? How do we confront him?"

"When we find out where he is, for sure, we'll have to bring a team to take him down. Or at least some sort of paralyzer. Not that I think he'd put up much of a fight," Dave shrugged.

"Okay. That's the next step. I'll try to get it done as soon as I can since I need that meteor. There's already some equipment I can use in my bedroom, so I'll work on it there and continue testing the kids once we get it out of the way."

Aaron was walking to cheerleading practice with his sister that same afternoon. "You know, even though only bad shit is gonna come out of this, we can still try to have a little fun."

"There's nothing fun about sweating and jumping around," Lisa's arms were folded as they approached the wired fence which would take them to the field.

"You're such a buzzkill. I think that if you feel the music, you'll enjoy yourself. And maybe you should try getting close to some of the chicks on board. Coulda swore that Chantalle was giving you eyes on Saturday,"

"You make it sound strange. And are you referring to the girl we have to annihilate?" Lisa whispered at the entrance of the field. People were gathering already. School had ended just ten minutes ago.

Aaron laughed. "Wouldn't hurt to get to know someone before you make 'em kick the bucket," he did a gesture where his finger cut his neck, and he acted dead.

Lisa's face screwed up when her idiotic brother began laughing. "You-"

"Lisa, you're here early," Annalise appeared before them. She waved at Aaron before smiling at the short girl. "We were thinking of something involving you. Come on," her eyes kept moving to Aaron as if uncomfortable.

Lisa was good at picking up nuances. Was Annalise nervous about something? *Hard to tell.* "Okay," she jogged after her to the field when she started walking away.

Aaron waved with his fingers. "Have fu-" his phone suddenly started ringing in his bag. "What? People call me?" the guy grunted as he pulled it out. *Shit.*

He ran to the field, tossed his bag aside, and then hid behind the bleachers to answer. "Old man. Hey. Thought you'd give us a call later," he was staring at him and Lisa's father, sweat forming on his brow. *He found out that Reymond knows, and now he's calling to chew us out. Shit, shit, shit.* Aaron struggled to read his face.

James sat in his large chair once more. He held clasped hands at his front. "I've been dreaming and thinking a lot these days about everything we discussed."

Aaron saw dark circles under his eyes. "Is it like when you get all powered up on resentment to work harder?" he asked cautiously.

"You could say that," James was enamoured by the idea of destroying everything Reymond had built. "Now, what's your grand plan to get rid of the problem?"

Aaron detected so far that he knew nothing of the fiasco of Reymond finding out. *Good. It's not like he'll actually find him, so we don't need to tell him anything.* "Lisa and I came up with it already. She's just gonna make it look like the wheel on our bus on the school trip blew up and caught the thing on fire. She'll make sure that the problems get burned alive."

"Nice. Why did I think for a second that you two had gotten sidetracked?" James sounded pleased. "And as for me, I've just been working on something that will take care of Reymond. My friend turned enemy," he whipped out something from next to his chair to hold in his lap.

"Is that a bomb? You're gonna blow him up?" Aaron asked in horror. "Whatever happened to poison, or I don't know- being discrete?"

"I'll give more details when we reunite. I'm planning to visit after you take care of them. Trust me, it's going to end beautifully."

Aaron narrowed his eyes. "I don't think you should blow him up. Is that what you mean by ending things beautifully? You're gonna bring a bomb to his office after we confirm things are done and blow up the whole thing? We already said getting rid of those kids will look fishy. That's gonna look even worse. People are *definitely* going to be suspicious when we're ready to get our names out there."

James seemed angered. His brain replayed his days of building things from the ground up by himself after what happened between him and Christopher. The frustration, loneliness. He even saw his childhood. So much of the same thing, but only with Chris there to give comfort when necessary. Years had gone by, and he was still alone. Desperately clinging to the idea that one day his pain would amount to something. He deserved a break, and everyone who caused a delay for him to get there needed to pay big time. "Do you need to be reminded of who's in charge here, Aaron?" his voice was steady, painfully calm.

Aaron used his hand to wipe his face. "I know that you are, but we all also know that sometimes you . . ."

"I what?" the man was not at all pleased. He increased his volume on the question.

"You lose sight of logic when you get too worked up," Aaron darted his eyes to the side.

"Are you calling me insane?"

Aaron swallowed thickly. "No . . . sometimes you-"

"Focus on what you're there for, and allow me to focus on what I must do to fulfil my destiny," James hung up.

Aaron sighed. *He'll click back to reality; I know it.* For now, he was just high on ideas. They had seen it quite often as kids.

He walked onto the field to see Lisa being lifted in the air by a group of girls. "Would you look at that?" he laughed to himself.

Chantalle was one of the girls lifting her. "Then we put her back down like this?" she and the five others allowed Lisa to stand on the ground again.

Lisa was glad to be on steady ground.

"Yeah. This is just an idea, though. If Lisa's not into it, we can hoist someone else up," said Annalise.

Jun stood on the sidelines with Alex, shaking his head. "She really thinks her idea will work," he tsked. "Chantalle is full of it,"

"If she is, then you're overflowing," Alex laughed. "How has your spying been going anyway?" he had noticed a change in the lights at school today. Not just the surge that made them go extra bright earlier but also in the noise they made. As in, they made a noise now. Like a soft buzz akin to a bee. *Lights do that sometimes I guess.*

"I . . . I'm gonna spy tonight, hopefully. They talk a lot when they're alone, so we'll find out what we need to know if we listen in," Jun could see Aaron sitting at the bleachers and smiling.

Lisa shook her head at her brother's stupid grin.

Aaron seemed to be telling her to have fun by mouthing the words.

"Lisa?" Chantalle asked carefully.

The girl faced her. "I don't mind," she would prefer to stick to the ground but being hoisted in the air wasn't the worst thing.

"Aww," all the girls squealed.

Lisa startled. "You're suddenly noisy. Why?"

Chantalle smiled. "I guess they're happy you have a big role."

Lisa rubbed her arm awkwardly. "The people carrying me have a bigger role."

"You think that because we haven't told you what you'll be doing after we raise you up. How flexible are you?" asked a friend of Annalise.

Lisa had been banished to the sidelines of all practice to do stretches with Annalise on a safety mat. The practice was over now, but her muscles were still strained. "Oh my God," she lay on her back.

Annalise didn't want to laugh, but she was being cute. "Everything hurts now, but by the time we're done, you won't feel a thing and raising your leg up high will be nothing,"

Lisa frowned at her. "I won't feel a thing because my legs would have fallen off."

Annalise found it difficult to keep up appearances all day, but now it wasn't so hard. She still thought she and Devon should tell the principal, *especially* with the crazy stuff that thing was doing with the lights, but Devon was hellbent on keeping far from all of that. *Now he wants to mind his business. When the issue is his business.* If things got to an all-time low, she was telling. "You'll be fine," she sat next to Lisa.

Lisa sat up. "I need water."

"I can get it- hey, Chantalle's coming up," Annalise waved.

Chantalle held two bottles of water in hand. "Would our star gymnasts care for some refreshments?" she smiled nervously.

"Thank you," Lisa snatched one to drink.

Chantalle watched her gulp down the whole thing in seconds. "You're not used to physical activity, are you?" she handed the other to Annalise.

Lisa tossed the empty plastic across the mat. "What gave me away?"

Annalise showed a relaxed smile, but it vanished as she remembered that the very people she was speaking to now had some sort of problem going on with them. They had never confirmed whether Reymond was abusing them or not, but she could not just ask.

"You okay there?" Chantalle had not seen Annalise all day until practice. To her, the cheerleader was just a little less chipper than usual.

"I'm fine. I just . . . saw something over the weekend that upset me," Annalise did not know if it made sense to lie. What was the worst thing that could happen? They would tell Reymond what she and Devon did. Had they broken the rules? *Having that weird orb get stuck in the wall and mess with the lights is pretty bad. Especially since we probably weren't supposed to be down there.* She gulped with eyes on Devon. He had just finished football practice on the other side of the field.

Lisa used her top to wipe her mouth. "What was it? You're usually always chatting and smiling," she noticed the person Annalise was looking at. "Did he do something to you?"

Chantalle was watching Devon too. Come to think of it, he had not been all over them today like he had been last week.

"No," Annalise's guilt was painful. "Hey, the girls and I thought that after the cheer offs that everyone could go out to eat pizza or something. To celebrate our hard work?"

"What if we fail miserably?" Lisa played with the bottle in her hand.

Annalise laughed. "That won't happen. Come on. Be optimistic."

Lisa's eyes went slowly from her bottle to the girl standing before them.

Chantalle did not know what that look was about. She could not read it. "Or maybe we could try a sleepover? The girls of the squad, of course. Having boys would make the whole thing . . . weird," she spotted Jun and Alex swatting each other in some sort of silly fight, which she was sure was over nothing.

Annalise completely snapped out of her funk. "That sounds amazing! I hope the guys won't feel left out."

"Sleepover?" Lisa thought of what she had to do to the girl in front of her. She was sure that the last thing anyone would want to do after that tragedy played around in a bedroom.

Chantalle smiled at her. "Yeah. Ever been to one? It's just an event where girls go to one girl's room and talk and laugh and just have a lot of fun all night. Sometimes they don't even go to bed," she giggled.

Lisa was startled by the short laugh.

"It's incredible. *Have* you been to one?" Annalise asked.

Lisa turned from Annalise's smiling face to Chantalle's. *She'll be dead.* But the girl did not know that. Here she was, making plans for a fun night. Lisa did not pin her as the type to enjoy such things. Why was she . . . "No. I've never been to a sleepover."

"This would be the perfect chance for you to have your first one," said a beaming Annalise.

Lisa blinked her eyes. "I'm not sure if . . ."

"If you want, we can just invite some girls from the squad. In case it sounds a bit intimidating. Or heck, maybe just Annalise and I can come to your room," Chantalle would try to get closer to her through practice as well.

"Um . . ." Lisa did not know how to tell her that that was a horrible idea. "Fine," the girl would be dead, so it would not matter. The plans would just automatically cancel.

"Great," Annalise got up. She really liked that Chantalle proposed that. *And included me.* Did Chantalle see her as a friend? "That means we gotta make sure we do our bests at the cheer-offs so we can have reason to celebrate," she began to walk off but stopped. "I-if there's anything that you two ever wanna talk about, you can uh . . . come to me, okay?" she displayed a soft smile after saying this.

Lisa scratched her head. "Okay?"

"Sure thing," Chantalle was not sure where that came from.

Annalise walked away.

Chantalle remained with Lisa. "You're okay with the whole sleepover idea, right? I just felt that maybe you might want to get a bit closer to some people here? I know things are crazy, but we can try to act like they're not. It's what I did after I got enhanced,"

Lisa was silent.

Chantalle was not sure what to say. "Do you agree with that?"

Lisa looked at her and nodded.

"Leese, I saw you out there doing your thing," Aaron walked onto the mat. "Looking like a true cheerleader," he had a good laugh. "Oh, and you're here. Does Dr Reymond want us for something else? I thought he said he needed time to figure out 'the next best course of action'. Which basically means he's blank about all this."

Lisa rolled her eyes.

"No, I was just talking to your sister," Chantalle took this as her cue to leave.

Aaron tilted his head when Lisa stood up. "What was she talking to you about?"

"Sleepover and other stuff,"

"Huh . . . anyway. Dad called, and he seemed riled up. I told him about our plan."

"Riled up?"

"Ah, he'll calm down, I'm sure. We'll talk more later, okay? Let's get our stuff packed," Aaron walked over to the sidelines.

Lisa remembered the girls smiling just now and their sleepover idea. *People* . . . She just shook her head.

CHAPTER
NINETEEN

For the past couple of months, Dr Reymond could not catch a break. It had made it nearly impossible for him to get to work on the x-ray machine, but despite all odds, he got it done.

Dave lifted it off the scientist's desk that Thursday night when all students and teachers were off the compound and in their rooms. "How does it work?"

The frazzled doctor walked around his desk to hold it. "You point this end at what you're looking at, and this screen will show you what's through it," they had gotten an electrician to look at the lights last month, but the man had not been able to find the problem. He had been bringing in different professionals to investigate the issue. Dr Reymond had not had time to see about that because of all the appearances he had been making as well as the work piled up on his desk. To this day, the lights would go extremely bright, and just yesterday, they had started blinking. Reymond made a note to look into things himself because from the reports given, it seemed as if something strange was interfering with the school's circuits. The back of his mind told him that the orb contained behind that glass may have a lot to do with it, but he had not given it a look in a while. His focus was elsewhere.

"Seems pretty sophisticated," Carla pushed a red button next to the screen. "Comes on pretty fast . . . is it waterproof?" she could see through the flooring.

Dave moved it to point at Reymond's desk.

"Of course, it is," Reymond told them to turn it off. "I don't want you seeing my skeleton right now," he sat on his desk. "When do you think you can take it for a dive? It's been too long. I'm surprised nothing insane has happened while we've been working."

"The kids haven't caused any trouble, and neither has the orb. Guess because it's contained again, and they know they're in safe hands," Dave did turn it off. "Tomorrow's kind of an off day, right? Can we go then, or do you need us here?"

"It's an off day?" Carla had not heard of this.

"The cheerleaders will be leaving for their cheer-offs, and I told the other students they could dress casually, remember?" Reymond reminded.

"Oh right. I've been so overworked I forgot. I don't know. Maybe we should do a Saturday. I'm the secretary," she said to Dave.

"I'll have to go by myself then because I don't want to delay this any further. I'd even suggest we go tonight, but the marine centre's probably closed. Wouldn't wanna break-in," Dave was holding the x-ray machine in one hand.

"Carla, you can take the day off. I might need to as well. I'll tell the vice principal to take care of things," Dr Reymond had a headache. "And the electrical problem. You two think it's got something to do with what's downstairs?"

Carla hummed. "But it's behind protective, indestructible glass. How would its energy reach the wiring of the building?"

"Something could have happened," said Dave. "But if it did, wouldn't things be worse?"

"Maybe we should encase it in steel and see what happens. Dave, can you go check on it tonight and try to whip something up?"

"Okay. And Carla, tomorrow we're leaving to do what we gotta do as soon as possible," Dave gave the x-ray machine to her. He went to the door.

"Okay, but I have to finish some stuff first. I'll try not to be long," she called as he walked out.

WHISTLING THROUGH THE underground hallways made this experience less disconcerting.

Dave was never a big fan of travelling through abandoned labs at night on his own or checking on unstable scientific creations, but tonight, he flat out hated it.

The old friend of Reymond stepped slowly down with brows furrowed by the unnerving sense he got. Why was the hum audible here? Why were things pulsing? Were the walls buzzing with something?

His saliva became difficult to swallow. *The orb.* If he could feel its presence from here, then Reymond may be onto something about it messing with the circuits.

He had five more steps to reach the desired room when all the walls around him suddenly flickered with purple electricity. "Jesus Christ," he stopped in his tracks while holding his chest, eyes glued to the walls.

Dave came closer to see if what he saw had been real. *It was floating behind glass. The walls on the floor around it were covered in the same material. I made sure it was foolproof.* Had its field of impact grown or something? Did it destroy the glass that surrounded it?

Dave noticed burn marks on the walls while inspecting them. He touched for a split second, then gazed upon the open door.

In a second, he was running inside to see for himself what development could have unfolded behind their backs.

He ceased all movement when he stood before the glass wall.

The orb. It was . . . not floating where they left it. Not floating but fixed in the wall behind it. He only noticed because of the glow coming from the hole it left and the cracks branching out. They all glowed, and this room seemed to hum the loudest.

"My God . . ." Dave breathed in both awe and horror.

He stepped back to see what else had broken. The glass sounded like it was shaking but held up rather well. He looked away from it to focus on the orb in the wall. One of the cracks led right to the ceiling and continued above his head. Another ran to the ground and made a trail on the floor. Dave stood next to it.

Kneeling down gave him a better idea of the damage done. Purple light glowed from here, too, and it seemed to run from the floor in this room to the one beyond it. He heard the hum from it too. *I need to get it out.*

Dave pushed a button on the wall, which made a portion of the glass raise so he could get behind it.

Getting closer made him feel this intense pressure against his body that he was not at all comfortable experiencing.

Dave stepped out and closed the opening once more to just observe from where he was standing. How could they get it out of there? *How did it get in there?*

The man ran to Reymond's computer to get a reading on things. *Why is it open?* He asked after using the mouse to get the screen out of sleep mode. Reymond had not been here in two months. Had someone done something? Who and how? *One of the kids . . .* Was it James' children trying to sabotage the school? *I don't have time. Reymond and the others have got to know about this.* He dashed out of the lab to give his report. In a moment, he was sure that not only the circuits would be their problem. The whole building may very well come down.

JUN WOULD NOT DENY it. This uniform made him feel stupid.

"We got our own jerseys and uniforms. Man, do we look good," Alex walked back and forth in front of Jun and Chantalle the morning of the next day. The cheerleaders would leave for their road trip at nine, but for now, they were in the hallway before classes soaking in the joy of all students.

There was a good luck banner hanging in the main hall for the cheerleaders, and the building was decorated in the school's colours. No one wore uniforms, and once again, students at Reymond high got to express their individuality.

"I don't know about Jun, but you look amazing, Alex. Ten out of ten," Chantalle could not remember the last time she wore a skirt this short. Her locks were in a ponytail, and she wore a ribbon that matched her uniform. Part of her wanted to cringe over it, but another part felt pretty and kind of excited. They had practised so much. She wondered how things would go.

"Aw, thanks," Alex was as pink as a strawberry. "Uh you . . ." he had wanted to say this since seeing her come down the hall. "You-"

"Look amazing. Like a model actually," Jun blurted out to beat Alex. "Even if you don't think I make this dorky outfit rock, you do."

Chantalle did not expect that from him.

Alex scowled with folded arms. "I was gonna say that-"

Jun covered his mouth and smiled nervously at Chantalle.

Chantalle stopped herself from smiling. "Thanks. And I didn't mean to insult you. You actually *do* make the dorky outfit look good," the boys wore long pants with sweaters similar to what the girls wore. "Truth be told, I think you both look adorable."

Jun gushed internally, but Alex did so out loud.

"Well, I don't know about th- h-hey, maybe we can take a picture together," Alex held up his phone nervously.

"Uhhh . . ." Jun and Chantalle said together.

"Sure," Chantalle hesitated because this was the first time any of them proposed this.

"I don't know. This is already gonna be televised. Do I really need more evidence of me dressed as this and . . . doing this?" Jun accidentally said out loud rather than in his mind.

Chantalle rolled her eyes. "Your 'cool friends' aren't gonna see a picture on Alex's phone."

"Huh? That's not what I-" Jun waved his hands.

"Actually, I was thinking of making it my first post on Instagram. Not that I have many followers . . . apart from my mom. She'll see," Alex smiled.

Jun did *not* want to be on an Instagram page of a kid only followed by his mother. "Okay fine, but . . ."

"I can't believe you're still fretting over this," Chantalle had had to put up with him interrupting all their practices not only to request that he be kept away from Aaron but also to ask to be placed at the back. Apparently, one of Jun's female friends would be there with her own cheer squad, and he did not want them catching him prancing around. That was what she discovered after overhearing him on the phone after practice once. She had confronted him about it, and his argument sounded shallow to her.

"Hey, you don't know what it's like to work hard to get yourself to a certain status and to have it all in jeopardy of being lost, okay?" Jun argued.

"Dude, you made it sound so serious," Alex was laughing.

Jun rolled his eyes. "Because it is. To me," he waved them off. "You guys won't get it."

"Won't get what?" Aaron and Lisa walked up to them and kept a distance of six feet. They had learned through trial and error that this was the best way for Jun and Aaron to avoid having a reaction. Alex, Chantalle and Lisa were in the clear in terms of that.

Chantalle smiled a little. "Hi, Lisa."

"Hi, Chantalle," Lisa's eyes kept away from the taller girl's. She did not know why, but Chantalle insisted on acting kindly towards her. Lisa would try to squirm away when it just started, but after a while, she realised that it was not so bad. She would never admit that out loud, but both Annalise and Chantalle's care for her made her feel . . . kind of nice. Normal in a sense. *But what must be done must be done.* It would be done as well. Today was the big day.

"I'm here too, you know," Aaron pointed to himself. *We gotta get rid of them.* He kept having nightmares where his hands would be covered in blood. They did not intend to fight these yahoos like that, but the point remained that they would have blood on their hands. *The old man is crazy.* He and Lisa had not spoken to him in a while. Aaron was kind of worried. People like James Foster were not the best to stay in isolation too long.

"We see. We just don't care," Jun muttered. How was it that Aaron made this uniform look less unflattering than he did?

Alex did not know what to say to them. Jun's spying had only gotten him caught and them nowhere in terms of knowing if they were up to anything behind their backs, while Chantalle's kindness towards Lisa had not caused the girl to reveal anything. *Guess that means we're in the clear?* "Are you guys excited?" the five of them were in this mess together, so Alex had thought it best to try to be courteous whenever they were around. Even if Aaron did scare the shit out of him.

Aaron and Lisa hesitated in giving an answer.

Lisa opened her mouth to supply him with something in order to not appear suspicious, but at the same time, to their confusion, they were all called to the office.

"I FAIL TO SEE HOW THIS is our problem," Aaron spoke dryly to the doctor and his partner after they laid down the situation.

"This is crazy! Do you think it'll crack the whole school? How did it get planted *in* the wall?" Alex was the only one excited about this.

Dr Reymond had seen it for himself when Dave brought him underground to have a look. His observation led him to believe that someone had indeed tampered with his laptop to get the orb to lodge itself in the wall. As for who did so? Dave's guess was James' kids, but Reymond did not want to jump to conclusions. "That's what we're trying to figure out."

Dave was rough in comparison. "Which one of you found yourselves in the abandoned section to play around with our equipment, huh? Did you think this would be funny? I know it was one of you because nobody else knows about that place,"

Jun gulped. This guy was mad. "We didn't do anything," he stood at the end of the line they formed with Aaron at the other end. "We've been focusing on cheering," the embarrassment.

"I don't know; your sidekick's acting a little too excited about this for us to not rule him out," Aaron narrowed his eyes.

"Me?" Alex slapped a hand over his breasts. "I've been way too busy with school and extracurriculars to find myself in that creepy lab,"

Aaron mouthed 'lies' to Reymond, then laughed.

Dave fixed his face in a frown at the boy. "If this is some kind of sick revenge plan on your part, come clean. I know that you guys claim to not know of James' intentions, but it's not impossible that he contacted you to mess up everything Dr Reymond worked for."

Lisa and Aaron grew silent.

"David, come on," Dr Reymond's voice was soft. "They're just children-"

"Who was raised and possibly brainwashed by James. If he was willing to experiment on kids, then he's lost it, so for all we know, he could have contacted one of them to get them to destroy the school," Dave spat.

"And why would he get them to do that by lodging a rock in a wall? They have powers. They could just burn the place down with them," Chantalle defended.

Lisa blinked at her. "She has a point. It wouldn't make much sense now, would it?"

Dave glared at them.

"Calm down," Dr Reymond heard the bell ring.

The tension in the room was tangible to Jun. "Uh . . . we gotta meet the other cheerleaders now . . ."

"Go ahead," Dr Reymond dismissed them. "We'll find out who did this. Don't worry," he smiled at them.

The kids filed out one by one.

Dave walked towards the wall. "Dr Reymond, who *else* could have done something like this other than one of them?"

"I have no idea, but it's not impossible that someone else found the underground area and accidentally pushed some buttons," the principal placed his elbow on his desk.

"What? Are you saying some *other* kids could have done this? How? By following me? I didn't see anyone-" Dave took a moment to think back to the first time he took the kids down there. He had been on the special lookout for anyone following them. Most kids had been minding their business and having fun since it was Saturday. *I mean, we turned a few heads, but . . .* he had seen that football boy a few times but had thought he was just heading in the same direction. *Hmm . . .* That was the only person who struck out. "We should talk to that football star."

"Devon?" Dr Reymond questioned. "He's going with the cheerleaders today. Isn't it great that so many boys are participating-"

"I highly doubt that he did this, but his face kept popping up when I was bringing the kids to the lab. I don't know. If we're considering all possibilities then . . ." Dave scratched his head.

"Hmmm . . ." Dr Reymond patted his fingers on his desk. "When they get back,"

CHAPTER TWENTY

D ave was still thinking of that Devon kid when he and Carla were suited up to dive later.

"It's always exciting when we get curious visitors," a scientist from the marine research centre was standing next to them. They were outside the building next to the sea. This was where Dave had seen James and those kids first emerge.

"Do you get those often?" Carla got her snorkel attached by a different scientist. She was surprised by how easy it was to get permission for this. These people seemed so excited about the work that they wanted to share it with the world.

"Not at all," the first scientist said before laughing. "I hope you two get a look at the new corals we discovered. They're like-"

"We'll be able to spot them once we're down there," Dave was not interested in getting another fish lesson. These people had not stopped talking since they had arrived. "Then we'll take a picture of it with this," he raised the contraption invented by the brilliant Christopher Reymond.

"That's the coolest looking underwater camera I've ever seen," the man who helped them get suited put his hands on his hips.

"I was just about to say the same thing," said the first guy.

Dave went to the edge of the concrete. "You'll pull us up when we yank on the rope?" they had ropes attached to them."

"Yesiree," said the scientist. "Will you show us your pictures once you come up?"

Carla smiled. "No. Sorry," she placed a heavy hand on Dave's shoulder. "You ready?"

"Let's get this over with," Dave dove in first.

The two swam with Dave holding the x-ray device to his face when they got close to the floor. He kept adjusting the settings to find something, but so far, it all just looked like a rock.

Carla watched Dave swim across the sea floor for a moment before taking in their surroundings. Would they have to go deeper to find something, or was this a waste of time?

She treads water in her immediate surroundings with eyes behind her, thinking of how terrifying the sea is. *If there's an emergency, all I have to do is tug this.* Plus, they were not too far from the concrete platform outside the centre.

The woman kept her eyes on the concrete that erected the marine centre in the ground. It was like a big block of rock under the platform. She tilted her head and then swam over to Dave.

Dave faced her and felt the contraption get taken from him. *Guess it's her turn?* He swam after her when she began moving back to the place they had come. What was she doing?

Carla directed the x-ray machine towards the underground part of the marine centre. She saw something after looking and turned to Dave with raised brows.

Dave could not see through her goggles.

Carla swam closer and pointed the machine along the sand that led to the concrete. It looked like a rock again. *Come on now.* She put the settings to maximum power. *I see it.* There was something like the outline of a massive tube displaying itself. She got Dave's attention to see for himself.

The man did, and he showed her his shocked face.

Carla let him take a look at the room within the concrete too.

Dave was not sure of the next step here. This did not tell them where James was. *I gotta break-in.* He swam up faster than he had done anything.

"Done already? Did you see the coral?" asked the perky scientist.

"Get me the biggest hammer you can find. A sledgehammer. Anything," the concrete under may have appeared thick, but they had seen through it easily. If he beat it hard enough, he could break into James' landing area and find something out.

"Why?" the men were lost.

Dave growled. "Just do as I say."

Carla appeared to his left. "What are you doing?"

"Breaking in,"

Dave got what he wanted and used all his might to pound the rock barring James' hiding place.

Carla found this futile. There was no way he could get in by doing that. And even if he did, wouldn't water flood the inside? *He needs to stop.* She swam over to him and held his shoulder.

Dave saw her shake her head. *But come on. We gotta get in somehow.* He persisted.

Carla was sure he had lost it.

Dave pounded ferociously until he removed concrete as wide as his body. Under it was this glassy material that he could see through.

Carla had gone up for a breather before coming back down to check on him. *Wow.* He must have been determined.

Dave broke right through the glass with a single swing and watched water rush in through it. The man pulled off his snorkel and air tank to fit his head into the hole and pushed the rest of his body in with the water.

Carla could not believe her eyes. She knew the inside would be filled with water soon, so she held herself across it with her body to try to ease the amount of water that came in. Would Dave even find anything in there?

Dave gasped for air once inside. His feet stepped in the water that came in when he broke through, and he had cuts on his face and body from the risky ordeal. *Now . . . what is this place?*

It was like a large circular room made of glass. Below his feet, he saw a tube leading underground. There was a glass seal over it. "What do we have here?" Dave stepped back as he observed. This was definitely the landing point for some kind of submarine. *But where would it come from?* He raised his head to look around for some sort of hint.

All that did was reveal a camera at the corner of the ceiling. *Shit.* Surveillance? James thought to put surveillance in here? *I should go . . .* There was water trickling in from the hole he left, but Carla's body stopped the place from flooding. *No, wait. Before I go.*

He came against the wall and tried to get a closer look at the camera. The man attempted to climb up to see it but kept sliding down. *Wait.* He noticed grooves in the glass wall that he could plant his toes and fingers in.

With much effort, Dave made it to the ceiling to look at the camera. He did not care if James could see him. He needed to know where this was made.

". . . Fairbanks-Tech-whoa!" he fell down and hit the back of his head. "Ah . . ."

Water burst through the hole he left while he lay on his back.

Dave took that to mean that Carla had grown tired. *Gotta go.* He forced himself to get up and ran back to the hole to force himself through despite all the water slapping his face.

Dave got out and immediately started swimming upward. He had no gear.

Carla came right after him. There was no way James would not know they had been there. The place was a mess.

JUN SIGHED WITH RELIEF after boarding the bus to get back to school. "Can't believe she didn't see me. I am *really* good at hiding."

The sun was setting on a joyous afternoon. Their team had won second place in the cheer-offs. Annalise had the trophy in her lap up front.

"You were being pretty obvious to me. Who were you avoiding again?" Chantalle sat next to him. Lisa had told the three of them to go to the back so they could stick together. Chantalle had not expected her to consider that, but she supposed it was part of the girl warming up to her. *Later we have that sleepover with Annalise.* She saw Lisa staring out the window as more kids filed into the bus happily. She seemed contemplative. Her and Aaron's seat was right in front of theirs.

"I don't think that's any of your business," Jun's phone buzzed in his pocket, and he opened it. "The point is that I- oh no."

Pictures of him in the background of their routine filled his old class group chat. Someone had been watching the cheer-offs live and had spotted him. His classmates and friends were laughing. Carter sent a message with laughing emojis asking if that was what Jun was up to at his new school. *No, no, no, noooo!* Jun's world crumbled. A sharp pain coursed through his chest. Why did he even agree to do this? Was there anything he could say to fix this? He started anxiously typing that some loser at the school forced him into it.

Alex was energized. "We rocked that place. I think we should have won, but that's just me. Guess I'm biased," the bus was starting. Jun sat to his left while Chantalle was at his right. "What do you think . . ." he happened to see Jun's phone. The message he sent to some group chat read; 'the fat kid next to me in the picture started following me on my first day and wouldn't leave me alone. He got me into this, I swear'. It ended with crying emojis. Alex went dead silent.

When they were driving off the cheer-off compound, Aaron nudged Lisa, whose eyes were glued out the window.

The girl faced him.

"When you gonna . . . you know? Do the thing?" Aaron asked through his teeth. Other students were singing silly songs and laughing. Sato and his gang were quiet, so he felt that they could catch them off guard. That Chantalle girl seemed to be trying to talk to the sidekick while Sato was just on his phone.

"When the time is right," Lisa had told them to sit where they were for a reason and was seated in her position due to the same fact. She took a deep breath with her eyes closed and let it out slowly. *Forget it all.* The fond memories of cheering with everyone and the idea of sleeping over with Chantalle and Annalise flew out of her mind. *Focus.* Their father wanted this, so they had to do it. *He expects it.*

Even though the coach and the driver told everyone to keep their seatbelts on and stay in one place, a lot of kids were kneeling in their seats to talk to friends behind them. Lisa did the same but put her head out the window.

She looked at the wheel a little under Chantalle and then checked to see if the coast was clear. They had just entered an isolated road.

With furrowed brows, Lisa shot the wheel with a pointed finger, and it erupted into catastrophic flames. She pointed that same finger to the window next to Chantalle's head to complete the plan, but . . .

"Does anybody smell that?" the guy across from Aaron said.

All noise ceased as the scent of smoke hit them.

"Alright, remain, calm everybody," said the swim coach. There was no cheerleading coach, so she was in charge here. "The smoke scent could be from anywhere-"

Lisa realised that it would look suspicious that she was staring out here and not reporting anything while the wheel had just caught flames, so she pointed and screamed. "The wheel is on fire!"

Aaron's mouth was agape.

"What?" panic spread across the vehicle.

"Pull over! Pull over!"

Chantalle stopped talking to a dismal Alex when she smelled the heavy amounts of smoke. It was right next to her. "What's going on?" she had not been paying attention.

"Fire!" a different kid pushed her head through the window and pointed at the flaming wheel.

The bus driver parked the transportation on the roadside as quickly as possible.

"Get out, come on," he said right after hopping out himself.

Everyone got up, and some people were nearly trampled as they sped off the burning bus.

Jun stopped texting in the middle of all the hoopla and got up right after Alex.

"Come on!" said the coach from outside.

Aaron stood in the central aisle and shoved Alex back before he could walk down. "Lisa get over here," he hissed at her. "I'll distract everyone outside. Say it spread rapidly out of nowhere," he ran right out to meet the coach and held her by the shoulders, pushing her back. "The fire is wild in there! It's spreading!"

Chantalle did not understand. "What did he just say?"

Lisa groaned. "Let's get out of here," she ran out before them.

Alex did not bother asking questions. He went after her, and the two others were on his trail in seconds.

When they were all outside and the bus driver was dousing his wheel with water, Jun whispered, 'I told you so' in Chantalle's ear.

Chantalle looked at Lisa with betrayal splayed across her face. *But she let us go.* Had there been conspiring going on behind their backs?

Aaron grabbed his sister and forced her to face him. "What the heck?" he whispered.

Lisa could not look at him. She did not know what happened back there.

THE TIME BETWEEN WHEN James had told Aaron about his bomb and now had given the scientist the opportunity to reevaluate how to address the situation at hand.

He was furious with Reymond for what he put him through and had harboured that fury for years while underground. That emotion had become an extension of himself. James was the kind of man who believed that anger towards those who wronged you was strength, but maybe this time around, he had jumped to a conclusion too quickly.

He had been sitting at his computer screen with the bomb he created placed on his desk, contemplating the task his adopted children had set out to do that same day. Was that the right way to handle this? The kids had brought up some good points on why this may not be best, but that same fury that anger had stopped him from seeing his point.

James was pacing his lab while wondering if calling off that whole thing was a good idea when his computer screen started blinking, and a window displaying someone in the landing area for his submarine popped up.

Quickly, he planted himself back in his chair to observe, pulse racing and heart alike. Had someone found him?

The feed had shown a man in a scuba diving outfit investigating his top-secret submarine base. James' lips had called many curses on the person who broke in, but his mind had been buzzing with questions. Who was that? What did they want, and what was happening?

His whirlwind of questions had come to a halt when the face of the intruder showed itself up close to the camera.

James' heart had nearly stopped when he made him out. That man in *his* hidden tunnel? This guy worked with Reymond now. What was he . . . doing?

At that point, something had died inside of him. Aaron and Lisa . . . had they told the enemy his whereabouts? Was that why they were brief whenever he called? He had gotten the impression they were hiding things, but this?

James had just finished packing the rest of his bombs into his bag and was on his way out.

He marched down the steel hall with a face of stone.

Calling the kids would be futile. He already knew what had happened. Reymond happened. He *must* have gotten through to them, and now they were on his side. *Would they really betray me like that?* Of course, they would! Everyone did eventually. He had been on his own from the start. It was like James Foster was destined to live in isolation. Not even his own children could remain by his side. *Makes sense, though.* Christopher was always more likeable. All he had to do was smile kindly, and people flocked toward him. James got the title of 'the cold one' between the two of them.

He ceased his motions before the exit elevator and stared at his feet. Once he did what the anger inside him was telling him to do, there would be no going back.

He opened his satchel to look inside at the glowing metal bombs. They were glowing with blue because he extracted energy from his own orb to create them.

James closed the bag and fixed his frown forward. *I don't need anyone but myself.* He pushed the button on the wall to get the elevator to open and walked in. There was another submarine he could use to get there.

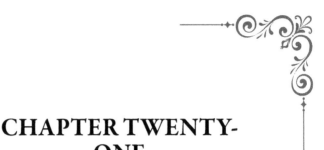

CHAPTER TWENTY-ONE

"You need to get out of my room," Lisa fluffed her pillow while kneeling on her bed that night.

"You can't just act like you didn't blow the mission," Aaron was leaning against her door with folded arms. He had been trying to have this conversation with her since they got back to school.

The bus driver had pulled out a spear tire after they got the fire to stop on the wheel. After installing it, the bus was good as new to take them back to the school compound. No one was sure of what truly happened except for the other enhanced kids. *And Devon.* Aaron had seen him glancing towards them again. He had been quiet and distant of late . . .

"I know what happened, and I know it was bad, but . . . something in me just couldn't . . . *murder* people. Sue me, Aaron. Sue me," Lisa sat in the middle of her bed.

"It's not about me, Lisa. I know this plan was bogus, but it was what Dad wanted, and he's . . . I don't know what he'll do after finding out we blew this. He's already been more unstable than usual," Aaron blew a raspberry with fingers combing his hair back. "And why do you want me to leave so bad? We're having a meeting,"

"Because . . . I agreed to have a sleepover in here," Lisa said to her shoulder.

Aaron blinked. "What . . . wait. The thing we were laughing about since we both knew that Chantalle would be dead before it happened?"

"She's not dead so . . ." Lisa shrugged. Between herself and Aaron, she would have never guessed that she would be the one who let her emotions disrupt their progress, but it was just hard to kill a person who had done nothing wrong and whose death may sabotage their dad's plan anyway. She and Aaron needed to talk to him, not fuel his insane ideals.

Aaron howled with laughter with arms wrapped around his stomach. "That's so messed up, but . . . didn't you see the way they were acting? Lisa, they *knew* what we were up to. I don't think Chantalle's gonna wanna sleep over after that. That was one of the biggest betrayals to ever betray."

She held her forehead. "I know, but . . ." she looked away. "I want to apologize but don't know how."

"You're not one to get attached. Damn," Aaron almost did not know how to deal with this. "Just say sorry. Sorry, I tried to kill you. My dad made me."

"It's not even just about the killing. There were secrets involved. Lies when she trusted me," Lisa hated how sappy that came out. "I don't know how I ended up here."

"You were just excited by the normalcy," Aaron held the door knob. "Happened to me too while we were cheering. I mean, we've lived underground our whole lives, and before we were adopted, we were broke and hungry."

Lisa did not say anything to that.

"Felt good," Aaron snapped out of it. "But now we got shit to deal with. Ugh," he thought of the old man. "Do I tell him it was a bust? What will he say?"

"We'll tell him that this needs to be approached differently. In a less brash and ridiculous way," Lisa was holding her pillow in her lap, squeezing it to ease her nerves. "But for now . . . please go to Chantalle's room to tell her I'm sorry," her voice was like a mouse,

Aaron hit his chest. "Moi? Porquoi?"

"Because you're the bold one!" she threw her pillow at him.

Aaron laughed when it hit. "I seriously don't have a problem," he opened the door. "I'll just tell her the truth. She seems reasonable," he stepped out the door and started walking in search of Chantalle's room.

Within five steps into his walk, the lights went out completely, and he stood in the dark,

Noises from confused girls in the rooms nearby filled the area until the lights came back on extra bright and in purple. *What the . . . they went back to normal after, but Aaron did not like the look of that. *Reymond hasn't fixed that yet?* A little gain and they'd have the whole school knowing about it. The rock in the wall.

". . . AND FOR ALL WE know, they could be thinking of some other way to take us down," Jun raised his voice over Chantalle's in her room.

Chantalle had a bag on her shoulder and a frown on her face.

Alex sat in silence on the floor.

"I'm pretty sure that whatever happened back there played out how it did because my kindness *changed* her mind!" Chantalle stomped. "You just wanna be right, but you don't even realise that your stupid spying plan couldn't pick up on what happened," Jun had called this meeting to discuss the fire and alleged betrayal.

"Yeah, well . . . at least I didn't trust the enemy," Jun said condescendingly.

Chantalle mocked his words.

"You're being such a-" a knock sounded at the door before they could keep arguing.

Alex got up with a sigh to answer it.

Annalise stood before him with a backpack on. "Hi guys . . ." she frowned in confusion. "Chantalle, why are Jun and Alex over? Do you guys do this often?"

"No, no," Chantalle forgot that she had agreed for Annalise to meet her here so they could walk to Lisa's room together.

Jun threw his hands up when she moved to the door. *Is she really still going to that sleepover?* Was he the only sane person in this room? *And Ale- hey. How come he hasn't been talking much?* This was completely out of character.

Annalise had seen the lights flicker and go purple. *Purple.* That colour made her sick. She and Devon had *really* messed things up. She was thinking of telling Dr Reymond tomorrow even though Devon feared expulsion. Things were just getting too out of hand. "Okay, well . . . are you ready?"

"I most definitely am," Chantalle gave Jun a sly look before stepping out. "You two are staying here?" she pouted at Alex. He refused to tell her why he was sad.

"No. I'm heading over to the boy's section so you can lock the door," Alex walked out and passed the two girls.

Jun did not understand. "I'll just go after him now," he ran past them and caught up with Alex down the hall. "Dude, what's with you?"

Alex tried to speed ahead.

"Hey Alex," Jun held his shoulder. Annalise and Chantalle were moving in the opposite direction behind them to find Lisa's room. "What's going on, man? You've been dead silent all day. That's not like you," he chuckled through his last sentence though worry eclipsed his heart.

Alex's chest hurt from the pain of what he read. He frowned harshly at Jun, then shoved him back. "I'm just a fat loser, huh? And I forced you to get into cheering?"

Jun staggered into the wall. "What?"

"That's what you've been telling your friends back home this whole time. That I'm this fat idiotic loser. I thought you were my friend, but you're just like everyone else. You fucking suck, Jun. You suck big time," Alex was marching off.

Jun gathered by now that Alex had read what he sent. *Shit.* "Alex, wait," He ran after him. "Man, it wasn't like that,"

"Then what was it like?" Alex demanded.

Jun opened his mouth, but a whistle at their backs caught his attention before he could speak.

"Am I walking in on a lover's quarrel?" Aaron was here?

The boys shared the same reaction. "What are you doing here?" Jun stepped in front of Alex.

"Relax. I come in peace," Aaron made sure to keep his distance lest an explosion came forth. "I came to apologize to Chantalle on my sister's behalf. You two know where her room is, right?"

"Apologize? For what?" Alex folded his arms.

"You know . . . for trying to kill her? Or did you miss that whole thing on the bus?" Aaron could sense a humming in the walls. *That's concerning.*

Jun felt it too. He heard it, actually.

"What's that?" Alex walked to a wall between two doors and pressed his ear against it. "This is linked to the lights, isn't it? And you know what? That got lodged in the wall downstairs," he was looking at Aaron.

"Definitely, but that's Reymond's problem, so I think we should focus on understanding exactly what happened earlier in order to move forward to be better people," said Aaron with an air of laughter.

Jun hated Aaron more and more as the days went by. "I don't know about Chantalle, but I will *never* trust you. There's no moving forward, okay? Just stay away from us."

"And you need to stay away from me," Alex stomped away from Jun.

"Alex, no," Jun grabbed his hand. "I'm sorry. I know I was being stupid and shallow. I know it. I . . . I was just . . ." he thought of how his friends laughed at him. "Chantalle is right about me, okay?"

Aaron was pouting. How adorable was this?

Meanwhile, Chantalle and Annalise knocked on Lisa's door.

Annalise sensed a humming around them that she did not like. *What's happening?* She looked up at one of the lights in the ceiling, and it emitted some purple electricity briefly. *Purple.* Vivid memories of that thing in the basement assaulted her mind. Her saliva was like gravel in her oesophagus.

Chantalle was sure Lisa would explain herself. *Maybe not around Annalise, but probably when we get some time alone. When Annalise is sleeping?* Was she the only one hearing that hum?

Lisa opened. "Annalise . . ." she locked eyes with the other girl in awe. "Chantalle."

"Hi," Chantalle winked at her, then entered first.

Annalise finally swallowed and then came in. "I like your room. It's so neat,"

"Thank you," Lisa closed the door. "Did you . . . run into my brother on your way here?" she asked Chantalle.

"No . . . was he supposed to tell me something for you?" Chantalle's head tilted.

"I-" Lisa saw the lights flicker with purple. They came back on. "I have a lot to explain, but I'll do it later."

They went from white to purple to nothing.

Annalise heard curses coming from the other rooms. What was going on? Why were things worse than usual in terms of the lights?

"Hmm . . ." Lisa picked up her phone and shone her flashlight upwards. "It's never stayed off this long . . ."

The guilt was killing Annalise. "They should really get someone to look into that, don't you think?"

"They did," Chantalle hoped they would come back on soon. "Okay, well, maybe we can tell scary stories fi-"

A blaring buzz followed by overly bright lighting startled them. The noise echoed all around, forcing the girls to cover their ears in horror.

It lasted for about a minute before the light bulb busted, and things went dark once more.

Chantalle could hear screaming from other rooms. She'd also heard faint cracks. "Are all the lights broken?"

Annalise could not take it anymore. "Devon wanted to expose you guys as having something up with you, so he led us down that secret elevator where you guys went off with the head of security, and we found a floating rock thing behind glass, and Devon pushed a button, and it rammed itself in a wall, and there was a crack, and now the lights have been going crazy for months!"

Lisa and Chantalle looked at her in the dark. "What?" Devon and *Annalise* were behind this?

Annalise was crying. "I know. We were scared of being expelled, so we kept it secret. I-I'm ready to confess now. Where does Dr Reymond sleep?"

"With everything happening, I'm pretty sure he isn't sleeping," Chantalle scratched her head. "We should probably talk to him about this for real, though."

"Think he'll expel me?" Annalise feared for her future.

"No. He found out what happened and has just been trying to fix this. Doesn't strike me as the type to expel people for something that was his responsibility anyway," Lisa left the room.

Chantalle went after her with Annalise. "Are we going to talk to Reymond about this? Think we can actually help?"

"Maybe. I don't know. But that thing needs to be out of that wall before this whole building explodes. I have a feeling you might be the best person for this. Considering your telekinetic abilities," Lisa used her flashlight to make it through the hallway.

"Lisa," Chantalle darted her eyes in Annalise's direction.

"She knows about the rock, so it doesn't matter," Lisa saw her brother and the other boys in the hall. "What do we have here?"

Jun had not gotten through to Alex yet. "Weren't you having a sleepover?"

"All of this is my fault. I'm so sorry. W-we're going to Dr Reymond for me to confess, but Lisa said something about Chantalle and telekinesis to get the thing from the wall?" Annalise wiped her tears, too ashamed to notice how ridiculous it was that Chantalle actually had out of these world powers!

"Wait, what?" Aaron had no idea what was happening.

Neither did Alex and Jun.

"Your fault? You put that in the wall? You know about . . . *what* is happening?" Alex's emotions made this hard to deal with.

"If you want this to stop, follow us, but if you'd prefer to sit this out, then stay where you are," Lisa led the girls away from them.

Jun used his phone to watch them. "Wait, but . . ."

"Jun," Alex had his flashlight on the wall.

Jun looked where his light was pointed and caught cracks coming in from the floor. Purple glowed within them. "Shit. Think we might be able to help?" was the school on the verge of blowing up or something?"

"I don't know, but we can try," Alex was still mad, but he would put that aside to deal with this. "Come on," he and Jun ran off.

Aaron did not want to be the only one left behind, so he followed. "All we gotta do is break the wall and the rock, right? It's not rocket science," he was some feet behind them,"

"I guess, but that'll take some force. Chantalle might be able to do this. But we should still join in in case something ridiculous happens, and they get hurt," Jun saw the girls on their way down the stairs.

REYMOND HAD BEEN DISCUSSING how they would find James with Dave and Carla when the lights went off, and the hum became audible even up here.

"Broke the light bulb," Dave pointed his flashlight towards the light over Reymond's desk.

"This has gotten completely out of hand," Carla walked back and forth, her hands placed on her hips. "I know that we said finding James needed to be the top priority, but we can't just have that thing wreaking havoc on the school from underground," anxiety crept up her spine. "We know where James is according to the label on the camera, so before we break in and get his orb, let's take care of the one that's been causing the lights to go crazy,"

"Saying it's making the lights go crazy is an understatement now," Reymond was not at ease. James definitely saw Dave on his security camera. *Alaska*. Should they really draw that conclusion? "The students must have the same issue with their light bulbs," he left the office with a flashlight of his own.

The principal pointed the light upward at the bulbs in the ceiling.

"Busted," Dave emerged from behind. "I don't know what it's doing, but whatever it is isn't good."

"How do we get it out of the wall without getting electrocuted or something?" Carla was at Dave's back.

Dr Reymond pondered with eyes on the damage.

"Dr Reymond,"

Dave shone his flashlight down the hall and caught a group of students advancing. "What the hell- oh, it's the mutated kids- wait, she wasn't part of it," he folded his lips. Had he just revealed what they had been hiding for months?

Annalise walked right toward the principal to confess. "Th-this is my fault. I'm so sorry, Dr Reymond but me and Devon, w-we came into your underground lab, and Devon accidentally pushed a button that sent that thing flying into the wall, and it got stuck, and now the lights are broken,"

Dr Reymond sighed, then looked at Dave. "You were right,"

"Can the controls on your computer really move that thing?" asked Carla.

"We used a computer to engineer it in the first place, so yes, it can," the scientist explained.

"Wait, so not only did that Devon kid find himself down there but you too? How did that happen? I didn't see you on my way to the elevator," Dave was pretty humiliated here. He completely failed at preventing students from finding the top-secret lab.

Annalise shrugged in a small manner. "It's complicated?" so they knew about Devon already . . .

Dave groaned, then pointed his light at all the kids. "Did you all come for her to confess? What's going on? This looks as suspicious as it is,"

Annalise spoke up first. "After I told Lisa about what we did, Lisa thought we could use Chantalle's powers to get the rock out of the wall. She has telekinesis?" she finally had that out of her system, so now her brain was processing this. "How did you guys end up like this, and what *is* that thing? What's going on?"

Carla had been moving the light of her flashlight along the wall when she noticed the cracks and slight glow.

"Annalise, it's quite a long story but thank you for telling me. That thing is highly unstable and clearly needs to be shot into the sun," Dr Reymond walked briskly down the hall.

"Where are you going?" Alex asked. They were right on his heels.

"There are cracks in the wall?" Carla caught up.

"Yeah, Alex and I saw them in the dorms too. I don't know what's happening, but I got a strong feeling that if we keep ignoring it that this whole building will blow up," Jun's main concern was getting back in Alex's good books. *I apologized a million times, and he still doesn't wanna look at me.* Was this the end of them? His heart splintered.

Dr Reymond stopped walking. "What cracks?"

They heard the pulsing of electric bolts from the broken lights overhead and saw purple sparks spluttering out.

"Oooooh . . ." Aaron was the least frightened by the recent events. "This is some serious shit."

Chantalle scratched her head. "I think I should definitely try to get it out tonight. We've left it in there long enough."

"Exactly. We need to stop stalling," Lisa led the party down the stairs.

Dr Reymond blinked at her willingness, then turned to Dave. "And you thought they were malicious,"

"Shut up," Dave rolled his eyes. "So, we're all going down to the underground lab so the girl with telekinesis can try to get the rock out?"

"I get the feeling it's not gonna be that easy," Carla muttered.

"That's the plan," Chantalle tried to psyche herself up for this. They hopped off the last stairs and were walking down the main hall.

JAMES STOOD WITHIN the surrounding walls of his old partner's beloved school with fewer bombs in his satchel than he had started with. Some security guards had been blocking his way when he got close enough, so he'd distracted them by blowing up part of the wall. While they were occupied, he wormed his way in.

The man scowled at the building in all its glory, then took long strides towards it, one hand in bag gripping yet another bomb. *Slowly.* Each section of this retched school would be blown up one by one by his doing. No reasonable thoughts traced his mind at this moment. All he knew was the sting of betrayal and the will to exact revenge.

He pulled the bomb from his bag and activated it with a push of a button when he saw the guards at the entrance shining their lights toward him.

"Who are you?" they asked together.

James threw the bomb towards the door that they guarded, and it blew up in seconds, flinging them in opposite directions and destroying the locked glass door in the process. "Christopher will pay for what he did to me," and so would his so-called children. After this, maybe he should let the world pay for how it treated him. He did not deserve to be dealt a bad hand in life. Why him? All he ever did was work for what he wanted. Why did life hate him?

He pulled out another bomb after walking through the blue smoke and threw it down the main hall.

It exploded just like the others, destroying whatever was near. *They will fall.*

DAVE HAD ENDED UP LEADING the way since he knew better than anyone how to find the secret elevator outside.

"With the kind of damage it's started doing, I have a strong feeling that it's gonna be a little difficult to get it out of there. For all we know, it could have made a network of threadlike electricity that embedded it into the walls. That thing was- JESUS!" he and the others went flying backwards when something circular landed before him a few feet away and burst into vicious blue flames and smoke before his eyes!

Reymond went as far as the staircase. He hit his back on it, nearly losing consciousness. Had it started? Jun had mentioned the school possibly exploding. Was that it? Had the boy's theory been correct?

He heard screaming faintly as his vision focused.

"*Cough, cough,* what was that?" Alex's voice.

"Everything's all blue; I can't see," Jun.

"That's definitely unrelated to the issue at hand. Is the school under attack?" Lisa.

"I didn't see . . ." Aaron.

Dr Reymond, Carla and Dave got to their feet quite some time after the students. Annalise was slow, too, holding her head when she walked forward to try to see through the smoke.

Aaron was frowning with his phone light directed at the blue smoke. *Blue.* "This is familiar,"

Lisa glanced at him.

"Somebody did this . . ." Alex had bruises on his body, which he would heal later.

"Seriously, *what* is going on?" Chantalle understood the crazy lights and cracks, but now a bomb went off?

The smoke was clearing, and with their combined lights, they recognized a silhouette. It held something blinking and blue.

"Am I interrupting a party of some sort?"

Dr Reymond stood straighter. That voice.

When all smoke was gone, and their lights were of more use, they not only saw the extensive damage to lockers and the flooring but also the owner of that sinister voice.

Aaron's shoulders fell. "Father," he breathed.

Jun glanced at him. Chantalle, Lisa and Annalise stood between them.

"That's your dad?" Annalise should probably be in her room . . .

After watching at a distance for so long with his identity concealed, James felt thrilled to finally be this close to Reymond as no one but himself. Himself at his purest. A man fed up with the way he had been treated for years. A man ready to take back control no matter the cost. He was . . . free.

Christopher cautiously moved his feet to take him toward the one he had been searching for.

Carla hated the entrance he made and the lights blinking in his hand. She had never met James Foster in person, but she knew of him. What she knew gave reason to believe he was not in his right mind. *The damage he's done after just stepping in here says it all.* Why was he here anyway? What was going on?

Christopher held a hand out as if trying to calm his old friend. Dozens of questions spun around his mind. "James . . . what are you doing here, and why did you bring a bomb with you?"

"Yeah, what's going on?" Aaron was pretty confused. He walked boldly up to their father. "Is this your plan in action? I-I thought you'd realise that that was way too risky. You can't just barge in here with bombs. There's security . . ." directing his flashlight down the hall and showed him the broken entrance and fallen men. "Wh-what's going on?" they had not told him they failed to execute the plan. *Well, he knows now.* If he could put two and two together, that was . . .

"Stay back, Aaron," James raised his voice.

Aaron frowned.

Jun, Chantalle and Alex were quietly exchanging glances in the dark. With the state of the lights and the school right now, they doubted that anyone had time for whatever grand reunion was about to occur here . . .

James gripped tightly to his bomb while directing it towards the teenage boy. "I know all about you all. *Everything,*"

"What do you mean by that?" Dave spoke up. "And how on earth are you only showing your face now after decades?" his eyes were on the blinking thing which they had all figured was a bomb.

"We know about what you've been doing," Carla spoke with a shaking voice.

Jun heard the broken lights buzzing. There was glass on the floor from when they exploded. "Maybe the grown-ups can deal with this while the rest of us see about you know what in the wall?" he would be much more freaked out by the creepy guy with the bombs if it wasn't for his fear of the school crumbling on everyone.

"But he's in the way," Chantalle whispered.

"I know, but . . ." Jun was not sure how to handle this.

"I know that you know," James turned up his nose. "Not even my own children can stick by me. It's as if I eventually repel everybody I ever meet,"

Dr Reymond shook his head. "James, you *know* why I gave up on the experiments. It wasn't . . . I know how hungry you are for success, but the entity is dangerous. As we speak, the unstable prototype is embedded in a wall and causing chaos. We haven't seen half of it, but so far, it doesn't look good," he gulped. "And using children as test subjects was just insane. You *do* know that, right?"

"And we didn't betray you. I mean, yeah, we told that little runt about you but not Reymond. The runt just ran his mouth, but we didn't sell you out exactly. We were even willing to go along with your bogus plan to kill those freaks," Aaron's arms were folded.

"What?" Dave, Reymond, Annalise and Carla said together.

"They uh . . . tried to murder us on that field trip," Alex just wanted the scary guy gone. "Are you gonna kill us all with that bomb?" he whimpered.

"Father, this is ridiculous," Lisa came up to Aaron. "Did you really come all the way here because-"

"I saw *him* on my security cameras for the submarine base, which means *you* told them about it. And how can you say you didn't betray me in the same breath that you reveal that Reymond found out about you and you didn't tell me?" James barked.

Chantalle could tell he was irrational. *And he has a bomb.* This man had lost it. He was high on anger and had a victim mindset.

Aaron gulped. "We just . . . we wanted to take care of the problem but didn't want to anger you. We didn't expect the runt to run his mouth, okay? It could have still worked,"

"The runt has a name, you know," Alex opened his arms in his terror.

"Humph," James laughed sardonically. "You're all just adorable," he walked past them and down a different hallway.

"James!" Dr Reymond started following him.

The terrifying noise of an explosion stopped him in his tracks, and he covered his face when the smoke reached him.

"What is he doing? Destroying the school?" Carla heard more explosions as the man descended the hall. She saw flames left in his wake.

"Shit. We don't have time for this," Dave muttered. "Somebody needs to stop him. Don't one of you kids have powers that can do that?"

"We shouldn't ask them to use those if it can be helped. It's dangerous," Dr Reymond would hate to exploit them.

"It *can't* be helped," Aaron sprinted after the mad man shaking the world around them. Someone in the dorm area must have been able to hear this.

Lisa's powers would not be useful in this setting, but she chased them anyway. "Father! Stop!"

"I'll go with them. Dave lead the others to the lab. Carla, take Annalise to her room and tell the students in the dorms to remain calm. I don't want them near the building," Reymond was already going after his old partner.

Carla held Annalise's hand and ran outside with her.

Dave was the first to begin jogging off. "Let's get this stuff done,"

Chantalle, Alex and Jun followed with their nerves wrapped around their organs.

CHAPTER TWENTY-TWO

" *What* is going on?" Ansel looked out his window at the school building. The only light making things visible was his lava lamp next to his bed.

"I don't know, but it's got everyone shaky. This is kinda cool, not gonna lie," Ryan had been in here to practice music. His guitar was at the base of Ansel's bed. They were both standing by the window.

Devon's thumbnail was as low as it could go without bleeding. Chewing it was a way that he coped with his nerves. "There's no way in hell that the lights blowing up, the walls humming, and explosion noises from the school building are cool," he just knew it. This was happening because of that weird thing that he and Annalise found, and Dr Reymond was probably close to finding out what they did. *Shit.* His body was covered in cold sweats.

Concerned voices flooded the halls outside. Ansel's door was open, and they could feel the presence of kids in the halls, asking questions in confusion.

Devon gulped. "I don't know how they're gonna fix the lights at this rate,"

"Forget the lights. There are cracks in the walls, man. *Glowing* cracks. This is like . . . an alien invasion or something," Ryan chuckled.

Devon walked briskly out of the room and squeezed his way through the confused guys inspecting a big crack which emitted purple light. *Gotta find Annalise. We did this.* Boys weren't supposed to be in the girl's section, but things were so crazy that he was sure no one would notice him weaselling his way in.

While running down the stairs with his phone flashlight on, Devon jolted at the sight of two people coming in the opposite direction. "Shhhit- Annalise!" he recognized the other person too. "And the secretary . . . ?"

"Where's the dorm overseer?" Carla had just been in the girl's section to provide some instructions on how to treat the situation. The overseer there had been telling the girls to relax when she had entered with Annalise.

"Uh . . . he . . . I saw him staring at the weird cracks with the purple and the-the . . ." Devon did not get to finish. The secretary walked past him up the stairs with determination. He was left here with Annalise. "Wait, why did she seem like she understood what was going on?" his brain caught on. "Shit. Did you tell her about this? She knows? What's going on? Are we all gonna die or what?"

Annalise brought him to the corner of the stairs. "I told her, Reymond and the security guy,"

Devon began to shake. "So what? Are you expelled now? Did you say my name?"

"No. I mean, I said your name, but I'm not expelled. Neither are you. Right now uh . . . they're gonna try to fix this," Annalise whispered.

"Who's 'they'? I haven't seen that Jun guy around during all of this," Devon could faint with relief at the fact that they were in the clear. *We're gonna get in trouble but just not that kinda trouble.* He would punish them if he was Dr Reymond too . . .

"And that's why. He's the 'they'. He and the others you saw that day," Annalise could faintly hear the secretary addressing the guys. "I think Chantalle's gonna use her powers to get the thing out so the school can stop being weird."

"Okay, uh, do they know what's happening?" Devon folded his arms.

"No. There were some theories, but I told them it was stuck in the wall, so she's gonna try to use her abilities to get it out. She has telekinesis," Annalise said. "Hopefully, all of this will be over soon,"

"Why didn't they let her get it out sooner? Feels like the world is ending. I do *not* feel safe in this building," Devon rubbed his arms as if cold,"

"Because they didn't know," Annalise agreed with him. "Some crazy guy came in with bombs and got in the way, but Dr Reymond, Aaron and Lisa are after him. Chantalle and the others are heading to the basement,"

"Wait, *that* was the explosions? Crazy guy? What the hell is happening?" Devon hissed.

Annalise wished she knew. "Things are getting crazy. I-I just hope it all resolves soon,"

Devon took a deep breath. "Me too," he saw glowing cracks appear on the wall behind Annalise . . .

"THIS IS LIKE ANOTHER planet," Alex jogged through the halls of the underground lab with the others. Cracks way wider than what he had seen in the dorms were everywhere he turned. They did not need their flashlights to see because the purple glow in the cracks was enough to illuminate their path.

"Don't step on the cracks. I don't know what's in that light," Dave jumped over one in the floor that must have been sixteen centimetres wide.

Jun hopped after him, and the others were right on his heel. "We gotta ask some serious questions here because how the *hell* is it doing this? It's like a virus. Even the dorms are affected. Does it have some kind of root system working underground or something?" in the midst of his fear, there was still discomfort towards him and Alex's fallout.

"We'll have to see. When I checked last time, it wasn't as bad as it is now. I don't know. The main word used to describe this thing is 'unpredictable'. I get the feeling that being embedded in another solid is somehow aggravating it," Dave led them into the room.

They all filed in and stopped in their tracks after doing so. This was the heart of the chaos.

Chantalle was in awe. "So much for indestructible," the glass concealing the anomaly was cracked up and the wall behind it the same. Breakage could be seen on the roof, and the room felt ready to cave in.

"Can you even see it?" Alex asked anxiously.

"Uh . . . I see its glow," Chantalle took steps forward.

Dave did not know about this. The pressure in this room was insane. Could this kid stop this with her mind? "Do you need to see it to try to get it out?"

Chantalle blew a raspberry. "Yes, but- I think that's it," she pointed.

Jun noticed the source of all the cracks. It was way in the wall but was the point from which everything came. "Yeah, that's the heart right there,"

"Should she get in through the glass wall?" Alex came up to it and touched it but had to pull back. "Vibrating . . . hot. Damn it,"

"It's like an overused charger or-or a chainsaw," Jun was at his side, using both hands to feel.

"Don't touch that!" Dave ordered.

Both boys stopped, looking at the man in the glow of purple. This really did feel like another planet.

"If the glass is vibrating, then does that mean going behind it will make me explode or something?" the weight of the situation was creeping onto Chantalle's shoulders. If she couldn't fix this . . .

Dave threw his hands up. "I have no idea,"

"Chanty, if anything happens," Alex held her shoulder firmly. "I'll save you. I swear on my mother's *life*," he enunciated.

Chantalle was moved until she played back what he said in her head. "Chanty?"

Alex's cheeks heated. "I ... thought it was cute?"

Dave rolled his eyes. "We don't have time to be cute. Look," he ran to the opening in the glass. "*I'll* go in first to assess the pressure," he opened the door and ran up to the wall.

Jun covered his eyes in case the man's head would blow up. "Is he dead? Is he dead??"

"No," Chantalle's voice came through to him.

Jun opened his eyes. "Oh ..." the Dave man was facing them near the wall.

"In here is hot and intense, but you can survive. Come on," Dave beckoned at Chantalle.

Chantalle took a deep breath and then turned to the boys. "Wish me luck,"

Alex's knees began buckling. "G-good luck. I'm sure you'll be able to end this no problem," he smiled, and it shook at the corners. *I don't know what's gonna happen.* But he had been told countless times that lying to yourself when you were unsure was a great way to get through trying circumstances. *Thanks, Dad.* He gulped.

Chantalle smiled anxiously at him before bringing her eyes to Jun.

"We can come inside if you want-"

"No. Stay here in case anything happens. Plan B can be Jun burning that thing to bits," Chantalle just did not want them risking their lives. *My stomach is so knotted it's crazy!*

The boys were uncertain. "W-well . . ." Jun was cut off by an impatient Dave.

"Come on. Let's see if you can get rid of this thing," called the head of security. His face was moist with sweat. *It may not be as hot, but I'd imagine the inside of a volcano to feel something like this.* His eyes were glued to the glaring purple shining in the middle of the massive cracks.

Chantalle gave them a firm nod and then ran in through the door.

She arrived at Dave's side and immediately experienced the severe pressure that came with being this close.

Dave had no idea how this would go. "Ready?"

"Ready," Chantalle raised her hand and kept her eyes on the rock.

Jun and Alex watched with bated breath.

Chantalle got hold of it and began pulling with her mind. "Gah!"

It was moving but not coming out. The wall had it stuck in this small hole it created for itself.

"Come on, Chanty," Alex whispered.

Chantalle had never had this much difficulty with her powers. This thing was *in* there!

Dave observed how the girl bit down on her lip and creased her forehead with an extended hand. "Is it moving?"

"A-a little but . . . it's like there's a force keeping it in," Chantalle grunted. "Shhhit!" she stepped back and raised her other hand to try to get it out.

Jun saw another crack emerge on the wall and could hear the sound of her struggle. "Damn. Are her powers supposed to make noise?"

"It's clashing with the hum of the rock," Alex's stomach was on his toes. "Chantalle, you can do this!"

Jun's ears picked up the strain on the glass. It would burst open soon . . .

Chantalle's head began pounding with the effort she was putting in. "Come on, you son of a b-bitch . . . get out of there!" did it have a mind of its own? How was it fighting with her to stay in?

Dave didn't like this. "We need to break the wall,"

"The wall's already b-breaking . . ." Chantalle's heart had never been faster. "Just let me do th-this . . . g-grr-guh! Uh-uh . . ." It was like a tug of war against a train headed in the opposite direction, nearly pulling her forward with its strength. "What the hell?" but she would not give up. "G-get out! Get out!"

Chantalle kept her feet as firmly planted on the floor as she could. *Shit.* She started being pulled forward.

Dave got down and held her ankles. "Just keep doing what you're doing," he was not sure it was working, but she seemed to believe so.

Chantalle struggled still, but the help of Dave made a difference. She was sturdier, so she had more of a chance. *Get out of here, you little shit. Get out! Get out! GET OUT!*

The rock pitched out of the wall!

"She did it!" Alex hopped up and down. "Chantalle for the wi-holy shitting on a shit ball! What the hell is that!" he pointed.

Jun had not rejoiced at all because he saw what followed their problem. "A-a network of energy?"

Dave's sweaty face grew sweatier as his eyes gazed upon the threads of glowing energy that came after the prototype. It was like a tree rooted out of the ground. He had been right.

Now Chantalle knew what had been pulling against her. "The roots are still in," only part of them could be seen behind the rock which she held some inches away from the wall. Her mind was the thing that grasped it. "I need to get them all out," she looked down at Dave.

"W-well . . . do it."

"I just don't know how far they go . . ." Chantalle could sense that they were pretty long. "That's why the problem spread so far.

It's embedded itself all over the compound. There are probably roots underground. It'll take ages to...."

"Chantalle, come on! You can do this!" Alex encouraged.

Chantalle looked at the guys through the glass, then at the pulsing purple rock. She didn't have a choice, did she? *I'll try something.* She got back into battle mode and continued using both hands and her mind to yank that thing and all its threads from the school's structure.

DR REYMOND COUGHED after running through clouds of smoke. His lungs were not in good shape. "James!"

Aaron and Lisa were ahead of him. They had just entered the classroom where their dad had blown up.

Lisa stopped when she found the man tossing a bomb to the ceiling. "You're in here too! You could die-"

The ceiling blew up, and rocks fell from above.

Aaron coughed into his elbow after the dust and smoke vanished, then tried to find their dad in the rubble. "What the hell is he thinking? Did he die?"

"Something must have hit him . . ." Lisa ran further in and climbed over scraps with the hope of finding the deranged man.

Dr Reymond used his hand to get excess dust and smoke away from his face. "J-James?" he saw what happened. Aaron and Lisa were tossing fallen rocks away to find his old partner in the debris. "J-James . . ." he ran to help them. *My old body isn't cut out for this.*

Aaron had to use his ice vision to get a lot of fires to vanish. He had been doing this since they started chasing. If the flames spread, then the school would be even more doomed than it was.

Lisa removed some brick and plastering, and below it was a face. "Father!"

Reymond crawled to look. His friend must have been crushed. "Get him out of there!"

Lisa climbed off the rocks and picked several of them up to toss aside.

Aaron helped once he outed the most worrying flames, and soon, they were helping their father to sit up.

Dr Reymond stared in horror at James' dusty injured form. "W-was that his intention? I thought he wanted to destroy the school. He's done a lot of damage but not enough to call it quits and commit suicide,"

"Come on, old man. Get up," Aaron was slapping his face. "I don't know why he did that. He's not . . . he's coo-coo but not *that* kind of coo-coo,"

Lisa shook her head. "He must have several concussions and broken limbs. I don't know. Maybe he wasn't thinking?"

Rocks and dirt were all over James's head.

Dr Reymond placed a finger under his nose. "We need to call an ambulance-"

James' eyes bulged open, and his body shot to a sitting position.

"Shit!" Aaron's heart leapt just now. "We thought you died. Why would you toss a bomb in the ceiling over your head?"

James got up but did not get far when he tried to limp to the door. His body was laced with pain, and his head spun. He fell to his front a few feet from the door. *Damn it.* Thinking straight had not been what he'd been doing when he threw that thing up. All he knew was that he needed to see destruction, so he would throw his bombs where ever he could. He wanted things to crumble, to fall to explode too. . . *I got caught in the crossfire.* He cursed himself while fighting to stand once more.

Lisa and Aaron came to him and forced him to stay put.

"Let me go! I know that you two are working with the likes of *him* now," James spat, making eye contact with his old partner.

"I should have seen it coming. Everyone who gets near him immediately becomes a follower. He was always the charming one. The one highly favoured. The one loved by life itself," his words were dripping with spite. "While I was cursed from the start."

Dr Reymond had heard him speak in this light before. Back then, he had sounded more sad than angry, though. *I can still hear the sadness.* "James, I know that things haven't been fair to you since the day you were born, but . . . you can*not* let it cloud your judgement and cause you to commit heinous crimes and-and go on a rampage!"

James freed himself from Lisa's grasp. Both kids held either of his shoulders to keep him still. He would not be able to move anyway. His balance was terribly off. "And why should I listen to you? You've had it all from the start! That was why you could just drop everything we were working so hard on. That was why. Y-you . . . you didn't have the pain to keep you going! You didn't!"

"My *son* had *died*!" Christopher exclaimed. "The thing we were creating *killed* my son! If that wasn't enough to convince me that it was dangerous, I-I don't know what would. How could you expect me to continue to work on something that *killed* my only child!" tears brimmed in his eyes. "That drove my wife away! It was unstable! It was-"

"It needed more testing. You didn't have the drive. Look at these two. They're the perfect example of what can happen if you *keep* pushing!" James still had that crazed look in his eye.

Christopher just shook his head. "James, those things need to be sent back to where they came from. You need to show us your lab so we can get rid of the rock and ship them off. Yes, your creation seems more stable, but that was how the prototype appeared before it *killed* Daniel. Why else would you let him near it? You thought it was safe, but it wasn't because-because we're dealing with something out of our world. We don't know where it came from, and now the prototype is . . . do you see the cracks in the walls? The ground? I know that its instability is due to my failure to destroy it. I know that destroying it halfway was what made it into this, but all of the chaos ensuing is what it's capable of. If we were to make others, they could possibly bring forth Armageddon!"

James's vision was failing him, and so was his hearing. "You're wrong. That only happens if it . . . if the power isn't harnessed properly. You're just too fearful of the unknown. And that mentality will keep you stuck the rest of your life, Christopher. The rest of your life,"

Christopher was stern. "Between the two of us, who do you think has been more stuck over all these years?"

James glared silently.

Christopher stared right into his eyes.

James' consciousness failed him before he could answer. He was out.

Aaron had not heard a more heated argument. "Thought you two were gonna kiss,"

Lisa pushed him by the shoulder.

"Ow. Sorry, it just felt that way . . ." Aaron started standing while supporting their old man.

Lisa stood too.

Dr Reymond told them to hand him over, and he placed one of James' arms over his shoulder. "He's gonna need a hospital," he started carrying him into the halls, which were slowly starting to turn purple from the glowing in the cracks which appeared more frequently.

"Will you call the police? He trashed most of the school," said Lisa. They walked quickly down the hallway at Dr Reymond's side. She always knew that the man who adopted her and Aaron was unstable, but his behaviour towards all this confirmed it. *Brainwashing* . . . Had he really brainwashed her and Aaron? Was that why they had not thought twice about what he sent them here to do in the first place?

"No. I'll blame it on the current disaster," Dr Reymond brought James to a staircase and let him lie on his side. "I hope this disaster ends soon," he fished for his phone in his pocket. "I wouldn't want paramedics at risk,"

"If they'd be at risk by coming here, aren't all the students in their dorms at risk too?" asked Aaron with eyes on their father. *Insane.* The man was insane. He didn't know who to trust anymore.

Dr Reymond thought briefly. "Keep an eye on things and if they get out of hand, tell Carla to escort everyone out; I need to check on the others," he started running off.

Lisa and Aaron stood close to their father in silence, watching Dr Reymond run through the broken halls to get to the entrance.

"So like . . . when will we know it's getting out of hand? 'Cause to me, it looks that way already," Aaron said to his sister.

Lisa thought about this quietly. "If the others don't come back up in forty minutes, one of us will go down there to check on things, and the other will talk to the secretary,"

"Forty minutes . . ." Aaron got his phone to set a timer. "Got it,"

CHAPTER TWENTY-THREE

Their problem was several inches away from the collapsing wall. At its back were threads of glowing energy just as long as its distance from it.

Chantalle's powers allowed her to get a sense of just what they were dealing with. These threads . . . she would be here all night trying to get them out.

"This is ridiculous," Dave grumbled, still holding her ankles. Right now, the orb was against the glass with long yards of zooming energy following behind it. "I don't even think there's enough space here to get it all out," he spoke over the deafening noises of pressure that seemed to be emitting from the purple threads. Pulling them out of the wall was making their surroundings even more unbearable.

"I know, but how else are we gonna stop this thing from destroying everything as we know it?" Chantalle's teeth were clenched while both her arms remained high, her brows furrowed over her squinted eyes.

Dave tried to think. "Cut the threads," it clicked.

Alex and Jun were staring at the way cracks formed gradually on the glass the closer the rock got to it. The shaking was at an all-time high.

"This thing is like something outta hell," Jun was stepping back.

Alex gulped when his eyes went back to Chantalle. "I don't know if this is a good idea!"

"I think we need to cut the energy threads," Dave spoke from the ground.

"What? With what? Scissors?" Jun was already against this. "That is a *bad* idea. I'm pretty sure that whatever we try to use will just end up exploding or-or electrocuting us, or I don't know, killing us? It's already dangerous enough as it is to have Chantalle use her powers on it, so I don't think that getting close enough to cut it would be any safer," he swiped his hand across the air.

"That might be the only way," Alex breathed.

Chantalle looked over her shoulder. "The threads are too long. If we cut them then-"

"They won't have their source of energy and will probably disappear," Alex finished for her.

Jun . . . "Or the person who tries to get rid of them will *die*! *How* are we going to cut energy strings?"

"The only thing I can think of is to use an energy source in the opposite direction of it. A bigger energy source. Something that will hit it in the perpendicular direction? Maybe Chantalle can . . . I don't know if her powers are good for that," said Alex.

"Bigger energy- this thing is so powerful it's destroying a building that spreads for like 200 miles. *What* bigger source of energy?" things were looking bleak to Jun, and he did not like that. Parts of the ceiling were falling.

"Can any of your powers focus in a straight line with extreme amounts of pressure? Maybe that can cut through," Dave shouted.

Chantalle's face was soaked. "Jun. Your fire. It's crazy strong. It's so intense that it's black and purple. The colour might have a lot to do with its potential. This thing is purple, so if you push hard enough, then you can overpower it,"

Jun's heart was on his toes. "I . . ."

Dr Reymond came dashing in at that point. "Have we gotten- oh my," one look at the lines of purple made him cease all movement.

"Dr Reymond, we wanna cut the threads. They go way into all the walls and underground. That's why the entire building is going haywire. Those roots slash tentacles slash whatever we're calling them have created a network for the energy from that thing to spread. Have you ever seen anything like this? Why is this thing so insanely weird, dangerous and creepy?" Alex whined with a little hop.

The scientist observed the rock high against the glass. It would come down to any second-

The glass shattered before their eyes.

"Shit," Jun nearly fell back by the pressure and heat that followed.

"Do you think we're onto something in terms of cutting the threads to stop this?" Dave shouted.

Dr Reymond's ears nearly popped. "Yes. I've never seen it do this, but if the orb is the source of energy, then cutting them away from it *will* definitely stop this,"

Jun's hands trembled. "Th-they want me to try to use my fire to cut through but-but like . . . it's energy. We can't touch it. The fire might just go through,"

"No. I'm pretty sure that if you focus enough, you can deteriorate the energy with something stronger. Dr Reymond, what do you think?" Alex was covering his ears.

Dr Reymond thought about it.

Chantalle and Dave stared over their shoulders to look at him.

Dr Reymond held the side of his head. "You can try. We don't have time so let's make this quick,"

Jun's body was rigid.

"I'll hold it still," Chantalle remained put.

Jun turned to Alex.

Alex nodded. "I know you don't like being a freak, but it just might be the thing that saves everyone here,"

Jun took a deep breath, shook his head then ran further in.

He stepped on the perpendicular side to the threads and raised his hands. "I-I don't have that much control, so I don't know if it'll be strong enough. M-maybe Lisa should do th-"

"It's too late to call her. The fact that you have no control can be a plus. You might go crazy enough to do what we need of you," Dave grunted.

Jun held his forehead. "Fine," he got back into position and looked right at the long, pulsing energy strings. *What the actual . . .* this was terrifying.

"Any time today Jun," Chantalle said.

Jun snapped out of his fear and started shooting fire out of his palms, right for the threads.

Dr Reymond tried to see if it did any good. The fire was hitting the wall after blasting through the energy. This place would set ablaze soon, wouldn't it?

"Stop!" Alex called.

Jun did so, and nothing changed. "I'm not strong enough!"

"No, no one of them cut through for a second. It just attached back. You need to be stronger. I think that if you cut them all with your flames and I tuck this thing away that we'll be in good shape," Chantalle told him.

"We need something to put it in," Dr Reymond ran to a different part of the breaking lab.

Jun looked at how Chantalle nodded certainly and then how Alex did the same. "O-okay, fine," he took a stance with his feet apart and raised his arms once again.

Jun bit his lip, then shot a straight, continuous line of fire from his hands again.

"That's it, Jun. Give it hell!" Alex needed this to be over and done with.

Dr Reymond came up to them, holding a cardboard box. He went under the orb suspended in the air and held it over his head.

Jun knew that Alex was only encouraging because they needed this to be done, but he appreciated it anyway. "How much longer?"

"You just started. Put your life into this Jun! Push everything you've ever buried into that blast! We *need* you to do this!" Chantalle saw the ceiling caving in above them as the fire spread towards it. That, paired with the pressure from the rock, was destroying this room!

"Yeah, come on! I'm pretty sure there's a lot you've got buried inside. Let it out with the fire! Let it out with the fire!" Alex clenched his fists.

Jun's face was dripping with sweat already. *Buried inside* . . . memories of being bullied in middle school. All the ridicule about his appearance, people making fun of his lunches because they were different, the shame he felt when the other kids called to him in mockery of Chinese, his things being destroyed, his body being shoved. All the pain that led him to be the coward that he is now. He was so scared of being different that he would shame one of the only people he could genuinely call a friend, all in the name of fitting in with kids who didn't even care about him. If they would laugh at him for trying new things, then they weren't friends. They were just people he sought the validation of. Horrible people whom he gave power over himself. Deep down, Jun hated that about him. Why couldn't he be more self-assured like Alex? Confident like Chantalle? Why was he . . .

Chantalle and Dave moved back when Jun's blast grew stronger. The heat was ridiculous, and around it was some sort of wave that fought with the pressure from the rock.

"Damn," Alex felt it too, and it was painful. "Th-that's it, Jun!"

Dr Reymond could see the orb shaking in the air. Shaking and sparking. Its threads glitching. "He's doing it,"

Jun hated himself for what he had become. He hated the shame, the pain, everything. He had superpowers, and he wanted to hide them even when they were needed just because . . . "Shit on me!"

His flames reached an all-time level of strength, causing the energy around it to overpower one of the rocks in a grating clash that sent everyone flying!

Jun flew into the wall a few feet behind him, Chantalle and Dave flew towards Alex, who was sent to a different wall, and Dr Reymond went with them.

As for the rock . . .

Dr Reymond nearly lost consciousness when his back jammed against a surface, but the crashing noise of the rock clashing in the place next to him made him open his eyes and fight the stun to scoop it into his box before it could create another network into a different wall.

It buzzed inside his cardboard box, but he held it to his chest anyway. "Sweet Jesus,"

Jun's eyes had closed down for a second, but they opened when a debilitating heat clutched his leg.

"Gaaaah!" his leg was on fire! *Because the lab is on fire!* His flames stopped the threads, but now the fire was everywhere!

A lot of the ceiling fell in front of him, and he began to cough. "Shit! Shit! Alex!"

Alex opened his eyes after the ceiling came down before them. "What the hell?"

Chantalle was on her feet. "We needed to get out of here yesterday! Where's Jun?" she heard faint screaming. "Did he get crushed?" she used her powers to toss parts of the ceiling out of her way as she ran to where she saw him get flung.

Chantalle knelt beside Jun when she found him. "Your leg!"

Jun winced in agony. "Alex . . . he can heal-" he heard the ceiling above them coming down!

Chantalle stopped it with her powers. "Come on. First thing's first, we *have* to leave this place," she used all her strength to send the ceiling flying away and then raised Jun with her mind. She ran to the others who were standing by the blocked door.

Jun was just floating behind her. "I-it's blocked, but you can unblock it, right Chantalle?" his leg was sizzling; he wanted to pass out so it would stop.

Dave did not like how much the flames were spreading. He coughed. "I don't know how much debris is blocking this, but it is a *lot*."

"Chantalle's powers can- oh, or Jun, can you use your fire? Shit your leg!" Alex went to try to heal it.

Chantalle let Jun lie down so Alex could do his thing, then started sending the rocks and plastering away from all of them. "Guh!" she cleared a path. "Let's go,"

Alex didn't finish healing Jun, but he did enough for the guy to not be in agony.

Jun was being supported by Alex through the door.

The fire was even in the hall!

"What the hell? Did that shockwave do this?" Dave said as they ran and jumped over cracks.

Some of the ceilings fell in front of them.

"Shit!" Chantalle found it difficult to focus on all this smoke and fire. "It's-it's . . ." she used her mind to move some away.

"Look out!" Alex and Dr Reymond shouted.

Chantalle got hit in the head with some of the ceiling and fell to her side.

"Oh my God! No! No!" Dr Reymond knelt next to her body. "She's gone,"

"No," Alex moved her away from the falling ceiling and sat to heal her head.

"We don't have time for this," Dave muttered.

"But Chantalle is the only . . ." Jun felt at fault here. The fires were black and purple like his. Was it really that energy clash that set this whole place ablaze? Did he set himself on fire too? Was that why his leg . . .

Alex healed Chantalle's concussion, but she was still out. "Chantalle, we need you!" he tapped her cheek. "Chantalle we-"

Dr Reymond dragged them both out of the line of the falling ceiling which had been coming down. "Dave, let's try to make some room," he hacked into his elbow.

Dave wiped the sweat from his face and ran to the fiery plastering in their way. "Shit. Doc I-I don't know if . . ."

Jun's eyes, his nostrils and his throat were burning. "Chantalle isn't getting up?"

"She should soon. I-I healed her . . ." Alex coughed.

They stood around, giving each other concerning glances, until Jun felt a shock erupt before him. "What the-"

Snow blew a hole through the fallen ceiling, and through it came Aaron.

"Aaron!" Alex immediately started sobbing.

He created a whirlwind of snow and ice that put out all the flames around them and made their area something like a winter wonderland.

Dave looked in awe at the snow particles floating in the air.

Aaron cracked his neck after doing so. "You guys ready to move or what?"

"Yes. Th-thank you so much-" Dr Reymond started. This boy saved their lives!

"Yeah, yeah, yeah. Let's go," Aaron went running down the hall first. It was all covered in ice and snow.

"Shit," Alex had snot running from his nose. "We thought we were gonna die! Thank you, Aaron!"

"Don't mention it. *Please*," Aaron led them to the elevator. "Lisa got Carla to tell everyone to leave the compound 'cause things were looking bad. I decided to come to check on everything because nothing was getting better, but then all of a sudden, all the shaking and cracking stopped, and the atmosphere felt . . . more or less normal,"

They filed in, and Jun tried to keep as much distance from Aaron as possible. Were they still glitching because he hated Aaron? *Not so much now. He saved us.*

"Then I got here, and all of you were frying in heat twice as hot as a volcano," Aaron said plainly. "So, I did my thing and viola. You're saved," he turned blandly to Dave. "You're welcome,"

Dave was holding Chantalle over his shoulder. They were all covered in soot and dust particles- not Aaron. "Thank you,"

Aaron smirked. "How did you do it, though?"

"Jun did it. He used his powers and cut all the strings-" Alex started.

"Strings?" Aaron did not want to hear more. "Anyway, the ambulance should be here, and I think someone called the fire department, so Doc, you're gonna have some explaining to do," he smiled tightly at Dr Reymond.

Dr Reymond was just glad they were all alive.

Alex looked at the box in Dr Reymond's hand. "W-wait. Is the thing in there?"

The doctor nodded.

Jun frowned, then pointed to Aaron. "Why isn't it going crazy?"

Dr Reymond opened the box.

They looked inside at the anomaly. It was like a flickering light and was vibrating inside.

"Usually, it starts clanging and flying everywhere when me and Lisa get close," Aaron shrugged. "Maybe it's running out of energy?"

Dr Reymond frowned. "I wonder . . ." this would require further investigation.

They got to the upper floor and walked onto the grass outside. The group went jogging to head for the gate so Dr Reymond could address the students and whoever else needed addressing.

"Thank goodness you're all alright!" Carla hugged Dave and then examined the state of their clothes and bodies.

Jun and Alex could see every single student staring at them in stun. The paramedics had taken Chantalle to the sidelines once Dave got close enough to them.

"What happened to you guys?" Ansel asked as he and a group of other kids got close. They were gathered on the street and sidewalk outside the gate. A few ambulance trucks were indeed here checking the vitals of students and dealing with security guards who had gotten hurt. Dr Foster was on a gurney being lifted into a truck. A few news reporters and journalists were on the scene too. First, there were mysterious fires on the compound two months ago, and now this? Glowing cracks in the walls, explosions and unstable lights would not be easy to explain.

". . . there was an issue with substances in the underground section of the school, but it's been handled, and once things are repaired, we *will* resume sessions . . ." Dr Reymond was answering some frantic questions.

"But what about the students' safety?"

"What were these substances?"

"What's going on?"

The old scientist opened his mouth to answer just as he saw James get placed in the back of an ambulance. The man's eyes were open, and his kids were watching him. "Excuse me," he walked away from the reporters.

". . . so yeah, we just got caught in the crossfire, really," Alex just told an elaborate lie as to why they were in their current state.

Ansel and Ryan frowned along with the other kids.

Devon and Annalise squeezed themselves through the crowds. "You guys uh . . ." Devon saw everyone peering in his direction.

"You got out alive, but is everything okay? Is Chantalle gonna be alright?" asked Annalise.

"I think she'll be fine. Probably just needs some rest," Alex spoke first.

Jun nodded. "Yes. Everything is completely fine. Dr Reymond has the thing, but it's weaker, so I don't think it can hurt us anymore,"

"What thing?" Ansel scratched his head.

"Good," Devon sighed with relief. "Damn, that was crazy. Are we even gonna keep having classes?"

"What were those explosion noises?" many questions were being thrown in their direction.

Jun raised his shoulders and let them fall. "This school used to be a research lab, so I guess some of the old equipment and experiments got out of hand?" he smiled awkwardly.

"Your leg is *messed* up," a guy pointed to Jun.

"Yeah, but it'll get better, I hope," Jun shifted his eyes to Alex.

"Yo. That was all *so* insane. I posted a lot of it online, and people are saying our school is cursed. Like . . ." the conversation among the other students took a different direction.

Alex wanted to go see Chantalle. Had she awoken? He started rushing to the paramedics who had taken her, but Jun held his arm. "What?" he snapped.

Jun drew back. "Alex I . . ." the shame was too much. "Look, man, on a serious note, I did *not* mean what I said to my friends. I was just embarrassed that they were laughing at me, but the thing is, if they were real friends, they wouldn't do that," he slowly retrieved his phone from his pocket. "I was bullied from elementary school to middle school, so I kind of tried putting on a persona so that wouldn't happen anymore, and I guess in the process, I became something like a jerk. I thought I had to be one way to make friends, but . . ." he half-smiled. "You showed me I didn't need to do that. You're so unapologetically yourself because you're cool and badass and being with you showed me that maybe I could be that way too. Plus, you liked my nerdy side, so . . . I'm sorry," he came to Alex's side to show him something. "Look,"

Alex frowned as Jun started typing a message in a group chat.

It read: Yeah, I was dancing around with cheerleaders at my new school. It wasn't because anyone forced me but because I wanted to be with my new friends. My real friends. Alex and Chantalle. I met Alex on my first day, and I love him like a brother. He's the coolest guy I have ever met. Cooler than any of you could dream of. I only said what I said earlier to stay in your good books, but now I don't give a rat's ass what you people think. Goodbye.

Alex gasped when Jun left the group chat. "*Dude,*"

Jun put his phone away.

"That was ballsy," Alex laughed. "Y-you're really dropping your cool squad for me?" his anger and embarrassment were ebbing away.

"Yeah. You're a real one, Alex," Jun said.

Alex teared up and hugged him.

Jun hugged back and rested his face atop his head. "Now come on, let's go check on Chanty,"

Alex giggled as they walked together.

James exhaled when his old partner was at his side.

"He's already feeling low. He doesn't need you rubbing it in," Aaron rolled his eyes.

"No, I'm not here to do that," Reymond held James' arm. "Are you okay?"

The paramedics seemed impatient. "Try to make this quick,"

James looked at him. "Where will you go from here?"

Christopher found the question out of place. "What do you mean?"

"I assume that the object glowing through that box in your hand is the prototype and that soon you'll go looking for my lab to seek out what I created. What will you do once you have them all? Make the ultimate enhancer?"

Lisa and Aaron both turned to Dr Reymond. He stood at the other side of their father's gurney.

Reymond shook his head. "I'm going to find a way to shoot them into the sun or-or something. This stuff is dangerous, and you must agree now that you got hurt by its hand,"

"I did this to myself," James' internal fire and anger were dying. He was just exhausted right now. He looked at Christopher. "You're a fool,"

Christopher sighed. "You need to rest, okay? And maybe once you're well enough, we can talk about everything we didn't over the last twenty years,"

James stared ahead as the paramedics got him into the back of the ambulance. "Take care of my children,"

They stepped away when the doors were closed.

Christopher looked down at the box that he held when the ambulance started driving off with his friend. *I'll find his lab and take care of it all.* But what about the kids? *I'll find a way to erase what was done to them.* "Aaron, Lisa?"

"We're fine," Aaron pocketed his hands. "Guess we're your problem now, uh old-timer?"

Dr Reymond smiled.

Chantalle had been revived with smelling salts. She sat at the back of an open ambulance truck. The workers were questioning students nearby.

"Chantalle!" Alex and Jun came up to her.

"Guys," she had an ice pack to her head. "They said they're gonna have to bring me to the hospital for some x-rays, but I'm pretty sure there's no concussion," she smirked at Alex.

Alex grew bashful. "Oh uh . . . Jun and I are friends again," he wrapped an arm around his pal.

"Aww . . . you guys stopped being friends? Is that why you were so quiet, Alex?" Chantalle asked pleasantly.

"I did some dicky stuff, so I deserved the way he treated me, but it's uh . . . it's all okay now," Jun was so happy to have Alex's approval again.

"Awesome," Chantalle looked past them at the bewildered students and the building beyond the gate and walls. "How long do you think they'll take to repair the place?"

The boys turned to face the building as well. "Not sure. There were cracks everywhere. I don't even know if parents will be okay still sending their kids here," Alex stated.

"We won't have a choice but to stay since we've got issues," Jun turned his palms to his face. "Think they'll ever go away?"

"Dr Reymond won't stop until we're 'cured'. I'm sure," Chantalle said pleasantly. "But in the meantime, we can have fun with this, right?"

"Or we could form a league of heroes. Dun-duh-duh-dun!" Alex gave a heroic stance.

Chantalle laughed. "Sure. Like in the comic books?"

"Yeah. I can be the healer, and Jun will be the main guy, and you'll be the rad girl character and.." Alex was going on and on.

Jun smiled at him and then took a deep breath. He had expected coming here to be a total bust, but it was okay. He nearly died a million times, but at least he had some fun and made friends, right?

He spotted Aaron, and the guy gave him a nod.

Jun rolled his eyes but nodded back. *Saved my life*. Having powers was scary, but he did find it interesting. Why *did* they still react that way?

He gave his palm a look and then clenched it into a fist. *I guess it's not so bad*. It wasn't so bad at all. "Alex, maybe there'll be an arc in our hero journey where we all set out on adventures and . . ." Jun started adding to Alex's wacky ideas, making Chantalle laugh.

Eventually, Lisa found herself among them, listening closely to a giggling Chantalle. Aaron was a few feet away, rolling his eyes but seeming invested nonetheless.

THE END

Don't miss out!

Visit the website below and you can sign up to receive emails whenever Laurie Bowler publishes a new book. There's no charge and no obligation.

https://books2read.com/r/B-A-LVUW-FZHMC

BOOKS 2 READ

Connecting independent readers to independent writers.

Also by Laurie Bowler

The Firaty Altar
Anima
Angels Blood
The War at Sea
The Shadow of Light
The Hidden Experiment

Milton Keynes UK
Ingram Content Group UK Ltd.
UKHW020137220823
427215UK00015B/825